I0831670

ADAM'S HEART

Other books by Mark Conkling from Sunstone Press

Prairie Dog Blues
Dog Shelter Blues
Killer Whale Blues
Honey Bee Blues

ADAM'S HEART

A Novel

Mark Conkling

Sunstone books may be purchased for educational, business, or sales promotional use.
For information please write: Special Markets Department, Sunstone Press,
P.O. Box 2321, Santa Fe, New Mexico 87504-2321.

Book and cover design › R. Ahl

eBook 978-1-61139-688-1

Library of Congress Cataloging-in-Publication Data

Names: Conkling, Mark, 1941- author.
Title: Adam's heart : a novel / Mark Conkling.
Description: Santa Fe : Sunstone Press, [2022] | Summary: "A tragic SIDS death, a childhood accident that killed his mother, and his double addiction could not destroy Adam Young's successful journey through hope, recovery, and the renewal of his marriage and family"-- Provided by publisher.
Identifiers: LCCN 2022038528 | ISBN 9781632933898 (paperback) | ISBN 9781611396881 (epub)
Subjects: LCSH: Drug addicts--Fiction.
Classification: LCC PS3603.O535 A43 2022 | DDC 813.6--dc23/eng/20220915

LC record available at https://lccn.loc.gov/2022038528

WWW.SUNSTONEPRESS.COM
SUNSTONE PRESS / POST OFFICE BOX 2321 / SANTA FE, NM 87504-2321 /USA
(505) 988-4418

Adam's Heart is dedicated to my brother,
Dave Conkling

"To live without hope is to cease to live."
—Fyodor Dostoyevsky

"...but those who wait for the Lord shall renew their strength,
they shall mount up with wings like eagles,
they shall run and not be weary,
they shall walk and not faint.
—Isaiah 40:31 NRSV

PREFACE

As a scourge on human life, addiction has no equal. Addicts have existed for thousands of years, as shown in Proverbs 23:19, "Those who linger over wine." We also find addicts in the future. In the Dune trilogy, the unending search is for "spice," a feel-good soporific. Being acquainted with recovered addicts, I find the topic to be fascinating.

Addiction is a doorway for evil to enter the world and ravage men and women—rich and poor, healthy and sick, and young and old. Addiction seeks out despair and sorrow, attacks, and then has its way with folks. Addiction often kills.

Opiate overdoses took over 100,000 lives in the past year, and ten million people misused prescription opioids; 1,600,000 individuals qualified for having an "opioid use disorder." Many are teenagers looking for thrills, and others are older folks wanting to change how they feel.

Alcohol is worse. Over 14 million people have an "alcohol use disorder." Over two million attend AA meetings worldwide. About 380 people die each day from excessive alcohol use—140,000 each year. Only about one in six alcoholics quit for their lifetime.

Yet, miraculously, hope and recovery exist out on the edge of despair and deep down inside of broken lives. How do people find hope? Why do some die a painful death and others recover?

I wrote *Adam's Heart* to show how a man besieged by drugs and alcohol finds hope and learns to surrender to powers greater than himself. For Adam, healthy relationships are the key to a healthy mind. Love and hope show Adam that surrender is a full-time job. Even in the worst of times, there is always hope and there is always love. Adam's story, though gritty and sometimes frightening, shows that "there is always hope." The purpose of the novel is to share that belief with others.

—Mark Conkling

ACKNOWLEDGEMENTS

I am grateful to my friends for their suggestions, encouragement, and support. Thank you, Bob, Dena, Kim, Mark, Mike, Pat, Peter, Rochelle, Tyler, and Vicky.

Carol Gaskin of Editorial Alchemy provided invaluable editing and story recommendations. Her talent is remarkable.

1

Until today, no one had ever seen Adam Young weep. Even at his worst times, he didn't shed tears. Instead, he choked down the urge, swallowed hard, gritted his teeth, and pushed out his square chin to meet the world—his familiar foe. His stiff posture created a barrier around his battered heart, and his frown let people know he was no-nonsense. He was fond of saying he was "physically fit and fearless," but somewhere in his heart, Adam feared two things: the loss of his strength and the force of his shame.

Maria walked past him jiggling her car keys. Lucas, their six-year-old son, followed behind. Always proper, his wife wore her necklace with a gold cross and turquoise earrings. "We're going to the store, and I should be back soon," she said. Lucas is coming with me. Ava is asleep, but I expect her to wake up hungry in about an hour." Adam smelled a waft of lavender and cinnamon as she passed by, Maria's everyday scent.

He yawned, stood up, and walked Maria to the door. It was a sleepy Sunday afternoon in April, and clusters of feathered, dove-gray clouds gathered in a washed-out blue sky. Streaks of dappled sunlight chased along the peaks of the Sandia Mountains, and the aromatic purple sage scattered throughout the Albuquerque Manor trailer park swayed in the breeze.

"Not to worry," Adam said. "I'll take good care of her. Hey, would you get some chocolate chip ice cream?"

Maria smiled over her shoulder. "Say please."

"Pleeease."

"I'll remind her, Dad," Lucas said.

Adam settled himself on their threadbare couch. Nacho, their golden retriever, looked at him through soft brown eyes and whined. Adam had bought Nacho as a puppy for Lucas's fifth birthday, and they had trained him together. Adam patted the couch cushion. "Come on up here." Nacho jumped up and settled with his nose on Adam's lap. "You're a good dog, a real sweet boy." Adam murmured, stroking the dog's soft head. Nacho took a deep breath and closed his eyes. The light at the window became a threatening gray. Dark clouds gathered over the Sandia Mountains, and it smelled like it might rain. Suddenly, strong gusts of the winds of misfortune rattled over the mobile home roof. Adam remembered the tires stacked in the back that he needed to pile on top of the trailer to stop that wind noise. Oh well, mañana.

Ava began crying. "Stay," he said to Nacho. "I'll be right back." Adam pulled up a chair by Ava's bed and gently rested his calloused hand on her gurgling tummy. The warmth of his hand calmed the infant, and after fussing a little she fell back to asleep. Adam smiled and touched her cheek—a miracle—Ava Camila Valdez-Young, their five-month-old daughter, sleeping sweetly in her crib, a blue ribbon with a blue bow tied loosely around her head. She had the same middle name as her mother, Maria Camila Valdez-Young, and had been born in Albuquerque on October 9, 2015, just one day after Maria's twenty-ninth birthday. Maria hated pink and saw it as a stereotype that branded girls, so she found soft light blues for Ava's sleepwear.

Maria should be home soon, Adam thought. Her grocery list included diapers, baby powder, Cheerios, and bread. Lucas loved Cheerios with milk and cinnamon toast for breakfast. He was a happy child, alert, blond, missing one top front tooth and one bottom tooth from his charming smile. He preferred watching football with his dad, but he didn't mind helping his mother with shopping, mainly because they both liked Klondike ice cream bars and would eat one in the car on the way home. But Adam also knew that Maria liked to get Lucas alone so she could quiz him about Adam's drinking when she was away. Typically, after a day on construction sites, Adam picked up Lucas from school and took care of him in the early evenings before Maria got back from the hospital.

Adam had gained respect as an outstanding framing contractor, finish carpenter, and lead foreman. He had trouble kneeling due to his various injuries, so he avoided cement finishing or flooring. But he knew an excellent job when he saw one and could manage subcontractors. After school, he would take Lucas with him to his latest job site to check the progress before going home. The boy enjoyed these outings, and Adam often talked with him about his life's dream.

"Someday, I'll have our own construction company, Lucas. I'll be my own boss and make more money. Then, we could have our own house and go on vacation, and I could buy you a new bicycle, a blue mountain bike with heavy-duty tires."

"Can we get two new bikes so we can ride together?"

Adam would smile and rumple Lucas's hair. "Of course. We can ride together on the Bosque trails." Then Lucas would give Adam a high-five. This conversation had become a ritual and a father's promise that delighted the child. They ate together nearly every night, and their favorite dinner was a giant burrito cooked in the microwave, bean with beef and cheese and green chili. Adam would tease Lucas.

"Okay, you be the chef tonight. Push that button that says five minutes, and I'll set the table."

Adam and Nacho settled back on the couch. After two beers and a ten mg oxycodone, Adam dozed off watching the Golden State Warriors and the LA Laker's game. Ten minutes. That was all. Adam awoke with Nacho whining and scratching both paws on Adam's knee. What's going on? He felt a painful twist in his heart, jumped up, and stumbled to Ava's crib—had she stopped breathing? Adam put his ear to her mouth. No breath, no sound. He felt the side of her neck. No pulse. He put his ear to her chest. No heartbeat. He grabbed his cell phone, called 911, and started gentle CPR on Ava's chest with his right hand. He held her head gently with his left hand and kept his ear to her mouth, hoping, waiting for a breath and the emergency response. He started gentle mouth-to-mouth breathing. The paramedics came quickly, sirens blaring into the trailer park, shrill noises bouncing off the trailer walls like an echo chamber.

The first responders jumped out of the ambulance. They trampled over Maria's yellow and purple bearded irises by the door, took over the CPR from Adam, and worked on Ava for twenty minutes. Her tiny body, the hair ribbon now dislodged, was unresponsive, eyes closed and her lips turning light blue like her comforter. Finally, the paramedic woman, eyes clear and moist, pressed her hand on Adam's shoulder. "I'm so sorry… She's gone."

Adam opened his mouth to speak and raised his fist, but no words formed as he closed his eyes, swallowed hard, pushed out his chin, and leaned back against the Disney cartoon wallpaper he had installed in Ava's nursery. He slid down the wall, knees up, and slammed his fists on the floor. Then Adam wept.

Over him—almost, it seemed, like a heavy thick fog in the darkness—time itself stopped. His heart filled with a scream, but his mouth would not open, and the swollen cry lodged in his throat. Scattered memories paraded through his mind. He saw the fire from years ago. He felt the heat. He saw his stumbling father and smelled acrid smoke. He heard his mother cry out. Then he saw Maria, radiant in her silky, white dress. He could smell the buckets of gardenias lining the altar. He could taste her minty kiss, the lemon cake, and the champagne from their wedding day. He felt himself flush, remembering his excitement at the birth of Lucas the following year, then felt numb from a drunken rage; he tasted his bloodied lip from a bar fight, and then sour bile from a wave of nausea remembering his broken promises to Maria. He shrugged his sore shoulders and felt Maria's grasping arms around his neck as their lovemaking brought new hopes that another baby would smooth out their rough marriage. Ava Camila Valdez-Young, the happy little girl, the soft bundle of life that nursed at Maria's breast and whose presence would heal their love—ripped away while under his care. Unfathomable.

Had he been awake, would he have heard her stop breathing? Would it have mattered? Although it would not happen until later, he knew now he would lose Maria. She would see him differently tonight, tomorrow, the untrustworthy father of Ava. Knowing he fell asleep, though only for a few minutes, would be too much for even her to bear. Oh, Maria was stalwart, and she would try, and so would he, but he could see the end at the beginning of baby Ava's life, in the desperate grasping and hugging and Maria's crying on the night they conceived Ava. "I know it will be better," Maria had whispered. "A new baby will bring us closer." Though unspoken, they both feared the end that night, but they'd gripped each other and held onto a fleeting hope. Adam was stubborn and never one to give up hope. "There's always hope, Maria; there's always hope." Desperation had brought tiny Ava into the world, but why was she taken out? Was the task before her too daunting? Perhaps so. No child deserved to be born with the burden of mending their parents' marriage. Then, without warning, time itself came rolling down, began again, and burst his reverie. It was about two pm.

"Does your wife drive a blue Honda?" the paramedic asked. Adam nodded his head. "I think she's outside. I'm going to call a chaplain and the medical examiner."

He heard Maria come crashing in, Lucas in tow, diapers, milk, and bread spilling out of a grocery bag. "What is it, Adam? Is it Ava?" she shouted. Rushing toward the bedroom, but another first responder blocked her way and said, "You'd better not go in there right now." Maria screamed and pushed him out of the way. Ava's blue comforter covered her completely. "What happened? What happened?"

"I'm sorry. Your baby is unresponsive."

"What do you mean unresponsive? Move. Let me see Ava."

"She stopped breathing. We think she died in her sleep."

"Died? She died?"

"Yes. I'm sorry; that's all we know right now."

"I need to see her."

The EMT put himself between Maria and Ava. "I can't let you touch her, not until our medical director gives permission."

Maria spun in a circle and dropped to her knees, pulling at her hair and clothes, and moaning with an unremitting cadence coming from the depth of her soul. Lucas ran to Adam, fell to his knees, and hugged Adam's leg. Adam reached out and tried to touch Maria, but she lashed out, screamed, and scratched his hand with two deep scratches that drew blood. The paramedic helped Maria up, sat her down on a chair, and ushered Adam and Lucas out of Ava's room as Maria put her head in her hands and sobbed, gasping for breath and groaning.

"Let's leave her alone for a while and get a bandage on those scratches." The paramedic washed Adam's hand with a wet blue towel from the bathroom sink and dressed the wound. The scratches were deep, painful, and would scar—a lifetime reminder of today.

"Our medical director just arrived," he told Adam. "He will examine you daughter. I see our chaplain driving up now, and she can talk with your wife."

Adam shuffled into the living room, dragging Lucas, who still held onto his leg, sliding on the floor. He collapsed onto on the couch and pulled Lucas up in his lap. Lucas put his mouth up to Adam's ear and hugged Adam's neck. "Daddy, did Ava die?"

"I'm afraid so. Yes."

"Why did she die?"

"I don't know, son. I guess she was sick."

"Am I going to die?"

"No, Lucas, you are not going to die."

"Are you sure, Dad?"

"Yes. You're safe here with me."

Adam hugged Lucas, made a place on the couch, and put Lucas's head on his lap with a pillow. He stroked Lucas's tousled hair and rocked back and forth. "I know it's sad, Lucas, but you'll be okay. We've got each other."

The woman chaplain came in and helped Maria as she stumbled into the living room and a chair. Maria's tearful brown eyes twitched with hate and confusion as she stared at Adam, black mascara streaking down her swollen cheeks. The medical director for the paramedics emerged from the bedroom and sat next to Adam and Lucas. He spoke quietly.

"This tragedy appears to be a case of sudden infant death syndrome or SIDS as we call it. It happens to about one baby out of every two thousand. I'm terribly sorry for your loss. I know it is devastating. She died peacefully in her sleep."

Adam looked at him, lips pursed, chin quivering. "What causes it?"

"No one knows. It is a medical mystery."

Maria glared at Adam and spat out, "Neglect?"

2

The medical director completed his notes and removed his glasses. He turned to Adam and Maria. "For now, I'm going to sign the preliminary death certificate and list the cause of death as 'apparent sudden infant death syndrome.' In New Mexico, for children under one year, the Office of Medical Investigator often requires an autopsy for sudden unexplained infant deaths. That will depend upon the investigation."

Adam raised his eyebrows. "Investigation?"

"Yes, the Office of the Medical Investigator, or OMI, will send someone in the morning to go over the circumstances, and he may want to do an autopsy. But frankly, there could be another cause of death."

Maria gasped and sputtered through her tears. "An autopsy? On Ava?"

"Yes, they may want one, just to make sure."

"Can they do that?"

"They can, if they suspect foul play, but otherwise, they will likely ask your permission."

Maria shook her head, pushing her fingers through her hair, biting her lip.

The chaplain took out a notepad. "Do you have a preferred funeral home? McClaren's is nearby. I can make a call, and they'll come now for Ava's body. I'm guessing you'll want a funeral?"

"What if the OMI wants an autopsy?" Adam asked.

"They can move Ava to the OMI facilities if they need to."

Adam nodded and looked at Maria. "McClaren's is okay, right?" Maria nodded.

The chaplain put her hands together. "Would you like to pray?"

Maria looked at Adam. He turned his eyes skyward and shook his head. Although Adam believed there is always hope, he could not imagine a reason to pray at this moment. Their little miracle was gone. Pray in the face of death? Seemed pointless to him. Maria dropped her face into her hands and mumbled incomprehensively. Then she raised her eyes and shook her fist at the ceiling. "Why, God! Why did you take my Ava?"

McClaren's Mortuary picked up Ava's body within the hour. The chaplain handed Maria her card. "Call me anytime, day or night. Is there someone you would like for me to call?"

"No, there's no one." Maria dropped the card on the floor, and then she shuffled into the nursery, crossed her arms around herself, swayed back and forth in the silence, and stared at the empty crib with glazed eyes, lips quivering. Her body shook from her sobs.

The chaplain turned to Adam. "I can call grandparents or friends if you'd like. I know you will both need family support."

"Maria's parents were killed eight years ago. She doesn't have any family—no brothers or sisters."

"Oh, I'm sorry. I didn't know."

"Run off the road, and they hit a tree in two thousand one, just after September eleven. It was horrible."

"And your parents?"

"You can call Jane Sullivan. She's my mother."

"Is there a grandfather, your father?"

"Yes, but I haven't seen him in a couple of years. Just call my mother. Here's the number. You could call Maria's friend from work, Carolyn Chapman. They're like sisters. She'll want to know. The number is by the phone."

"Okay, I'll call in a few minutes, but now I want to be with Maria."

Adam let out a deep breath he had held, it seemed, for a couple of hours. Thank God Carolyn would come over and be with Maria. It saddened him that, less than a year ago, her husband Doug would have come too, in support of Adam, but their friendship had blown up in the current political climate. He and Maria had gone to Carolyn and Doug's house for a cookout. Adam saw a flag flying from Doug's new yard flagpole as they drove up—a Trump flag. Adam pointed at the blue banner unfurled in the breeze. "Sonofabitch, it looks like Doug had a big gulp of Trump Kool-Aid. Wonder what happened. Maybe he lost his mind."

"Carolyn was apoplectic when he put up the flag," Maria said. "She said she was embarrassed to come home."

"That makes for interesting pillow talk," he said.

"She said things are tense."

"Maybe he'll tell me what's going on."

"Adam, don't worry. Carolyn's vote will cancel out his, and no one will be the wiser."

"Well, there's that."

"Right. Now be civil. You know Carolyn is my best friend."

Adam did his best, but both he and Doug knocked back several Jell-O shots while they were grilling hamburgers, and before the evening was over, they were red-faced and arguing about immigration and racism.

Doug pointed his finger at the south. "There's a caravan of illegals moving across Mexico to the border. Most of them take drugs and are gang members. If they cross the border, then there will be violence and rape."

"I heard that most of the people in the caravan are families. Why do you think they are violent criminals?"

"All you have to do is watch FOX News. Trump gave an interview, and he has proof. Plus, illegals will take our jobs, good white-folks' jobs. We don't need brown people mixing with real citizens."

"Now easy does it, Doug. My wife is Hispanic, and her dad was too. She's a Valdez. Her dad was a successful real estate professional before he died. Maria's mother comes from Irish heritage. They are all citizens of the United States, just like you."

"Maria is an exception," Doug said. "And she learned English, the language of Americans."

"She is an American. She was raised speaking English. Her father spoke a little Spanish, but English was their everyday language. You're making a hasty generalization."

"Don't add confusion to this," Doug said. "It's simple. We need to close the border once and for all. Building the wall is a great idea."

Adam took a deep breath and smiled at Doug. "We should just let this go. There's no sense ruining a five-year friendship over Trump. He's not worth it."

"You may think that," Doug said, shaking his finger in Adam's face, "but it is time to take a stand one way or another, and Mexicans don't belong here."

"Come on, Doug. Your wife was a Montoya before she married you."

"I know, but her father was from Spain. She's upper class, not Mexican."

"Okay, so be it. Let's change the channel and move on. What did you think about the Dallas game?"

"You can move on if you want, but I'm moving up with Trump. It's time to make America great."

Adam extended his hand. "Okay, but at least we can stay friends."

"Loyalty is more important than friendship. If we can't both be loyal to the same man, then we can't be friends." Doug ignored Adam's hand and showed Adam his back.

Adam threw both hands up in the air. "So, I'm not good enough to be your friend?

"No, you're not loyal enough. Things have changed, Adam. You're a liberal, and I can't waste my time with all your fake news."

Maria and Carolyn had gone for a long walk in the neighborhood, and when they returned, Adam was sitting in his truck with the motor running and a pint of vodka balanced between his thighs. He motioned to Maria. "Come on. Let's get out of here before I whip his ass." That night was the end of their friendship. To Adam, in one evening, Doug had become a stranger in the moment of Adam's deep need for a friend.

§

Adam shook his head as if to erase the memory and stood up. He carried Lucas to his room and rubbed his back until he fell asleep. Twilight veiled the windows, and the house became silent, as though blanketed by dense clouds, except for Maria's loud moans that broke through, like thunder rumbling through a fog. Adam paced up and down the hallway with his hands over his ears. His shoulders and biceps strained at his T-shirt as he breathed through his teeth and shook his head side to side. He paused when Maria came out of the nursery.

"Do something. Goddammit, Adam, do something!" Maria ran into their bedroom and slammed the door so hard the walls shook. Adam clasped his hands together and sat down.

"I called Jane," said the chaplain. "She's coming right over. And I called Carolyn and left a message to call me. So, I'll stay with you until Jane gets here, but Maria needs to be alone for a while."

Adam stood quietly, gazing out the window. "What?"

"I'll stay with you until Jane comes."

"No need for that. I'm okay. I'll heat some soup."

"You'll be getting a call from the OMI. An investigator will come by tomorrow. You should call and let people know you and Maria will not be coming to work. I know they will want to interview both of you. Please leave the nursery as it is. OMI will want to look things over."

"Do you think they're suspicious—of me, of us?"

"They look carefully at any unexplained infant death. That's their job. It's not personal."

Adam walked the chaplain to the door.

She took Adam's hand. "Please call. I'll stay in touch."

Adam peeked into the bedroom. Maria was asleep, fully dressed, and sprawled out on their bed, face in a pillow, and her dress up over her back. Her light blue hip-hugger panties made a wedgie. A streak of sunlight revealed she was still wearing her turquoise earrings from this morning. Maria is so beautiful, Adam thought. Even in this horrible time, she excites me deep down in my core. So, what's the matter with me? Maybe nothing. Maybe I'm crazy in love.

Adam moved to the couch, took a deep breath, and sat down with his head back and arms outstretched. Everything was too quiet. He went outside to his truck, grabbed a pint of vodka out of his toolbox, slipped off his work boots by the door, and tiptoed back to the couch. Four big swallows later, he fell into a hypnogogic sleep, images of little giggling Ava pushing him down into the darkness until he jerked awake at a loud knock at the door. "Adam, Adam, let me in!" He staggered to the door, opened it, and fell into the arms of his mother. "Ava died. She just died. No one knows why."

Jane put her hands on both sides of Adam's face. "I heard. I'm so sorry. Where's Maria?"

"Asleep in the bedroom."

"Lucas?"

"Asleep."

"You smell like a brewery. Are you drunk?"

"Maybe a little, but mostly just wiped out."

He dropped his head into his hands, and Jane sat beside him.

Jane Sullivan was a large, bony woman with a gentle smile at the bottom of her long, pink face. Her bright, attentive brown eyes were set far apart. She wore her light brown hair, now streaked with gray, short, and brushed back over her ears. At first glance, she seemed ordinary, except that her face radiated a captivating warmth. She had large hands, and they moved, touched, and held things with unmistakable compassion, as though her hands conducted music from her gentle heart.

Now fifty-six, Jane had never married, perhaps because her frame was gangly, because her hips were wide, because she didn't think much of men, because she cared more about animals than people, and because sometimes she smelled like a litter box. She owned a pet store and lived in a two-bedroom apartment above the store, Adam's childhood home after his mother, Margaret Sullivan, had died in the fire when Adam was nine. Jane was Margaret's older sister and had adopted Adam after his father Edward moved into a care facility. The fire had left him disabled, and his face featured deep scars from burns. Adam grew up with his new mother devoted to him, taking care of him, teaching him how to care for animals, and counting on him for repairs and maintenance. Adam became her companion and equally devoted son. Jane's clean and orderly pet store was bright and attractive. She specialized in rescued kittens and exotic tropical fish. She refused to sell puppies from puppy mills but always had a couple of healthy rescue dogs from the animal shelter available for the price of their vaccinations.

Adam glanced at his cell phone. "It's Carolyn; I should take this."

"Adam, it's Carolyn. I just heard from the chaplain. Maria doesn't answer her phone."

"She's asleep."

"I'm coming over. I want to be there when Maria wakes up."

"Sure, she needs you. See you soon. Just let yourself in. Maria's in our bedroom. I know she'd like you to be with her."

Adam looked at the floor. Jane held his hands. "Mom, I can't believe it. She was fine. She died while I was asleep—only for ten minutes—then Nacho woke me up, and suddenly, I felt a sense of doom, as though death itself came marching through the house."

They sat on the couch, and Jane turned to Adam. "The chaplain said the medical examiner thought it was SIDS. So, there's nothing you could have done."

"But I'm afraid Maria blames me. Maybe I could have done something."

"She's devastated, Adam. She's not herself. You were here when it happened, and she's lashing out."

"People from the medical examiner's office are coming to interview us. They say it is a suspicious death."

"Anytime a baby dies from an unknown cause, it is suspicious—but I'm sure it's routine. So don't worry; just tell them what happened."

"I will, but this is a nightmare. I don't know how we'll get through it."

Jane met his eyes, tears welling in her own. "You'll get through this the way you've gotten through everything else. There's always hope, Adam. You know that. You have to embrace the hope and live in it."

"You've said that for years, Mom, and you know I believe it. But times like this are so dark that you can't see hope. You can only wish you could see it."

"Stay in the wishing part. Don't let this pull you down so far that you can't see the stars."

The door opened. "I'm here," Carolyn said. "I'll go in the bedroom so I'm there when she wakes up."

Adam put his hand on his heart. "I'm grateful Maria has you as a friend."

Jane took Carolyn's hand. "I'll be here if you need me."

Carolyn let herself quietly into the bedroom.

Adam took a breath and turned to Jane. "Sometimes I wish I could be ten years old again, back when things were simple. We'd have breakfast together, sweep out the store, feed and water the animals, and help customers find a pet. And, with you helping me with homework, my school was a breeze."

"It might have seemed simple, but, believe me, that was a complicated year. First, we went to court so I could adopt you. Then, you were in and out of the hospital for surgeries every two months. That summer, I discovered that our tax accountant had made errors, and I had to go through an IRS audit. I spent hundreds of hours managing the insurance claims, attorneys, settlements, and trust accounts. There was barely time to sleep."

"I knew you were busy, but I had no idea of the burdens you carried."

"Maybe it is just as well. A ten-year-old boy who has lost his parents, who spent weeks in the burn unit, and was in constant pain, deserves to be loved."

"I vaguely recall that you had headaches all the time. If I'd known more, I could have been helpful."

"Having you in my life gave me hope, Adam. Every morning I would look forward to hugging you and having breakfast together. You were such a bright light for me."

"I am so grateful for you. I could have easily become a ward of the state."

"As your aunt, and with no other living relatives, the adoption process was easy. The hard part, Adam, was having to watch you deal with the pain from your surgeries."

"I remember you beside my bed rubbing my legs with lotion. You were so gentle."

"Yes, I put lidocaine gel on your burns every night. With heavy applications, you would fall asleep after about a half-hour."

"I still have the pain, and lidocaine gel still helps. The trouble is, and I'm embarrassed to tell you, I think I might have a drug problem."

"I know you have a problem, but I thought it was alcohol. You drink all the time."

"It's a dilemma, Mom. The alcohol helps the pain killers work better, and also dampens down my anger and resentment. I need both."

"So, you don't see any other way to live?"

"Someday, I have to face it. I don't know what to do about it."

"When things settle down after Ava's death, we can find you some help."

"I feel trapped. If I give up either drugs or alcohol, I am in such steady pain that I can't work. If I can't work, I can't provide for Maria and Lucas, and someday the unending pain would be my demise. I couldn't live that way. I would rather die."

"I think part of you feeling trapped is that you often carry other peoples' pain as well as your own. I think it was your twelfth birthday when we noticed that."

"You mean the day with that puppy?"

Jane nodded. "I remember I came into the office, and you were holding that little brown and white spaniel puppy. You had taken it out of the pet cage, and you were crying."

"That's the one we named Jupiter, right?"

"You thought about naming him after a star, but then you settled on a planet."

"He was whining, and he felt hot."

"You were frowning. You said you thought this puppy was in a lot of pain—that you could feel the puppy's pain in your heart."

"I saw the pain in his eyes first. I wasn't sure where it was coming from, so I felt him all over. That's when I felt his tummy. The pain was bad, worse than my legs."

"You saved Jupiter's life, Adam. We took him to the vet right away, and the x-ray showed a blockage in his intestine. The vet performed emergency surgery. If you hadn't felt his pain, the puppy would have died that night. Your ability seems to be both a blessing and a curse."

"I can control it better now. If I let in all of Maria's pain, it would paralyze me, so I keep it at bay and try to be helpful. I can feel my friend Ryan's pain over his broken relationships, but we don't talk about it. He keeps it buried, and I don't feel like bringing it up because he's my supervisor. And Doug's pain is so bad all he can do is be angry and belligerent."

"What about you? How do you feel about Ava?"

Adam groaned. "She was the salvation of our marriage and my precious daughter, so her death brings me double pain. She was such a sweet baby. How do I feel? Overwhelming sadness, and I feel a tear in my heart that won't go away. I can still smell her baby powder and formula. This sounds weird, but last night I dreamed Ava reached up, grabbed my hair, and doubled me over."

"I'm so sorry, Adam, but you've got to be strong. Maria will be inconsolable for a while, and then she'll soften—hopefully, she'll forgive you even though you did all you could. And she'll need to forgive herself, too, for not being here. Part of her will blame herself as much as you."

"I still wonder if I could've done more if I hadn't fallen asleep. Maybe Maria's right to blame me, and I don't see it."

"No, Adam, you did all you could. Ava was a SIDS baby, and guilt from parents is a normal reaction—if only I had done this, if only I had done that, the curse of 'if onlys.'"

"In a few days, I'll ask Maria to start marriage counseling with me, and we can work through things."

"She may need more time, Adam. You may need more time as well."

Adam yawned and stretched his arms out. "I'm starting to fade, Mom. I'm not sure I can sleep, but I'd better try."

"Your right. It's getting late. I'll check in with you in the morning."

"Okay, goodnight."

"Nite."

3

The morning following Ava's death, two women investigators from the OMI knocked at the door promptly at nine am. Adam let them in and offered them each a chair. "Would you like coffee or water?"

"We are terribly sorry for your loss, and we regret disturbing you at this difficult time. We have a few questions, but we won't take long."

They interviewed Adam and Maria extensively, visited Ava's nursery, took a few pictures, and then sat down at the dining room table. They both offered their business cards and shuffled papers into a folder already labeled "Ava Valdez-Young, SIDS Death."

The older of the two spoke.

"We want to reassure you that we do not see anything here that would raise suspicion. It appears to be SIDS death. No one is at fault. It is a mystery the medical community still does not understand."

"So, no autopsy?" Maria asked.

"There doesn't seem to be any reason for an autopsy. We will let McClaren's know they can prepare Ava for her funeral."

Maria put her hand to her heart, closing her eyes. "I didn't want anyone cutting up Ava's body."

"We can be glad for that," Carolyn said. "I wouldn't want that either."

The investigators left the house, and Maria and Carolyn went into the bedroom and closed the door. Adam wandered outside and sat in a lawn chair by two pots of golden chrysanthemums. He watched a rosy finch at the bird feeder. A roadrunner sunbathed on a large flat rock about thirty feet away, wings spread out in the gentle breeze. Maria still thinks I'm to blame, even though they said it is no one's fault. Can we ever get past this? Finally, after an hour of ruminating, Adam slammed his fist into his open palm, stood up, and went to the kitchen to make more coffee. He poured a large mug, added a generous splash of brandy, drank it, and then walked to the bedroom and stood by the closed door listening to Maria's soft crying and muffled speech with Carolyn. Adam knocked at the door and spoke loudly enough that they could hear. "I called McClaren's and made an appointment for one pm. They will have someone meet us so we can arrange a funeral. Are you up for that? I think it will help to get things organized."

"Okay," Maria whispered. "I'll be ready. But, until then, leave me alone."

"Do you want me to go with you?" Carolyn asked.

"No, we'd better do this by ourselves."

"Okay. I'll leave you alone. Call me if you need anything."

Maria hugged Carolyn. "Thank you. You're a wonderful friend."

Leave her alone? That was the last thing on his mind when he'd met Maria six years before, a day that sparkled in his mind. He shivered remembering the feeling of being smitten at first sight of her, an insistent flutter two inches under his heart that tightened his chest and made him skip a breath. He'd been standing in the kitchen, filling a hummingbird feeder with sugar water when they drove up. Ryan Withers, the sales manager for Albuquerque Constructors, had a customer with him. Adam and Ryan had worked for the company for over three years, and they became working companions. Ryan managed sales, customer service, and warranty callbacks. Adam was his go-to problem solver. Ryan was a somewhat portly recovered alcoholic with ten years of sobriety. He was a large man, about six feet two, 225 pounds, with short dark hair. Sixteen years ago, he'd been a star linebacker on his high school football team and voted MVP when they won the state championship. His round face featured an inviting smile, and his broad shoulders and kind hazel eyes suggested he could help carry whatever burden one might have. He ushered a spritely woman out of the car and escorted her into the two-bedroom townhome unit, where Adam was completing his final inspection and remaining tasks.

Adam stopped pouring the hummingbird juice, set the feeder on the counter, and stood with his mouth open. He was shirtless, and his tan, muscular body reflected glistening sunlight from the slight sweat on his chest and shoulders. Ryan's customer was a striking woman dressed in white shorts and a light green spaghetti strap top that showed silky, tan cleavage. Her brown hair was shoulder length with blond streaks. Laugh lines creased the corners of her bright brown eyes. She could be mischievous, Adam thought.

"I'd like you to meet Maria Valdez," Ryan said. "She's a registered nurse, and she's interested in renting one of the units."

Adam grinned, extending his hand. "I'm pleased to meet you." Her hand felt warm and soft in his own. He felt a surprising urge to pull her hand to him and hold it against his chest. Maria smiled, and they held their gaze for a moment until she looked away.

"Are you filling that feeder?" she asked.

Adam blushed. "Yes, there are a couple of rufous hummingbirds checking things out, so I thought I'd put up a feeder."

Maria cocked her head and smiled. "Seems odd, a construction worker feeding hummingbirds."

"I guess. Always have liked the little hummers." Adam gazed at Maria, returning her smile. "Beautiful and energetic."

"How about hanging it by that window?"

"Good idea," he said. He picked up the feeder from the kitchen counter. "I'll be right back." He stepped out onto the portal, tacked a small nail into a wooden roof beam, and adjusted the red, rubber-coated wire so the feeder hung in the middle of the kitchen window. Two hummers began buzzing and diving around the feeder as he stepped aside. They seemed gleeful, animated, and fast as a gusty wind. Adam stepped back inside and smiled at Maria. "How's that?"

"Great location," she said.

Adam turned to Ryan. "I've completed the punch list, so the unit is ready for you to show."

"Okay," Ryan beckoned to Maria. "Follow me, and I'll show you around. Our building company is keeping this four-plex, so there is no worry we would sell it out from under you."

Adam put his hands on the kitchen counter and dropped his head, eyebrows raised. He thought that Maria Valdez might be the most beautiful woman he'd ever seen. He caught a whiff of lavender and cinnamon as she walked by, and the blonde highlights in her hair captured rays of sunlight streaking through the window. Adam was glad he had used glass cleaner on the mirrored sliding doors on the bedroom closet. They shined and smelled like Windex.

"Maria," he called. "Be careful when you go in the master bedroom. Folks have said it is romantic in there, so watch out."

Maria looked back over her shoulder and raised an eyebrow. "I'll be careful."

Her pear-shaped hips in white shorts captured his imagination and his stolen glances. Her legs were shapely and tan like her bare shoulders. Adam wondered if she had tan lines or if the creamy beige tone of her skin was her actual skin color. Only one way to know, he thought. He fussed with his tools and wiped down the countertops until Ryan and Maria returned to the kitchen area.

"This is just what I'm looking for," Maria said. I'll be looking for a roommate from work. This townhome is the right size for two people, and you say it is six-hundred dollars a month?"

"Yes," replied Ryan. "Plus, your utilities. You have covered parking, and your courtyard is, as you can see, private and hidden from view."

"The courtyard walls are five feet high," Adam said. "Plenty of privacy for sunbathing or whatever." In his mind, he pictured Maria sunbathing naked. For a moment, the image took his breath away.

Maria adjusted one of her straps. "Great. I'll take it. When can I move in?"

"We require a minimum one-year lease."

"No problem. One year is fine."

"I'll get the paperwork ready," Ryan said. "Give me a check for your first and last month's rent, and you can move in this weekend."

Adam caught Ryan's eye. "The company provides a move-in service," Adam said. "So, I'll be here Saturday to assist."

"Yes, that's a new service the company is offering," Ryan said, winking at Adam. Ryan raised his eyebrows and nodded, as if to say I'm interested if you're not

"I don't have much to move," she said, "but I would appreciate the help." Her eyes lingered on his face and shoulders.

"Say nine am?"

"Okay."

Adam returned her gaze. For a moment, he saw pain deep in her eyes. Ever since he was in sixth grade, Adam had had the talent, perhaps the curse, of seeing and often feeling the pain in animals and other people. Maria's pain felt dull and heavy, as though it was old, and it was constant, like a slow drumbeat with no breaks. It was so strong that Adam thought the pain could pull her down low, perhaps keep her down if she gave in to its power. However, she was so beautiful that he knew an admiring world would continue to lure her forward. The pain would remain a few steps behind, a burden to pull along, not the face of tomorrow. She would never see herself as a victim, he thought. She's too strong for that.

"Will you have to drive far? I have a truck and can come to your place."

"Not far. I can put everything I own in my Prius. Later, I need to go to a good furniture store and pick out a few things."

"Do you work nearby?"

"Yes, I work at Presbyterian Hospital downtown." She smiled with pride. I just recently graduated. This is my first job." She walked to the door with Ryan, turned, and looked back and waved. "Okay, then, I'll see you on Saturday. Is there a fee?"

"For you, there's no fee," Adam said. "It's on the house for beautiful women."

"Great," she said, clearly ignoring the compliment. "Goodbye for now."

On Saturday, Adam had stopped by Walgreens, bought a Mr. Coffee on sale, and took it to the townhome. He had a fresh pot brewed when Maria drove up with her Prius stuffed with boxes and plastic bags.

"I've got fresh coffee," Adam said. "Would you like some before we start unloading?"

"Sure." Maria walked a few steps ahead of Adam to the coffee pot on the counter. She had dressed in blue jeans and an oversized white T-shirt with "I AM WOMAN" emblazoned on the front. She sure is, Adam thought, as he stood next to her, filling their cups.

She had a medium build, five feet five inches tall, size ten or twelve, ample breasts cushioned in a light beige bra that showed through her shirt, and solid and shapely arms likely developed from swimming or playing softball. She had tied her hair back in a ponytail and pushed it through the back of a white baseball cap. Now, this was one fine woman, a sight to behold.

Maria turned toward Adam and looked into his eyes. "I appreciate your help with moving in, but we need to clear the air."

"What do you mean?"

"I'm worried about saying too much. Are you open-minded?"

"I like to think so."

"Okay, then, please drop the flirty, teenage behavior. It makes me feel degraded."

"You are a beautiful woman. I'm just offering compliments."

"You don't see me as an equal. I do have a mind, you know."

"Of course, we are equals."

"Yes, but you are more focused on my body, and I can sense that—the way you look at me, as though you're undressing me. I don't like that."

"Well, now I'm confused. You're a woman with a beautiful body. I can't help it if I'm attracted. What's wrong with that?"

"Plenty of men ogle my body, but I want friends interested in my thinking, beliefs, and moral stance in the world. In my work, I care about the safety of children and families. Too many families suffer violence and abuse. Healthy families. That's what's important. Not my butt and not my boobs. Please drop the leering gaze."

Adam felt his face turn bright red. He extended his hands toward her, apologetic. "Sorry, I don't want to diminish or embarrass you. I want to get to know you better. I guess I was born with a roving eye."

"You know you can move past that. You do seem different, not like most men."

Adam, put his hands behind his back, trying to appear harmless. "Sure, I'll try to stay tuned in." Move past that? How do you change what you see?

"If we are going to be friends, we need to start with a new normal—shared beliefs about what is important with families and the moral world, you know, what's right and wrong, good and evil, compassion and indifference."

"Okay, let's start a new normal right now. Tell me about your family, your parents."

Maria looked down at the countertop. When she looked up, tears glistened in her eyes. "Both of my parents are deceased. My father was a heavy drinker, and one rainy night two years ago, he skidded off the highway and hit a tree. The highway patrol said they both died instantly. I've always hated that my father's drinking killed my mother. She loved him until the end, but I can't tell you why. I keep working on forgiveness, but I can't seem to get there."

Adam frowned. "I'm so sorry, and I understand. I lost my mom—really, both my parents—in an accident when I was nine."

Maria's eyes went wide. "A car accident?"

"No, we went camping. Our trailer caught fire. Mom was trapped, and my father and I got burned. He almost died but wound up disabled and lives in a care facility. Nurses in the burn unit saved my legs." Adam pulled up his pants legs and showed Maria the jagged folds of scar tissue on his shins and calves. "I've had a dozen skin grafts to keep up with my growth, but the scars hurt all the time. It hurts too much to be on my knees, so I can't work on floors or foundations. The scars make me ugly. You may want to reconsider a friendship with me. As long as we're being open and honest, you need to know that I have a lot of defects."

Maria wiped her eyes with a paper towel. "I don't see anything ugly. I see the damage and healing from a disaster, a traumatic accident. I'm sorry for your painful challenges."

"Thank you for your concern. I guess we both understand pain. We share the suffering of a major loss. Perhaps we could share the joy of friendship."

"Do you believe in God?" Maria asked.

"Yes, but I have questions."

"Do you believe God can heal pain?"

"For me, that's complicated. Sometimes pain brings us closer to God, and other times the pain becomes anger. I worry about my anger most of the time—can't seem to get away from it."

"I like the idea of being friends and sharing ideas. Maybe having a friend can ease your anger and help you along the way. Is that possible?"

"Perhaps. I must admit, I've never met a woman like you." Adam grinned. "Any chance you're a curandera?"

"Oh, for heaven's sake, no. It takes years of training and study to learn to be a traditional healer. I'm a registered nurse. That's all. However, my father told me that my great aunt Juana, my tia abuela, was a curandera. I never met her. He said she visited from Oaxaca for two weeks and cured his mother of pneumonia with herbs. So, I guess that's possible."

Adam shuffled his feet. "Well, nurses are healers. Maybe some of Juana's skills got passed down to you."

"Perhaps so."

Deep in his bones, Adam believed that meeting Maria on that happy Saturday had set his life on a new course. He had climbed up onto a new path that led to a better way of knowing a woman, a way that helped him temper his adolescent behavior. Adam treated Maria with respect. He tempered his expression of sexuality and generated conversations about values, attitudes, and beliefs. That led to frequent dating, long discussions, weekends together, desire wrapped in privacy, thoughtfulness, and candlelight, and a kind of love that covered him from head to toe with comfort and excitement—a shield, he imagined. He had proposed to Maria under a down comforter one cold night in January 2009, and they were married on Valentine's Day. Maria was a tiger in bed, and she calmed him with her soft lavender smell. She didn't have tan lines.

§

Adam strained as he gathered torn memories from those days, recalling details that warmed him and, at the same time, sent utter fear into his heart. He swallowed hard to push back the ache in his throat. Little had they known at the time that their union would be a marriage of the walking wounded—he would persevere, however, because his love for Maria and Lucas was as strong as Hercules and filled with a powerful hope. With them in his life, he could always see the sun and the stars through his constant pain. Polaris, the North Star, never failed to shine for him and to send tiny slivers of light toward his next challenge. Deep in his soul, he imagined that starlight beaming down and connecting him to a reservoir of hope, and in that hope was the light needed for the dark path ahead.

4

McClaren’s funeral home featured soft carpets, velvet purple drapes hung on ornate brass rods, the mixed smell of lemon air freshener, day-old flowers, and quiet, insipid music. To Adam, the atmosphere felt too close and thick; there was not enough space to breathe. His feet sank into the thick carpet and padding, which kept him a little off balance. No other customers were there. A gray-haired man in his sixties dressed in a dark blue suit greeted them and ushered them into a private room with a table and chairs. “I’m Charles McClaren,” he said, extending his hand.” I’m one of the owners, along with my father and brother. Please have a seat. I am so deeply sorry for the passing of Ava, and we will do our best to honor her. Would you like coffee or a soft drink?”

“No, thank you,” said Maria. “Let’s go ahead.” Adam squinted and nodded in agreement.

“The first thing we need to decide is whether you would like to choose a casket and prepare Ava for burial or cremate her and save her cremains in an urn.” He opened a notebook and turned to a page of small caskets. The facing page featured an array of urns. “These caskets run from eight hundred dollars to five thousand. The tall urns are six-fifty, and the shorter ones are a hundred twenty-five each. Sometimes people buy several small, pewter urns to distribute cremains to family members. The small ones are available at sixty-five dollars each.”

Adam turned to Maria and raised his eyebrows. “We haven’t thought much about it,” he said. “This was so unexpected.”

“Yes, unexpected and tragic. I’m so sorry.”

“I don’t know what we are supposed to do,” Maria said. “Do we need to buy a cemetery plot?” Maria asked.

"Yes, or you can buy a niche in one of our memorial walls."

"A niche?" she asked.

"It is a small compartment in a wall where we can put the urn. The niche will last in perpetuity. Or you can take Ava's cremains with you and keep the urn in your home."

Maria wrinkled her nose. "Do people do that?—keep ashes in their homes? That seems morbid."

"How much is a cemetery plot?" Adam asked.

"We have a few left for three thousand dollars," he said. "We have arranged the infant graves in the shade under a cottonwood tree. It is a peaceful location."

"How much is a niche?" Adam asked.

"There is a one-time charge of a thousand dollars."

Adam wiped his eyes and then touched his thumb and forefinger to his chin. "So, if I understand, if we buy a casket and a gravesite, we will spend about four thousand dollars. Or McClaren's would cremate Ava and provide an urn for about six-hundred-fifty. How much is the cremation?"

Maria gritted her teeth and pursed her lips, turning them white. "Money is the last thing we have to worry about." Tears ran down both cheeks, and her nose dripped. Adam handed her a tissue. She blew her nose. "Think about honoring Ava. The money be damned."

"I know," Adam said, "but I want to get out of here. This place gives me the creeps."

"Please slow down," Maria said, wiping her eyes. "I need to understand what's happening. Don't you get it? I've lost my baby."

"You mean our baby," Adam said. "She was my daughter, too."

"You can't possibly feel as devastated as I do," Maria said.

"I know we feel pain differently, but my pain is just like yours. I feel like someone pulled my heart out." Adam reached for Maria's hand, but she pulled it away.

"The cremation is one-thousand eight-hundred," Mr. McClaren said. "Plus, if we conduct a funeral with music and flowers in the sanctuary, we will add twelve-hundred-dollars for that."

'I don't want a funeral," Maria said. "I've decided just to have a memorial at our house with friends. So, forget the funeral expense."

"So, either way, it would be about four thousand more or less, "Adam said.

"Yes," said Mr. McClaren. "Unfortunately, the state also charges sales tax."

"This all feels like something's missing. Do we have other choices?" Maria asked.

"Yes, we have another possibility. Have you ever seen a LifeGem?" He turned the notebook page to an array of precious stones of various sizes and colors mounted in rings, earrings, and pendants.

Maria leaned in and studied the photos. "What are these?"

"We have an arrangement with the LifeGem company. We send them the ashes from cremation, and they use heat and heavy pressure to create a LifeGem. It lasts forever, and you can wear the jewelry so that Ava is always with you."

"There are different colors and sizes?" Maria asked.

"Yes. Depending upon the heat and pressure, the company can make yellow, green, blue, and clear white. In addition, they can vary the sizes from a quarter-caret to a full three carets."

"Are they expensive?" Adam asked. The roses and daylilies on the table smelled sickly sweet. Some red and white petals had dropped on the table from drooping stems. Adam adjusted himself in the chair, crossed his ankles, and clasped his hands together, interlocking his fingers. Well, here we go. Here comes the sales pressure, he thought.

"Well," said Mr. McClaren, turning the page. "This one-quarter caret green stone is three thousand; this one caret yellow one is ten thousand; and this blue rectangle shape, a full three carets, is twenty-five thousand. So, any one of these would honor Ava, don't you think?"

Maria shook her head and pointed at the blue one, the three-caret rectangular gem. "That's the one we want. I want it mounted on a white gold ring."

Mr. McClaren took a breath and spoke softly. "You realize that this cost is in addition to the cremation costs, right?"

Adam inhaled a deep breath and let it out slowly. "So, about twenty-seven thousand altogether?"

"Yes, plus the state sales tax at seven percent."

"Well, McClaren, you sure saw us coming—do you make this much on every baby death?"

They gray-haired man offered a reverent dip of his head. "I'm sorry for your loss and the sadness you feel. I'm aware that this is a difficult time for you but rest assured that our job is to perform a service, not fleece people. This LifeGem seems to be Maria's choice."

"Yes," Maria said, slapping the table. "That's what we want."

"I don't know," Adam squirmed. "Do you offer financing?"

"No, I'm sorry," McClaren said.

Maria scowled at Adam. "Excuse us for a minute." She motioned for Adam to join her in the hallway. They stepped around a corner. "This is what I want, Adam. Don't you hear me?"

"Yes, but we only have four thousand in savings. It would take me six months to make twenty-seven thousand if I was busy every day with side jobs."

"You can probably borrow it somewhere, maybe the building company or the bank. I want the blue LifeGem mounted on a white gold ring."

They returned and sat down at the table.

"We want to go ahead with cremation and the blue sapphire LifeGem," Maria said.

"If you wish," Mr. McClaren said. "I need a two-thousand-dollar deposit and the balance upon delivery. We will also need the eighteen-hundred cremation fee this week. I'll prepare the paperwork."

Adam wrote out a check for three thousand-eight-hundred dollars. "I need to transfer money from savings to cover this check," he said.

"Sure. I'll wait a couple of days before I put it in the bank."

McClaren completed the paperwork. They both signed, received copies, and told Mr. McClaren they would stay in touch and provide a short obituary for the newspapers.

Adam opened the truck door for Maria, and she climbed in. He took his seat on the driver's side, started the engine, and turned toward Maria. "I have no idea how we are going to cover this. Where are we going to come up with twenty-four thousand?"

Maria frowned and crossed her arms. “Figure it out. It’s your problem.”

“My brain is in a fog. Figuring things out right now is beyond me.”

“Okay, here’s a start. First, we’ll use my salary for everyday expenses and your truck payment. After that, we’ll deplete the savings account, and you can find extra work. Or you can talk with your father and see if the Trustee can let loose of some money.”

“The Trustee?”

“Sure. We will need money for Ava’s funeral and grief counseling. Those are medical expenses, and your settlement includes all medical costs related to your accident. I’ll bet you can convince your father to go along with that. It won’t cost him anything.”

“I haven’t seen him for a long time. I don’t know if I can face him. He should’ve died.”

“Well, he didn’t die, so you need to go make the best of it.”

“I hate it, but I’ll go see him.”

Maria began sobbing and shaking. She dropped her face into her hands, moving her head back and forth. Adam went inside and brought her a paper cup of water. “Drink some, Maria. It will help.” She slapped it out of his hand. “I don’t want water, and I don’t want you. I want my baby. Take me home.”

5

By choice, Adam had not seen his father for two years. Neither cared much for the other. Edward Young was disabled, badly scarred, and confined to a wheelchair in a care center without any discernable future. Like his father's, Adam's lower legs had also been deeply burned. The many surgeries since the accident had resulted in ongoing pain that he dealt with it every day. Alcohol helped some, and OxyContin helped some. Nothing helped completely. Adam's mind and body had both come to associate his father with pain. Edward was the cause of the pain, and his visage loomed in Adam's consciousness whenever pain radiated throughout his thoughts and actions. The association of his father with pain had been born in anger and nurtured in resentment. Adam's steady irritation helped him carry the pain, but the anger robbed his energy and focus and created a layer of darkness and confusion between his intentions and actions. His ongoing pain haunted him, gnawed at his sleep, and led him through his life as though he were being towed by a beast of burden.

Adam parked his truck under a shade tree in the parking lot. White billowy clouds gathered above the Sandia Mountains as if the clouds were alive and protecting the sun-bleached peaks from any malevolent forces that might be at work. Two crows jumped and flapped and fought over a shiny aluminum gum wrapper. Their "caw-caw-caw" sounds upset the quiet surroundings until one crow flew away with the prize, and all fell quiet again.

Adam leaned his head back on the seat and closed his eyes. He'd been nine years old when it happened. His parents had taken him camping in a twenty-four-foot camping trailer in Pagosa Springs. They parked on top of a grassy hill east of town overlooking a stand of pine trees and a fast-moving stream. His mom stepped out of the car and turned to admire the view. She clapped her hands together and smiled. "This is a perfect spot. We can hear the stream, but it's not too loud for sleeping, and the view is breathtaking!"

"I'm glad you like this place," said his dad. "I thought you would. Adam and I will gather some wood for a campfire, and we'll get our fishing gear ready for the morning."

When they got back, his father built a fire, then wrapped some new potatoes in an aluminum foil packet and put them in the ashes to roast. His mom opened a couple of windows to air out the camper and heated chili she had frozen earlier. Adam laid out marshmallows and Hershey bars on the kitchen counter to make s'mores after dinner. They ate quietly, enjoying the views and the nightfall that crept over the trees.

Adam took charge of the s'mores. He and his dad cut some branches off a nearby tree, and Adam roasted the marshmallows. "These are wonderful," said his mom, smiling and hugging Adam. "You are certainly handy to have on a camping trip."

They played scrabble as the evening wore on, and Edward talked about the finer points of catching trout from the stream. At nine-thirty, just before going to bed, Adam asked his father for some hot chocolate. So, his dad fired up the propane stove, heated some milk, and stirred in five dripping tablespoons of Hershey's chocolate syrup.

"Thanks, Dad, this is good," Adam said. He downed the hot chocolate, crawled into his father's hand-me-down sleeping bag, and bunched up his favorite pillow that his mother had brought. The bag was over six feet long so Adam could nestle down inside. The musty old fabric reminded him of the smell when they open their spare bedroom closet.

About twenty minutes later, his mom walked to the stove. She whispered so as not to wake Adam, but he heard her. "I think I'll make some tea. Would you like some?"

His dad stood up. "No thanks. I'm going to tend the campfire and walk around a bit."

She struck a kitchen match to light a burner, and suddenly there was a loud whoosh, almost an explosion, and the stove, her nightgown, and her slippers erupted in flames. His father had not turned the propane off all the way. It had been leaking for twenty minutes, settling on the cooktop and the floor. As his mother screamed, his dad beat on the flames with a couple of bath towels. Then his mom's hair caught on fire, then the curtains and his father's sweatpants and hoodie.

Adam had twisted in the sleeping bag, and he couldn't get out as the stuffing caught fire. He struggled to escape the flannel lining. His dad grabbed him, pulled him out of the trailer, and rolled him in the wet grass to put out the flames. He peeled the burning sleeping bag away from Adam's legs, and then he ran back into the burning trailer to pull out Margaret. The heat was too intense, and the skin on his arms was afire as he let her go in the doorway. He fell out of the trailer and then rolled in the grass to extinguish the flames of his burning clothes. Several people came running from other campsites, but by then, the trailer was burning brightly, lighting up the moonless night and sending embers high into the starlit sky.

When the sheriff and a volunteer fire truck arrived, the trailer was smoldering ashes. Adam's mother was dead, his father was almost dead from burns, and flames had burned Adam's legs almost to the bone.

"We need a couple of ambulances here," the sheriff said on his radio. "This is a horrible accident. It looks like three people all burned up." Two ambulances and four EMTs transported the family to the Pagosa Springs hospital. Margaret was pronounced dead on arrival. The ER doctor sedated Adam and his father, and the following day they were transported to the Presbyterian burn unit in Albuquerque. It all happened in a whirlwind, and confusion and otherworldliness dogged both Edward and Adam for several days, abetted by a haze of pain and opiates.

Then, one evening, when they seemed conscious enough to understand, the burn unit physician let them know that Margaret had died in the fire. Stunned and broken-hearted, both reverted to blank stares and intermittent moans from the ever-present agony of their injuries. pain every day, sometimes intense and other times low-level, but always there.

Volunteers had helped Adam and his father attend Margaret's memorial service. They were in wheelchairs and barely conscious from pain medication. The casket was closed. Adam felt as though he was underwater, separated from the reality of her funeral, struggling to breathe, wondering if God had decided that he and his family were unworthy. His mother's death created a profound absence in his heart as acute now, at age thirty-four, as he'd felt it as a child of nine. And now, to lose Ava…

Adam opened his eyes and shivered as he pushed the memories away and swallowed hard. Anger and resentment forced their way up into his throat, and he gritted his teeth and slammed his fist on the steering wheel. He took a couple of deep breaths, got out of the truck, and walked to the lobby of the care center. That no-good son-of-a-bitch blames me, Adam thought. If he dares to say one more time, "If you hadn't wanted hot chocolate, your mother would be alive," I'll wipe the floor with him once and for all. How could that bastard blame a nine-year-old boy for his own mother's death? Adam wondered. From what he'd heard, his father had left one of the stove burners partially on—at least according to the EMT said in the ambulance. "One match was all it took," he'd said.

Both father and son had their medical expenses covered by financial settlements from the camper trailer company, stove, propane tank, and valve manufacturer. The insurance payments projected a lifetime of disability for Edward and years of annual surgeries on Adam's legs to keep up with his growth. In addition, he had numerous skin grafts from his thighs and buttocks to supply the extra skin needed for his lengthening calves and shins. A third-party Trustee managed the settlement money. The Trustee created investment accounts, managed the earnings, and paid out funds for Edward's residence and treatment at the care center and Adam's surgeries and follow-up medical care. That was the resource Maria thought they should use.

Adam sat at a table in the dayroom, and his father sat in his wheelchair across from him. A shadow of the energetic father Adam had known as a kid, this man appeared shriveled and gray before his time.

"What brings you here" Edward asked with a grunt. Haven't seen you for two years. You must need something."

"Your granddaughter Ava died. The Medical Investigator said it was a SIDS death, nobody's fault."

Edward gave a short nod. "Who found her?"

"I did. I watched a football game, and when I checked on the baby, she had stopped breathing. Maria was at the store with Lucas."

"That's bad news. How is Maria doing?"

"Not well. She's withdrawn and blames me for Ava's death."

"Was there something you could've done?"

"No, it just happened. No one is to blame."

"How about CPR or mouth-to-mouth? Did you try those?"

"CPR until the paramedics arrived."

"I can see why Maria would blame you. She comes home to a daughter who died, and you are the adult on site. This whole thing reminds me of our accident and your mother's death. Being responsible is not one of your strengths. Are you ever going to amount to anything?"

Adam took a breath and waited for his father to blame him, but Edward looked down at his hands and did not continue. He must have sensed the silent communication that fought to appear from under Adam's bitterness.

"I don't know if our marriage can make it through this," Adam finally said.

"You should probably prepare to be alone. Most marriages don't last through the loss of a child. She's always going to blame you, so get ready."

It was Adam's turn to nod. He gazed up at the ceiling. "We went to the funeral home. Maria selected a LifeGem as a daily memory."

"A LifeGem? Sounds weird. Never heard of such a thing."

"There's a company that makes jewelry from the ashes of cremation—'cremains,' the funeral director called them. They put the ashes under extreme pressure and make stones that look like diamonds, rubies, and sapphires."

"Well, what do you know. You learn something new every day."

"The company does the same thing for dogs and cats. As a result, their market is growing like crazy. They even make cat earrings."

"Cat earrings? No shit?"

"Yeah, they are shaped like a cat and have a stone for the cat's eye."

"So, they have a cat's eye created from the ashes of a cat?"

"Yup, quite a business, huh? Maria chose a three-carat blue sapphire ring. I need twenty-five thousand dollars."

Edward whistled. "Wow. It sounds like someone saw you coming! Do you think, even for a minute, that I have that much money? You know better. I have a weekly allowance for bullshit purchases, and that's it. Do you want a candy bar, a soft drink, or shaving soap? That's what my budget provides—bullshit purchases.

"No, the money wouldn't come from you," Adam said. "I'm going to ask the Trustee for the money, and I want you to support my request."

"Will that cut into my medical care payments? I don't want to end up on the street. And, by the way, I don't think much of a twenty-five thousand sapphire ring made from burned-up baby ashes. Come on, Adam. This idea is ridiculous."

Adam shrugged. "It's what Maria wants. I'm going to tell the Trustee that the money is for medical care since it will help with my grief and the health of my marriage. After all, my daughter is dead. If you support me, I think he'll write checks to the funeral home and a counselor. Maria is going to need help. Probably me too."

Edward picked at a fingernail and chewed his lip.

"Tell you what. I'll sleep on it and let you know tomorrow. Call me after lunch."

"I need the money. That's all there is to it. So don't screw with me. We have it, and I need it. Don't you understand?"

"Yes, but I want to sleep on it. That's a lot of money."

Adam got up out of his chair, put his hands on the table, and leaned close to his father. "Well, don't die in your sleep." Then, head down and hands balled in fists, he strode out to his truck and got in. "I guess it is true," he mumbled to himself. "Every family is miserable in its own way and having an asshole for a father is our way."

Adam shook an OxyContin from his prescription bottle and washed it down with vodka from a pint he grabbed from under the seat. He smelled electricity in the air—ozone, announcing a storm. More clouds marched over the Sandias, a brisk wind came up, trees bent, leaves fluttered, and the rain and hail came. The noisy clatter of hailstones on the truck rooftop made Adam feel trapped inside tin can. He waited a while for the rain to subside, then picked up Lucas at school, and went home to cook dinner. He welcomed Maria home with a small glass of hearty burgundy, her favorite wine.

"I saw my father and asked for his support for my money request."

Maria pursed her lips. "Any chance he was helpful?"

"I told him there wouldn't change his healthcare—that all he had to do was support, and all he had to do was support my request for grief counseling and funeral expenses, including the LifeGem."

"Did he say he would help?"

"No, he said he needed to sleep on it, but I think he'll come around. He just wanted to piss me off, which, of course, he did. What an asshole. He will die angry."

6

The gray, overcast dawn emerged from the darkness and peeked through the kitchen window. Maria had not slept and paced through the house most of the night. Adam had tossed and turned on the couch, got up a few times, but could not get to sleep either. He heard the coffee pot brewing and shuffled to the kitchen in his gym shorts. Maria was sitting at the table. Her eyes were red, and she ran her fingers through her tousled hair. She got up and poured herself a cup of coffee. "This is too much, Adam."

Adam nodded. "Yes, this is hard," he said, "but we'll find a path through it. We always have."

"You don't understand. I feel like everything is coming down around me, and my stomach is in knots. Every day gets darker."

"Should I look for a grief counselor?"

"No. You should move out, and you should stop drinking. Last night, when I put Lucas to bed, he said that when you drink too much, he gets scared, and he doesn't know what to do."

"Move out? But Maria, we need each other."

"Maybe so, but right now, I need to be alone."

"But why?"

My bereavement leave is only three days, and then I need to go back to work, and I need all my energy. Being with you is a lot of work."

"A lot of work?"

Maria took a deep breath, folding her arms in front of her. "When I had Ava, it was okay. Now, being with you is overwhelming. It takes all my energy."

Adam gaped at her. "But I need you, Maria."

"Perhaps, but I can't be around your drinking and pain pills. You are an addict, and you need to take care of yourself before taking care of this family. I'm at my limit, Adam."

"What about Lucas?"

"You should come and get him for school, pick him up after school, and make dinner."

Adam gazed out the window. The sunrise pushed through the clouds and burned away the gray, leaving blue skies on the eastern horizon. Soon the sun would rise above the Sandia Mountains, and Lucas would wake up.

"So, you mean I don't sleep here?"

"I can imagine you might need to sleep over occasionally, but not with me."

Adam glared and clenched his teeth. "So, I should move all my stuff out?"

"At least take your clothes and things out of my bedroom."

He nodded toward the bedroom door. "Your bedroom? That's our bedroom and has been since we moved in here."

Maria put her hands on her hips. "Well, things have changed. I need time alone, and it is now my private sanctuary."

Adam slammed his fist on the table. "What will we say to Lucas? This will tear him up."

"Tell him we are too sad about Ava for us to be together. We need some time apart, and we love him very much."

"He'll be awake soon. Why don't you tell him? You're the one who wants to be separated."

"We can both talk with him. I know that if I don't get back to work, I'll come out of my skin. So maybe you could stay with Ryan since he lives alone."

Lucas came into the kitchen dragging his blanket. He sidled up next to Adam. "Are you and Mom fighting?"

"No, we are not fighting," Maria said. "But we are talking about some changes."

Lucas frowned. "Changes?"

Adam pulled out a chair. "Here, Lucas. Sit down, and I'll get you some cereal and orange juice."

Maria reached out and put her hand on Lucas's arm. "We both love you dearly. You know that, right?"

"I know, Mom."

"We are both very sad about Ava, and we need some time apart to get better."

Adam poured a glass of orange juice, then put a bowl of Cheerios in front of Lucas. "I will still take you to school and make dinner," Adam said. Then, after Mom gets home, I'll go to my place to sleep."

"Where is your place, Dad?"

"I haven't got a place yet, but I'll be looking today."

Lucas began crying. "This is a bad idea."

Adam put his arm around him. "You need to be strong. This is a hard time for all of us. I think it is a bad idea, too, but we all need to help each other get through this, and Mom needs time alone. I'll see you every day."

"What about Saturday and Sunday? Can we watch TV together?"

"You can come to work with me on Saturdays, and we can hang out some on Sundays."

He looked at Maria. "Right?"

"Sounds like that will work." She stood up and hugged Lucas from behind, resting her chin on the top of his head. "When you take your bath, ask Dad to wash your hair."

"Okay, Mom, I will."

"It will be okay," Adam said. "Whatever happens, it will be okay." He turned and watched the sun as it moved above the Sandia Mountains, casting shadows and bright patches in the cedar and pinon trees. "There's always hope, Lucas. Remember that. There's always hope."

7

Ryan Withers and Adam came to work for Albuquerque Constructors three years ago in April. Though hired for different tasks, Adam quickly became Ryan's craftsman of choice to take care of customer callbacks and other complaints. Adam had a charming way with people, especially women, and his competence impressed the men he worked with on construction issues. Ryan had previously sold health insurance, so he was trained in public relations and marketing and creating perceived value. With his linebacker build, Ryan could be imposing, but his smile radiated beyond his round face and usually put people at ease. If his smile wasn't effective, then his sheer size seemed to ward off inappropriate, complaining behavior from customers. His girlfriends over the years had come to see him as a big teddy bear with hazel eyes, ready for hugs and cuddling. His muscular arms could hold a woman with gentle strength, making her feel protected and admired.

Adam pulled his truck under the carport and knocked at the door. It was about five pm, and Ryan had gotten home a little while ago. He opened the door. "Hey, Adam. Welcome to my humble abode."

"Thanks. This whole thing sucks, but I'm grateful that you don't mind if I stay with you for a while. Our separation probably won't last long, and I'll be going back home soon."

"I hope so, but you should know you're welcome."

Adam began carrying boxes. He hung up a few shirts and pants in the closet, emptied a suitcase of T-shirts, underwear, and socks, unpacked a box of books, and then brought in a couple of toolboxes.

"Is it okay if I leave my tools in here? I worry they'd get stolen out of my truck."

"Sure. Take whatever square footage you need, and I have two assigned parking spaces for my apartment. Your truck should be safe right outside the door and next to mine."

The last thing Adam brought in was a twelve-pack of Budweiser. He pulled two cans loose and put the rest in the refrigerator. "I brought us beer," he said, extending one to Ryan.

"No thanks. You may remember that I don't drink. Although, to be honest, I'd prefer we don't keep alcohol in the house."

"No problem, Adam said. I guess I forgot." He frowned, retrieved the rest of the twelve-pack, took it out to his truck, and stashed it in the back under a black, plastic tarp.

"I'm going to order pizza," Ryan said. "Is sausage and mushroom okay with you?"

"That would be great."

The pizza came. Ryan turned on the TV, watching the news while they ate.

"Shall we check out the sports channel?" Adam asked.

"Adam, you know I'm your friend, right?"

"Right."

"And you know I care about your health."

"Yes."

"Then, I want to talk with you about substance abuse."

"You mean my pain pills? Don't forget, Ryan, I've had prescriptions for pain pills ever since I was nine years old. The surgeons say that the scar pain from my burns and skin grafts is unremitting, and I have to live with it."

"Yes, I understand. It's not so much about the pain meds as it is alcohol. You continually self-medicate with alcohol on top of your pain pill. The combination can be deadly. You seem to drink more when you're anxious. Have you noticed?"

Adam nodded, trying not to sound defensive. "A shot of vodka settles my nerves. Since Ava died, my nerves have been ragged, and now it's even worse because Maria wants us to live separately. It all sucks."

"I get it, but I worry that the alcohol is like a tripwire, and when you stumble, it will be bad. I don't want to be taking you to the hospital with a stroke. That would end your career in construction. And you could bleed from your esophagus. That's a death sentence."

"Don't worry so much, Ryan. I have it under control. I only drink occasionally to calm down the anxiety."

"You might think so. But the alcohol mixed with the OxyContin makes you more anxious—and paranoid, and angry, and on edge. So, you should do one or the other, but not both."

"I can moderate, and I will, as soon as we get past the memorial for Ava."

"Well, in the meantime, out of respect for my sobriety, I have a rule that there is no alcohol in my house, not even a beer. So, anyone who wants to drink must leave and go to a bar or somewhere else. You can't drink here, and you can't be drunk here. Is that clear?"

"It is, but I think you are way too severe. I might need just a swallow or two to calm down after work or to get to sleep. What should I do about that?"

"You can do lots of things. You can learn to meditate, or you can go to the gym and workout, but you can't drink in my house."

Adam sighed. "Okay, I've got it. I won't be here that long anyway because I think Maria and I will be able to get back together after the memorial service when Ava's death is behind us."

"I hope that's true, for your sake. Now let's check out your pockets and belongings. I want all the alcohol gone."

They went into the bedroom. Adam took the one pint of vodka from his bag and handed it over to Ryan. "That's all I have here."

Ryan tipped his head. "You'd better not be lying to me. You know the saying. How do you know an alcoholic is lying? His mouth is moving."

Adam felt his temper rising. "I'm not lying, damn it. I'm not a liar."

"If you are, and if I find alcohol, friend, or no friend, you'll have to move out, and Maria will find out why. She's no fool, and she can't live with you the way you are now."

"What do you expect me to do?"

"We can go to the gym in the evenings—I can give you a guest card—and work out hard enough that you're tired. Then we can sit in the steam room and sweat out the poison. When we get home, you'll fall asleep right away."

"I might have a drink or two elsewhere before I come here."

"Hey, that's your call. If you want to keep risking your marriage, and for that matter, your job, drink however much you want wherever you want except here. It's your life to screw up. You're the boss of your misery."

Adam sat heavily on the bed and dropped his head into his hands. He cried softly. "I don't know if I can do it," he whispered to Ryan. "I just don't know." From behind him—almost, it seemed, with living breath sounds—long shadows crept over his back and fell onto the floor before him, as though they were searching for a place to hide from the fading light coming through the window. "I just don't know."

8

Ryan received a callback list each day and made appointments to visit homeowners. He went by himself to verify the complaints and the work, and then Adam or another finish carpenter would meet him at the house to perform the job. The issues were typically annoying but not monumental mistakes. Most of the time, Adam adjusted doors, trimmed out and replaced sloppy baseboard joinery, made sure he keyed all the entry doors alike, caulked the edges between the cabinets and walls and the trim carpentry and walls, tightened up plumbing joints against drips, adjusted bifold closet doors, replaced defective cabinet hinges, and touched up the grout in floor tile and tile backsplash. If he had time left in the day, he would help homeowners with picture hanging, shelf paper in the kitchen, window shades, installing shower curtains, and sweeping out the garage. Homeowners typically called the office or talked with Ryan about Adam's great job. "He's a keeper," they often said. "Don't let that guy get away."

When Adam was not attending to callbacks, he was the first choice for a finish carpenter to trim out a house. Both Ryan and Adam had worked themselves up in the ranks at Albuquerque Constructors, and before long, Ryan was the supervisor of public relations and sales and was Adam's supervisor. Adam was a construction superintendent and finish carpenter. Framers were not allowed to start until Adam had laid out the house and struck chalk lines on the finished slab. When Adam did the layout, there were rarely errors, and the company owners realized his value. Because of his consistent talent, they overlooked Adam's mild impairment, even if he smelled like vodka. If he and Ryan were attending a callback, Ryan always had breath mints on hand to cover up and sweeten Adam's breath. Adam never staggered or stumbled, and customers were never the wiser.

Now, as they approached a home, Ryan gave Adam a couple of breath mints. "You know, as I've said, the day will come when you need better ways of handling your pain. As long as I've known you, you've taken Oxies for the pain in your legs, and then you added alcohol. Not good."

"Don't keep harping on me. I've been moderating some, and I've got it under control," Adam answered, begrudgingly popping a mint in his mouth. "I just can't work without my meds. The pain and anxiety are overwhelming. But I know what I'm doing. So don't worry, Ryan. I won't let you down."

"I'm not worried about that," Ryan said, shaking his head. I'm worried about you. You're going to be thirty-five next month, and I've never seen you completely sober. Sometimes I wonder what you would be like if you were not under the influence."

"I would be my old, sweet self. Nothing changes."

"Have you ever quit drinking for even a day?"

Adam had to pause to consider. "The day Maria and I were married, I didn't drink all day, not until evening, and then only a couple of drinks. After all, we were toasting."

"Have you ever been without your pills?"

"No, my prescription is pretty much a habit."

"I don't want to be offensive, but as I've said, I think you are an alcoholic. It seems driven by physical pain and psychological demons. That's what makes it hard. You have to control the constant pain somehow."

Adam snorted. "I have my share of demons—you've met my father. Edward is the demon-asshole of all times. If you needed a reason to drink, having my dad is a good reason. That's the only way I can stand to be around him."

A smiling middle-aged couple answered the door. They both had red hair and he leaned on a cane favoring his right leg. Both were dressed as if they were on their way to church except that she wore an apron and house slippers.

"Hello, thanks for coming. I see that you have your list."

Ryan held out his clipboard. "Yes, this is the list we went over last week, and today Adam is here to help take care of things. Adam, these folks are the Williams, Ruth, and Dave."

"Hello," Adam said. "It is nice to meet you. If you don't mind, I should get to work right away. This list will take most of the day."

"Let's walk through again," Ryan said. "That way, I can point out things to Adam as we go down the list."

"Sure," Dave said. "Right this way."

As Ruth, Dave, Ryan, and Adam toured the house, Ryan was careful to say out loud what he had offered in the way of repairs so Adam would know what required his attention care and how much. Ryan had learned to set expectations ahead of time so the repairs and adjustments always matched what he said the company would do. He always pointed out that dissimilar materials could change somewhat and cause separations. For example, when an exposed beam was next to sheetrock, weather changes would cause the wooden beam to twist slightly or pull loose from existing caulking. Those areas, he would caution, require maintenance on an annual basis. He typically left a tube of the correct caulking and showed homeowners how to strip out the old caulking and put down a new bead.

"I'll get going on the list," Adam said. "I'll start with adjusting the bedroom doors. They always move a little with the first change of weather."

"Okay," said Ryan. "I'll leave it to you and be back after lunch to check on things. I've got some other folks to visit."

Dave followed Adam as he set to work.

"Somebody should have installed these doors correctly in the first place," Dave said. "Who hangs these doors and puts on the hardware for you? They need more training."

"The company buys the doors prehung and predrilled. So, I installed the doors and frames as units and then put on the hardware. Unfortunately, it is not unusual for the doors to move a little after they hang for a while, especially with weather changes—the rain we've had. Plus, the hinge screws sometimes loosen a little."

"It hasn't rained that much," Dave said. "Looks like you screwed up when you installed them."

Adam answered in an even tone. "Not to worry. I'll adjust the doors, and they'll be working fine before I leave."

"I guess you've heard this before, but it is a lot easier to do things right the first time. That's what I stress at the plant."

"What kind of work do you do?"

"I'm the manager of a cabinet manufacturing company. I supervise twenty employees and handle quality control. The cabinets have to get by me to get out the door."

"That's impressive," Adam said. "Finish carpentry and cabinet making are nearly lost arts in our building culture. So many times, things get slapped together by rough and ready laborers."

"Yeah, like these doors?"

"No, not like these doors. I'm careful with my installation. Put a level on that doorframe, and you'll see the bubble is perfect."

"We paid a lot of money for this house," Dave said. "I expect things to be done right or fixed."

"By the end of the day, all the doors will stay open wherever you leave them and close without a squeak. I'll tighten the hinges as well. You'll be pleased."

"I'm not sure about that. Every time I open or close one of these doors, I'll think about the poor workmanship. It takes away from our enjoyment of the house."

Adam took a deep breath. "Please understand. These are normal adjustments. Adjustments are part of the construction process. You've already paid for my work when you bought the house."

"If that's true, then we overpaid."

"I'll let you know when I've completed the doors, and then you can check them out."

"I'd rather watch you work."

"Dave, it makes me nervous with you standing over my shoulder. But I'm a professional, and I'll let you know when it's time to look things over. So just let me do my work, please."

"I hope you don't mind. First, I'm going to take videos of your work and offer comments along the way. After that, I may need to show your shoddy work to an inspector or an attorney."

Adam struggled as his voice rose. "Shoddy? There's nothing shoddy about my work. You're out of line. I'm one of the better finish carpenters and construction superintendents in Albuquerque. You are the recipient of some outstanding work by a good company with good warranties and outstanding references. Now let me get to work."

Dave left the hallway and returned a few minutes later with a video camera. He turned it on and focused on a door latch Adam was adjusting. Adam took the hardware out of the door, tweaked it a bit, so the lever handles matched perfectly on both sides, and then replaced the hardware back and checked the closing mechanism. Finally, he tried the privacy lock to make sure it worked and would open with an emergency tool he stored above the door on the door trim.

"Did you get a video of this one?" Adam asked. "It's right on the money."

"No, it's still off a little. The handle on the inside is about a sixteenth of an inch from horizontal. Looks odd."

"Most people, I'd say ninety-nine out of one hundred, would see this door and hardware as a perfect installation. One-sixteenth of an inch is clearly within tolerance, and the door and frame are true and level."

"Should I report the error to Ryan or call the office?"

"There is no error. Show it to Ryan and see what he says, but I'm done with this one."

Adam continued with his work, adjusting all the bedroom entry doors and the bifold closet doors. Dave trailed along behind him and videotaped each of Adam's tasks.

"Does the company have any other call-back people?"

"No, Ryan and I are the team. He reviews the issues with homeowners, decides on a plan, and then shows up and does the work. Why do you ask?"

"I want to request someone else. You don't seem to understand the level of excellence I expect. But unfortunately, I'm not going to be able to sign off on most of these things, especially the finish carpentry."

Adam spoke slowly and patiently. "Well, there's no one else available, so this level of excellence is what you will receive. You can't nit-pick these things to death. Doors open, doors close. Bifold doors fold open and unfold to close. If they are true and level and the hardware is correct, then that is what we call complete. The work you see is what it is, and that's what you get."

Just then, the doorbell rang, and Ryan pushed open the door. "Hello everyone, how are things going?"

"Not well," Dave said. Your man here is not performing at the level of excellence that I expect in an expensive house, and he's argumentative."

Ryan looked at Adam and raised his eyebrows. He smiled straight into the conflict. Ruth left her kitchen tasks and scurried into another room.

"Adam does great work," Ryan said. "We get compliments and good reviews all the time. So, I can't imagine your concerns."

"Come with me," Dave said. "Let me show you some shoddy workmanship."

They walked down the hall, and Dave pointed at one of the bedroom doors and opened it.

"See what I mean?"

"Sorry, I don't see," Ryan said. "It opens, its level, the hardware functions, and the hinges are tight. What is the problem?"

"Well, if you paid attention, you would see that the handle on the inside is off horizontal. So, it dips a little."

"By a sixteenth of an inch," Adam said. "He's freakin' upset about a sixteenth of an inch."

"I expect excellence," Dave said.

Ryan put the door between his knees, grabbed both handles simultaneously, and twisted so that they were perfectly aligned. "There you go, Dave. Now it's excellent."

"All you did was bend it. I'm afraid I will have to ask you to replace it with a new one."

"Let's continue," Ryan said. "The handle is not bent. It's adjusted."

They walked through the house, checking off the items on the callback list until they came to the kitchen.

"I want these cabinet doors aligned," Dave said. "Some of the double doors do not meet precisely."

Adam set about adjusting hinges, tightening screws, and aligning the doors. He used a level on the top of pairs of doors and on the single doors.

"Looking good," Ryan said. "You're right. When they installed these doors, they should have adjusted them at the time. They look great now."

"Not so fast," Dave said. The cabinet knobs are a little off on these four doors, which is an unrecoverable error. See how the knobs on the left are higher than the knobs on the right? You will need to order four new doors since these are already drilled for the knobs. You'll never be able to patch the holes without them showing."

"No," Ryan said. "That's just the light from the track lights and the light through the window. You always get a few shadows."

"Sorry, I need new doors and new knobs, and while you're at it, let's get all new hardware for the bedroom doors."

"Dave," Ryan said, "we're doing everything we can to make things right here, but you also need to be reasonable. We are not building furniture here. Your home is a house of good quality, and that's what you get. We want to help, but you need to meet us halfway."

"I know what I want. I know what I expect. I was worried, so that's why I had the title company withhold ten percent of the price until the callback list was complete. You will not receive one dime of that money until I am satisfied with your work."

"I'm sorry that you are disappointed," Ryan said. "We're doing our best to make things right."

"Well, you are not doing enough. Ruth, could you come in here?"

Ruth came into the room and looked down at her shoes. She wore her hair tied back in a bun, and her apron was soiled from the chocolate on her hands from making chocolate chip cookie dough, remnants of which were still on the kitchen counter. On her feet she wore pink house shoes adorned with white rabbits.

"Ruth, tell Ryan how disappointed you are in the installation of these cabinets."

Ruth raised her head. Her face was gray around her eyes, and she frowned.

"Ryan," she said, pointing. "I am disappointed in the kitchen cabinets." Then she grabbed her apron with both hands and hurried away.

"See?" Dave said. "I told you. We are both disappointed."

"Yes, I see," said Ryan. "Let's be reasonable. If we do agree to replace all the hardware and the cabinet doors and knobs, that would only be about fifteen hundred dollars at the most. You have thirty-four thousand dollars held in escrow, and the company needs it for payroll and other operating expenses. Let's be reasonable. So, keep three-thousand dollars in escrow and release the other thirty-one thousand. That way, you are still covered. We'll check with the owners about replacing things, and I'll get back to you tomorrow."

"Sorry, I'm not releasing any money until you complete everything according to my satisfaction. I don't care how long it takes." He pointed at Adam. "And I would prefer someone else to do the work. This man's work is shoddy, and he has a bad attitude."

Adam gritted his teeth. Ryan raised his hand to caution Adam in his response, but Adam had had enough.

"I'm proud of my work, Dave," Adam said. "When you find someone better, I'd like to meet him. This is as good as it gets, and dozens of people have hired me to work on their homes. I don't want to get confrontational, Dave, but the truth is you are out of line."

Dave raised his cane and pointed it at Adam. "We'll see about that. You guys need to leave. I may just hire other people to complete these callbacks and pay them out of the escrow I've withheld. When I'm satisfied, then your company will get the change."

"Your purchase agreement expressly forbids that," Ryan said. "We do the work with our people. We are the contractor. You are the customer. You don't hire people. We do."

"Then, call nine-one-one and get the police out here to arrest me because that is what I'm going to do. Tell the police they can charge me with the crime of fixing my own house. By the time your management and lawyers get around to doing something, I will have hired my help and paid them, and the house will be the way I expect it to be."

Ryan went over to Adam and took his arm. "Let's get your tools packed up and get back to the office. This conversation is no longer productive."

"That's right," Adam said. "It's no longer productive because that fucking Dave is a nit-picking asshole."

Ryan gripped his arm harder. "Easy does it."

"Yes, we don't want to add assault to shoddy workmanship," Dave said, grinning. "Watch your mouth, Adam. You're starting to annoy me."

Ryan wrapped his giant-sized his arm over Adam's shoulder and pushed Adam toward the door. "Come on, it's time we leave. Other people will sort this out."

At the door, Adam turned. "This is not a threat," Adam said to Dave. "But if I ever see you on neutral ground, I will whip your ass until you can't crawl home. You get the prize for the worst fucking customer we've ever had. Do you want to fix something? You can fix this." Adam grabbed his framing hammer from his toolbox, and before Ryan could intercept him, he swung the hammer and smacked a knob on a cabinet door, putting a massive hole through the door and shattering the shelf and plates and wine goblets. The door fell on the floor in splinters, and the knob bounced on the tile floor and disappeared under the refrigerator. "Now you don't have to worry about that knob, you piece of shit. I should take that knob and put it where the sun don't shine."

Dave dropped his cane and covered his head with both hands. "Out, out, get out of my house, or I'm calling the police." He took out his cellphone. Ryan grabbed the back of Adam's neck, forcefully ushering him out the door, picking up Adam's tools with his other hand. He pushed Adam into his truck. "Hey, friend, what was that? Have you lost your mind?"

"He's an asshole, Ryan."

"I know, but you blew up. You lost it. Now you're an asshole."

" He's been harping on me all morning, following me around with a danm camera. Can't say I'm sorry."

"Sorry wouldn't be enough anyway, Adam. You may have cost the company thirty-thousand dollars with your big mouth."

"He pissed me off big time."

"I can see that. But let's face it. You lost it. You could lose your job and cost me mine. That's the last thing we need right now. We're done for the day. You're too drunk to work."

9

The day after the blowup with Dave Williams, Ryan and Adam met with Rocky and Jim Olander, owners of the company. They sat around a conference table with mugs of coffee and the unrolled floor plans of Dave and Ruth's home. Jim Olander, the financial manager, used a red pencil to mark the areas corresponding to the callback list.

"I looked things over," Ryan said, "and it seems to me that everything he's upset about could be fixed for under twenty-five hundred dollars, even if we hired another company."

"That seems about right," Jim said. "There's over thirty-one thousand in escrow, so it is unfair. I called our attorney, and he will file a contractor's lien on the house by the end of the day. We'll keep the lien in place until he pays. Our attorney said to offer him a check for three-thousand dollars so Dave can hire whomever he wants. We just want Dave out of our hair."

"I'm the one who takes care of callbacks," Adam said. "That asshole should not have free reign to hire another company."

"You've taken care of enough on this one, Adam," Rocky said. "It's going to cost us no matter what, and you've messed things up beyond all recognition. Every heard of FUBAR? Well, that's what you did. You're typically quite charming with customers, but you lost it on this one. I understand you are grieving, but you are one angry young man. Stay away from that house, Adam."

"You should not go back there," Ryan chimed in. "I'm not even sure if I should show up myself. Rocky, maybe you are the peacemaker on this one."

"We should all stay away," Jim said. "I'm guessing Dave is not one to let up or give in. He has to win to be satisfied."

"So, what do we do?" Adam asked.

"Well, the first thing we do is send you home. You've been like a loose cannon for the past couple of weeks. I know you are drinking on the job. We accepted you on board, knowing that you had a prescription for pain pills for your legs. We didn't say you could drink on the job, though, and your problem is getting worse."

"Go home?"

Jim paused and took a slow breath. "You've had a rough time, Adam. You need to take your bereavement leave, a few days of vacation time, and find a counselor to help you with your drinking problem. We are deeply sorry for your loss of little Ava—we can't even imagine the pain—but you need some time to take care of yourself. Your need to mourn Ava's death and get control over your drinking."

"Am I fired?"

"No, let's just say you're taking a break—you're on leave. You can't be around customers in this condition. If this happens again, though, you will be fired. Think of this incident as a wakeup call."

"I'm one of your most talented people," Adam said. "It will hurt the company if you fire me."

"Yes, it could," Rocky said. "But you may have cost us thirty-thousand dollars today, and that hurts the company big time."

Jim settled back in his chair. "Ryan, I think we'll let the attorney handle all the conversations with Dave and Ruth. He can offer them money, offer another company to do the work, and call in an inspector from the Construction Industries Division to give an opinion. It might cost us four or five-thousand-dollars altogether, but after ten years and two hundred customers, I can see that Dave and Ruth are people we should not engage with. Let the legal eagle take care of them."

"I agree," Rocky said, "although it is tempting to help assholes like Dave to learn some manners."

"I don't mind talking with them," Ryan said.

"No, we are walking away from this one," Jim said. "No further contact. If Dave Williams calls, refer him to our attorney."

"If that's all," Ryan said, "I'll see to it that we reassign Adam's callbacks and that he gets squared away. He's staying with me for a while."

"With you?" Rocky said.

"Maria and I are separated temporarily," Adam said. "She's so sad and worn out from Ava's death that she wants to be alone for a while. I don't think it will last too long, and then we'll be back together."

Rocky and Jim stood up. Jim put his hand on Adam's shoulder. "Is there anything we can do? You've been through hell these past weeks."

"Well, you could call Maria and tell her that Ava's death is not my fault. She thinks I screwed up and could have saved her. While you're at it, tell her my heart is broken, too. It's our daughter that died, not just hers.'"

"Didn't the doctor at the OMI rule it was a SIDS death?"

"Yes, that's what they said."

"I guess Maria doesn't believe them."

"I guess," Adam said. "Please don't fire me. I'll get things together soon."

"I think you will," Rocky said. "You're strong and determined, and shall we say, stubborn as a mule."

Adam drove his pickup, and Ryan followed in the company pickup. They parked under the carport by Ryan's place, out of direct sunlight but next to a stand of sunflowers waving in the breeze. Ryan unlocked the door, and Adam carried his backpack into the spare bedroom. He took a pain pill, chased it down with a couple of swallows of vodka from a pint in his pack, stretched out on the bed, and promptly fell asleep. When he awoke in the night and fished around for his vodka, he discovered it was gone. Ryan had no doubt found it. Adam took another pain pill and fell into a troubled sleep.

§

Maria looked out the kitchen window and saw Ryan picking a handful of white daisies from the neighbor's garden. He knocked gently at the door. She answered the door as she pulled her robe closed and cinched it with the terrycloth belt. The dark circles under her eyes did little to diminish her beauty. He handed her the daisies.

"Oh, hello, Ryan. These are lovely, thank you. Adam is at work, I think."

"No, I left him sleeping at my apartment. He's not doing well. The company sent him home because he was drinking on the job and blew up at a customer. The owners want him to stay away from work for a week or so."

"Oh, I see. Figures. He screwed up again. Would you like to come in for coffee?"

"I've got time for a cup. Are you sure I'm not interrupting?"

"Interrupting? No, I'm alone here and wouldn't mind some company."

They sat down at the table. Maria poured two cups of coffee and set out cream and sugar. "I can't remember. You take cream and sugar, right?"

"Just sugar, please. I need to maintain my sweet self." Ryan smiled, his light blue eyes twinkling. "How are you doing, Maria? I'm so, so sorry for your loss. Can I help with anything?"

"It is comforting to know that you care."

"Of course, I do. Adam is my friend, but I've always been partial to you. He's a lucky man to have married you."

"Well, I'm not lucky to have him in my life. His drinking is out of control, and he's not dependable. He could've saved Ava if he had been alert."

"You know that's probably not true, Maria," Ryan said gently. "She wouldn't have made any sound. Adam gave her CPR and called for help the moment he became aware something was off."

Maria shrugged, as if no words could change her mind. "I need to be alone to maintain my sanity, and Adam should learn to take care of himself."

"Are you going to get divorced?"

"I don't know, Ryan. We'll see how it goes, but unless he straightens up, there's no future for us as a family."

"I'm sorry to hear that. Let's hope Adam hears that loud, popping sound soon."

"Loud, popping sound?"

Ryan smiled bigger than his face. "You know, that sound it makes when he pulls his head out of his ass. Pardon my reference, but that's what needs to happen."

Maria felt herself smiling. "I hadn't heard that one before."

"It's an old AA saying," Ryan said.

"You go to AA meetings?"

"I used to go. I haven't been to a meeting for a couple of years now. It has been over ten years since I've had a drink." He fished in his pocket for his ten-year medallion and showed it to Maria.

"Wow, ten years. So, I gather that you don't have a problem anymore?"

"Right. I'm a non-drinker, a sober man with a happy life."

"You've never mentioned a girlfriend. Do you have one?"

"Not now. I had a girlfriend, but we called it off about a year ago. She had problems with drugs."

"And you can't be around drugs or alcohol, right?"

"I could probably handle it okay, but she had some other issues as well. She stole money out of my billfold at night."

"For drugs?"

"Yes, thought she was hiding it from me, you know, like all addicts. She thought she kept it a secret, but I knew, and so did everyone else who knew her. I offered to get her into a rehab program. That's when she packed up and left. I haven't seen her since."

"I guess a little like Adam, huh?"

"A lot like Adam. He doesn't think he has a problem. He doesn't think people know he's always impaired. But, as I said, we're waiting for the loud, popping sound."

Maria felt a whisper of cold air and noticed her robe had fallen slightly open. Ryan was staring at her ample right breast. She flushed, and pulled her robe closed. "That was awkward," she said, smiling demurely. "Wardrobe malfunction."

"Not a problem. You're beautiful, no matter what malfunctions."

Maria finished her coffee and ushered Ryan to the door. They stood quietly for a moment. She wanted to take a step back, but something kept her still.

"Would you like a hug?" Ryan asked, opening his massive arms. She watched the skin around his light blue eyes crinkle with a smile.

Maria didn't answer but settled into his arms, her head against his chest. She took deep breaths and lingered for a while, feeling his warmth. She allowed a full-frontal hug, knowing her breasts pushed against him through her robe. His hips moved toward her as she felt him becoming aroused. She took a couple of quick steps backward. "Thank you for stopping by. I appreciate your kindness and friendship."

"Sure, I'll keep in touch. Call me if you need anything or just want to talk."

"Okay and thank you for taking in Adam. I'm sure you will be a good influence."

10

On Saturday, a week before Ava's memorial on May 28th, Adam had arranged a meeting with his father and the Trustee of their medical settlements, Lawrence Olson. They met in a visitor's office at Edward's assisted living center. Since they were meeting with the Trustee, Jane Sullivan—Edward's sister-in-law and Adam's de facto mother—insisted on attending as well, to support Adam.

"This is an unusual request," Mr. Olson said. "Twenty-five thousand dollars is a lot of money for memorabilia, let alone a funeral. And, this is not for you, Adam, or you, Edward, right?"

"In a way it is for me," Adam said. "The LifeGem jewel is for my wife, Maria, and it is not just memorabilia. They form the gemstone from Ava's ashes pressed into the shape of a sapphire that lasts forever."

"A frigging waste of money," Edward said. "Why can't she have a traditional funeral? It would be cheaper."

Adam narrowed his eyes at his father, his voice tight. "Maria does not want a funeral for Ava, just a memorial gathering at our house. The LifeGem is not your issue. It won't affect you."

"It damn sure is my issue. It takes away money set aside for my healthcare."

Adam turned to Mr. Olson. "That's not true, right?"

"Of course, it is not true," Jane said. "The corpus of the Trust varies from week to week, depending upon the market. Olson has done a good job investing, so this shouldn't affect you at all, Edward."

Mr. Olson chimed in. "The market has been up the last few months, and your account has grown by over eighty thousand dollars this past year.

I could release some of the earnings, but I need to know more about the medical reasons."

"The medical reasons are clear," Adam said. "Ava needs grief counseling. She's out of her mind with despair. We need marriage counseling if we're going to keep our marriage together. I'm depressed and angry all the time, and some people think I drink too much. The LifeGem gives Maria an anchor and a daily reminder that Ava, in some form, is still with her. That means our marriage has a chance of surviving."

"Will you have a funeral as well?"

"No, just a memorial gathering at our house with a few friends."

"So, this would be the only expense?"

"Yes. We'll take care of the rest."

"We've organized it all," Jane said. "Maria's friend Carolyn and I are preparing all the food, and we hired the Cheery Maids to clean the house the day before. The LifeGem is the only expense."

Mr. Olson took a pen from his pocket. "Can I get a doctor's recommendation, say from your marriage counselor?"

"We don't have one yet."

"How about your grief counselor?"

"Haven't found anyone yet."

Edward turned his wheelchair toward the hallway. "I'm against it. I won't sign off on the LifeGem. It's stupid."

Adam stood up and walked around to face Edward. "I need your help on this."

Jane clasped Edward's forearm. "This will not have any impact on your healthcare. You heard Mr. Olson say we could use the earnings."

"I will agree to the counseling, say three or four thousand dollars, but not the LifeGem." He looked up at Adam, grinning. "It's time you learn about the value of money. Good luck." Edward wheeled himself out of the room.

"Hold on a minute," Jane called. Let's be reasonable about this."

"Sorry," Edward said. I am reasonable, and the LifeGem is freakin' stupid."

Adam slumped back into his chair, then slammed his hand on the table. Mr. Olson put his hand on Adam's shoulder. "I'm truly sorry for your loss of Ava," he said, "but I need both signatures indicating approval and full disclosure. I will approve if both you and Edward recommend it."

"He won't."

"Then, I can pay for counseling but not for the LifeGem."

Adam made fists with both hands. "I'm going to lose my marriage over this. You've got to help."

"I'm afraid my hands are tied as Trustee."

Adam closed his eyes and opened them. "Could the Trust loan it to me if I sign a note to pay it back?"

"There is a loan provision in the Trust documents, but I haven't read it. I can check when I go back to my office and let you know. I'm not optimistic."

They both looked up as Edward wheeled back up to the table. "What are you doing back here?" Adam asked.

"Aren't I supposed to sign off on the counseling? Don't want you to get crazy or anything."

"I don't have the paperwork ready," Olson said. "Today was just a preliminary meeting. I'll draw something up and bring it back for your signature. You approve of both grief and marriage counseling, right?"

"Right, but no LifeGem. No way will I sign off on that—it's a rip-off."

"Come on, Edward," Jane said. "How can it matter? These folks are in a world of hurt with Ava's death, and they need your help."

"I said I would sign off on counseling. That's what they need."

Adam glared at him. "You are a real sonofabitch. Is there any compassion left in your dark, nasty soul?"

"Guess not. You're no prize yourself, you know. Your selfishness killed your mother and burned us both nearly to death. You've never even thanked me for pulling your ass out of the fire."

Jane rose, putting her hands on her hips. "That's uncalled for, Edward. If my sister could hear you, she would roll over in her grave."

Adam knocked his chair over backwards and started around the table with his fist raised. "You bastard, I'm going to whip your ass good."

"Yeah, come on ahead and attack a cripple. Burn me and then beat me up. That would be like you. Way to treat your father."

Mr. Olson pushed his way between them. "Easy does it. We don't need an altercation here."

Adam gritted his teeth and stuck out his jaw. "Fuck you, Edward. You are bound for hell, and I hope soon."

"I'll see you there, you ungrateful asshole. Remember, you'd be dead if it weren't for me." He spun his chair and wheeled out of the room. At the doorway, without a backward glance, he raised both middle fingers. "Whip up on these," he said.

Mr. Olson sat down and let out a breath. "That was a close call. I haven't seen this much hate between you before."

Adam rubbed his temples. "I'm sorry you had to see that. It's been building up over time, and now it's overflowing."

"Please check on the loan provisions," Jane said. "There's got to be a way."

Mr. Olson nodded. "Give me a couple of days, folks, and I'll review the loan provisions. Call me Thursday."

Adam choked back an angry scream. "I wish he'd died in the fire. He's been a major thorn in my side for over twenty years. I'm sick and tired of it."

"You've had some tough times, Adam, more than most men," said the Trustee. I'm truly sorry for your loss and your suffering. I'll see what we can figure out."

Adam shook his hand. "You've stayed with me for all these years. I appreciate your help, Mr. Olson. I'll call Thursday."

Jane took one of Adam's hands in both of hers. "Don't lose hope, Adam. This will work out. You'll see."

"I believe you, Mother, but losing Ava hurts more than I can say."

11

People gathered at Adam and Maria's mobile home before noon on Saturday, the second week in May. The sky was clear blue with a few floating clouds and a gentle breeze from the South. Carolyn and Jane had come early, baked chocolate chip cookies, and made several plates full of finger sandwiches. Lucas helped by trimming the crust from the bread and arranging the white bread on one plate and whole wheat on another. Adam had vacuumed, and Jane brought several floral arrangements, including orange flowers from nearby Trumpet Vines and purple sage from her planter boxes. Jane also set out blue cornflowers supplied from the neighbor's garden; the color so pure that the most valuable sapphire is known as 'cornflower blue.' They smelled earthy and fresh with a hint of black pepper. Maria put a large photo of Ava on an easel in the living room. The chaplain from OMI had agreed to come by and offer words of encouragement and say a prayer for Ava.

Adam learned from Mr. Olson that he could sign a note with the Trust, provided he paid it back within five years. He called Jane, told her the good news, and then went by the funeral home, arranged payment for Maria's LifeGem, and got a receipt. It would be a month before the LifeGem was ready, so in the meantime he received a small urn for himself with some of Ava's ashes. Ryan arrived and motioned to Adam. They stepped into a bedroom. "Did you get the LifeGem?" he asked.

"Yes, I paid for it this morning. The Trust loaned me the money."

"Did your father approve?"

"No way. That asshole kept saying the LifeGem was a rip-off."

"What do you think made the difference to the Trustee?"

"Jane was a big help. Since she was the one who led us through the lawsuits, the Trustee was open to her opinion, and the Trust had earnings that the Trustee could loan.

"That's great," Ryan said. "Maria has been counting on it, and she was worried you couldn't find a way to pay for it."

"She told you that?"

"I stopped by to offer condolences, and we visited for a while. I've never seen Maria this miserable. So, I hope I can be there for her as a friend, you know, a friend to both of you."

Adam cocked his head slightly. "That's kind of you."

The chaplain arrived, and Carolyn's husband, Doug, came in a few minutes later. "Sorry for your loss," he mumbled to Adam. Doug was wearing his red MAGA hat and appeared drunk.

Adam shook Doug's hand but did not let go. Instead, he pulled Doug toward him and whispered loudly in his ear. "Normally, people remove their hats when they're inside. Do you mind, please?"

Doug backed up, pulling his hand loose. "Yes, I mind. This hat is now part of who I am. The hat goes where I go."

Adam threw up his hands. "Whatever, but if you can't take off your hat to honor Ava and Maria, then you need to leave."

Doug turned on his heels and stormed out the door. "I don't have time for people who can't understand. Tell Maria I'm sorry, but I can't put up with her stupid husband."

Adam started for him, teeth gritted, and his right fist clenched at his side. "You ready for a piece of me?"

Carolyn moved quickly from across the room and stood in between them. "Doug, move along now. I asked you to show up here in good condition, and here you are drunk and belligerent. Today is an important day, and you need to go somewhere by yourself. You're not fit to be with other people, especially me."

Doug glared at her, then stomped off to his truck, his hand in the air with the one-finger salute.

Carolyn slammed the door shut after him. "And Adam, you know better than to pick a fight with Doug, especially when he's drunk. If you do, you are no better than he is. You need to be here for Maria and Ava today—and for yourself. We are all here for you, too."

§

Carolyn, Jane, Maria, Ryan, Adam, and Lucas gathered by Ava's photograph. Nacho paced, whined, and then settled next to Lucas. The chaplain offered a prayer that the open arms of God would receive Ava and that God's Holy Spirit would come and comfort family and friends. Then, each person provided a few words of encouragement and sympathy for Adam, Maria, and Lucas. After a period of silence, Adam extended his hand and took Maria's hand in his. She was frowning and wary but brightened up when Adam showed her the receipt for the LifeGem.

She smiled tearfully. "Oh, Adam, you figured out a way to make this happen. I didn't know if you would. Thank you."

"Sure. You're welcome. They said it would take a couple of weeks before delivery." He took the small urn from his pocket and put it high on the bookshelf. "McClaren's saved a few ashes for me to have an urn," he said, wiping his wet eyes with his sleeve.

"What's in there?" Lucas asked. He put his hand on Nacho.

"Some of Ava's ashes. They made other ashes into a ring your mom will be wearing."

Lucas's eyes went wide. "Is Ava all burned up? Why would you do that?"

"Instead of burying her body in the ground, your mother and I decided the funeral home should cremate Ava's body. Her soul, her spirit, went to be with God. Her little body was just a container for her soul."

"I don't want them to burn me when I die," Lucas said.

"Well, you have a lifetime to think about it, and you can decide what you want."

"I'm really sad that Ava is gone," Lucas said. "I thought I had a little sister I could help take care of." He dropped to the floor, still hugging Nacho, and began crying. "Dad, would you burn Nacho if he died?"

"We would decide together, but we would probably bury him and make a nice grave marker."

Lucas wiped his eyes with his shirt. "That's what I would want. Don't burn him up."

Maria gathered him up in a hug. "Okay. We won't."

Lucas sighed. "I guess I'll take care of Nacho since Ava's gone."

"We understand you wanted a sister," Adam said, reaching for Maria's hand again. "We all wanted that, but sometimes things don't work out the way we would like. Just remember, Lucas. There's always hope, and when someone you love leaves your life, someone else will come along for you to love. Always remember, love never ends, and hope never ends. They go on forever."

12

The day after the memorial, Adam gave Maria her space. Maria packed a small suitcase. Carolyn had arranged a one-week trip to Santa Fe so the two women could have a change in scenery. The sky was overcast with a smoky, brown tone from forest fires far in the West. It was hard to breathe; Maria wore a cloth mask. Adam remarked that the smoke would likely thin out as they gained altitude driving from Albuquerque to Santa Fe, and the afternoon clouds and cool showers would clear out most of the haze. Maria made no response, and he couldn't tell whether she had heard him.

Maria hugged Lucas on her way out the door. Adam opened his arms, inviting a hug, but Maria kept her head down and hurried past him, holding her suitcase in front of her, leaving Adam standing with his arms open to nothing. Then, as she opened the car door, she paused for a moment. "Lucas, mind your father. I'll will be back next Sunday, and we can have lunch at Subway."

Lucas took Adam's hand. "We'll be okay, Mom. Dad said I could go to work with him. Adam waved as the car pulled out of the driveway, but no one waved back. Did he still belong to this shred of a family? Thank God for Lucas and Nacho. Adam squeezed his son's hand and then leaned down and scratched Nacho behind his ear, glad to be home.

§

Maria and Carolyn checked into the Eldorado Hotel and went to the restaurant for lunch. The two women worked together as registered nurses at Presbyterian Hospital, and they had been friends for ten years.

Maria felt a surge of gratitude for her friend, Carolyn, a strong, plump woman of forty-five with short salt-and- pepper hair swept back over her ears. She often wore a practiced bureaucratic smile on her perfect oval face, an expression that would quickly become a smirk if she found someone annoying or warm and inviting when she felt comfortable. Maria admired her compassion and openness to the plight of marginal people. As a nurses, the friends had seen more than their share of human misery. However, the suffering brought on by the death of Maria's baby had shaken their world as nothing else could. Carolyn leaned closer across the table, her eyes glistening with tears.

"I'm so sorry, Maria. I know this the cruelest thing you've ever known. It isn't fair, and I know you feel like your heart is shattered."

Maria stifled a sob. "It doesn't just feel shattered once. It breaks, again and again, every time I think of Ava. It keeps getting worse."

Carolyn took Maria's hands in hers.

"Are you angry with Adam?"

"I told him to move out."

"Move out? You're separated?"

"At least at night. He helps with Lucas during the daytime and cooks his dinner."

"So, he's still in the picture?"

"Sort of. Mostly the routine is helpful, and Lucas likes to be with Adam."

"Do you blame him for Ava?'

Maria shrugged. "They say it was a SIDS death, but there were things he could've done, don't you think?"

"He gave Ava CPR and mouth to mouth, right?"

"But if he had started sooner?"

"Well, perhaps."

"He was asleep. Nacho woke him up, for God's sake. I know he was zonked with pain pills and alcohol. A few minutes sooner could've saved her life. You live with an alcoholic, so you know how irresponsible they can be."

Carolyn nodded. I do. But the medical investigator said there was nothing anyone could've done. Don't you believe him?"

"I'm not sure. The doctor didn't know Adam was impaired."

"Yes, he hides it well—better than my husband."

"Not from me. I can see the dullness in his eyes, and he grits his teeth and seems distracted."

"Well, I pray there is hope for you and Adam. This tragedy will be a test of your marriage. We both know that more than half of marriages don't last after the loss of a child. And, Lord knows it might be time for a change."

"Ava was our hope for mending our marriage and finding the joy we had in our early years. Now, what is there? I have a husband who's an addict and a dead baby girl. What do I do about that?"

"That was a big step telling him to move out. Now you need to detach from the behavior you can't stand. Detach with love, as they say. You could come to Al-Anon with me. It's been a lifesaver, the only way I can stay married to Doug."

"Right now, I'm too fragile and not myself. I can't see past this moment or make decisions. So let's talk about something else and find a shoe store somewhere—maybe there's a sale."

The murmurs in the dining room were interrupted when a couple at a nearby table began shouting at each other. The woman cried out, and Maria jumped in her seat, her knee hitting the table and spilling her water on the table and all over her lap.

"Are you okay?" Carolyn asked.

"I'll be fine. Loud arguments frighten me." She held out her shaking hand. "Check it out. Takes me a few minutes to recover."

"Oh, Maria, I didn't realize you were still dealing with that. Are you still seeing your therapist?"

"Yes, occasionally. She says it is a stress or trauma disorder, and it may take years to overcome."

"Please, Maria, start attending Al-Anon with me. I'm sure it will help. Or, you could try an ACOA meeting and see what you think. There are more adult children of alcoholics than you realize—some twenty million people come from alcoholic families. You'll meet people with similar issues, and they offer so much support. We've talked about this before, but you are battling two demons—your family of origin and

Adam's addictions. That's more than any mother should have to bear."

"I know, but I'm never sure about what to do" She lowered her voice. "I'm afraid of other people and their judgment."

Carolyn offered a rueful smile. "So was I, and so are the other people you will meet. Believe me, they are accepting. They understand. We have a community of shared suffering. We talk a lot about fear and isolation and anger—issues we all work on. Most of us had a family history with alcoholics or addicts before we married one. Or a parent with depression and rages. Or something like that."

"Yeah, that's how I was raised—living with constant anger and shouting. That's where I learned to walk on eggshells. My family life came straight from the depths of hell."

Maria closed her eyes, took a deep breath, and raised her face to the ceiling above, hands trembling. Suddenly, she had a vivid memory of peeing in her underpants when she was eleven. The acrid smell of her own urine seemed present. She felt her face flush with embarrassment, and her hands came together in prayer as the memories came.

Maria took a deep breath. "There's a lot about my family that you don't know. When things got loud and scary, I would run into my closet and hide back in the corner, shaking, keeping quiet as a mouse, and hugging myself. I was literally scared speechless. Usually, there was only shouting and some broken dishes, followed by crying and apologies and make-up sex, I learned later. But sometimes my father hit mother across the face. I could hear the smack through the closet door. When she cried out, I would pee a little in my underpants. That made me furious. I mean, what eleven-year-old girl kept clean underpants in a shoebox in the closet so she could change? Does that suck or what? Scared and mad. That's what I was. I wanted to be invisible. I was so ashamed that I wanted to disappear forever. I prayed that God would take me away."

Carolyn leaned in closer. "I can remember my parents fighting, but nothing like what you've seen. Did things ever settle down?"

"No, but things changed when I grew up. I don't remember when it began—perhaps about age fourteen—but somehow, it became my job to make excuses for my father and sometimes for my mother. I kept their drunken secrets from others and covered for my father when he didn't know he had embarrassed himself. I made excuses for Mother when she missed teacher conferences or my dental appointments"

Carolyn put her hand on Maria's. "So, you became the adult, the responsible one."

"Yes, but I didn't even know what to expect from one day to the next. I couldn't invite friends to our house for fear of my father's drunken behavior. He would be passed out on the couch, or he could be pleasant and friendly if it were early in the day. He ogled my girlfriends and made them uncomfortable, although, to his credit, he never touched anyone or hit on them. He just stared at their boobs and smiled. Weird, right?"

"Very weird," said Carolyn.

"I got some relief going to school, and I was a good student. I wanted to be a perfect student, but at school, people saw me as the strange girl with the weird father—far from perfect. I couldn't stand that, so we lived in the bubble of the secret. Oh, I loved him and wanted to help, so sometimes I put a cool, wet washcloth on his face when he was asleep on the couch. Sometimes he would open his eyes and mumble, "Thanks, sweetness. You are a wonderful daughter." He said I was wonderful, but all I felt was shame."

"Was your mother aware? Did she ever comfort you, encourage you?" Carolyn asked.

"My Mother was clueless. She made excuses for my father, said he was trying to sober up, but he had a lot of pressure from work. He was a salesman on commission, and he only got paid when he made a sale."

Carolyn shook her head. "Did your mother drink, too?"

"She would drink with him, and sometimes she wouldn't even get dressed for days. I remember her bloodshot eyes, raggedy bathrobe, and dirty green flip-flops. She would even forget she had curlers in her hair. She said that part of her job as a wife was to be a good companion and to bolster his self-confidence. But Mother, I would say, you argue and fight and he even hits you sometimes. She explained that my father was her soulmate and they always made up after fighting. She said my job was to be a dutiful daughter and to help protect our family from scrutiny and judgment.

"Carolyn, please understand. I lived in fear every day. Maybe they would gather up and leave me alone in the house one day and never come back. How would I cover for that? Mother thought it showed weakness if I cried, so I learned to hold back tears and change the subject in my mind—you know, get busy with something, imagine something different, and cast aside what I was feeling. What if I lost control? What if I wasn't responsible and adorable? What if people disapproved of me? Life would be over, that's what. So, I figured it was too dangerous to feel anything and closed down my heart. Didn't need the pain."

"So that's when you shut down your heart and your feelings?"

"Yes, I learned to ignore them. I became good at isolation. I came to enjoy being by myself, ignoring my father's ogling of my body and I grew super responsible—the wonderful daughter doing things perfectly. I did laundry, always added dryer sheets, often cleaned up the kitchen, kept a grocery list, anticipated what my father might need from day to day, and more or less managed our household. Of course, I wouldn't say I liked it. Actually, I hated it, but it gave me a sense of satisfaction and a purpose, you know, a way to live on top of the chaos, a way to keep my faith and sanity."

Carolyn took a sip of water and wiped her eyes with a napkin. "You had a major burden to carry, you know, being a perfect daughter. When you met Adam, did he remind you of your father?"

"Yes, but he was different. Adam could exercise self-control, behave appropriately, and have low expectations about my ability to sustain a loving relationship. He was forgiving and respectful. Yes, he drank, but he had a reason. Yes, Adam took painkillers, but he had a reason. He went to work every day and was a good provider. Although I don't understand why, Adam believes that I'm beautiful, intelligent, gracious, and competent. I know he loves me. He often looks to me for leadership. Imagine that. Leadership from me! Oh, well, sometimes he doesn't know what he's doing.

"Carolyn, you're my best friend, and I'll always be grateful for how you stood by me at the funeral. I was so devastated when my parents were killed—you remember, a single-car accident on a moonlit night with no rain or snow. Dad was driving—no doubt drunk. I had managed to detach from my family somewhat, but I was afraid and in pain. I loved them, but I didn't like them."

"I wish I could have done more," Carolyn said, "but at least I could be there with you."

"Thank you again for being with me through that. I'm sad that you have to go through this again with Ava but know that I'm deeply grateful."

"I'll be with you no matter what, and Adam seems to want to support you. I remember when you had a bout of depression, Adam stood by you."

"That's so true. He had tremendous compassion. I wanted desperately to love him better, but I didn't know how—maybe I still don't know how. But now he's drinking way too much and has become undependable. Perhaps our time together has come to an end—that's what I think now. I feel nauseated when I think of how Adam has changed—sick to my stomach—wrenching despair from the meltdown of a hopeful and, yes, sensual marriage. I've always enjoyed making love with Adam. He's tender, thoughtful, and he knows what I like. I shiver to think about it. But, and this is important, I should put a heavy blanket over it all and forget about it. I know how to do that, and that's what I should do now."

"You are going through a rough patch, Maria. Folks wiser than me say you shouldn't make any big decisions when you're grieving."

"Oh, I know, but that's how I feel." Maria looked at the time on her phone. "Sorry, Carolyn, I've been yammering way too long."

"You needed to talk," Carolyn said.

Maria looked down at the table. From a skylight, rays of sunshine spread over the polished wood, making the spilled water glisten and display a little rainbow. Standing up, Maria raised her eyebrows and wiped her tears with a napkin. "Okay, Carolyn, enough about me. It's time to go. Let's go find a shoe store."

13

After Maria left with Carolyn, Adam had to make a trip to Home Depot for supplies. They got into his pickup truck and fastened their seat belts. Adam's legs hurt more than usual, distracting him. He shook out two OxyContin from his prescription bottle and washed them down with a couple of swallows of vodka from a pint he kept in the glove box, then stashed the remainder under his seat. He decided to take side streets to Home Depot to be less likely to be stopped for a traffic violation and clipped along at ten mph over the speed limit. As he rounded a bend, leaves from the trees filtered the sunlight and cast shadows on the road, random shapes that moved with the breeze.

Lucas turned to Adam. "Hey Dad, what are those designs on the road?"

"See how the leaves on the trees are moving?" He pointed up to a large cottonwood. "The sun shines through the trees, and the leaves make shadows. Check it out. Those shadows right ahead look like little animals chasing each other."

Watching the shadows dart here and there, Adam did not see the cement truck that pulled out into the intersection ahead. He came upon it fast. "Whoa, look out!" He instinctively threw his hand and arm in front of Lucas, jerked the steering wheel to the left, and jammed on the brakes. "Hang on, Lucas."

The truck jumped off the road and careened down an incline, bouncing off several trees before it came to a hard stop against a dirt embankment. Both airbags deployed, and Lucas screamed. His arm was smacked against his face by the exploding airbag, and his nose spurted blood. Adam's airbag broke his sunglasses but prevented him from slamming against the steering wheel. He pushed the bag away, shook his dizzy head, and moved over to Lucas, pushing his airbag away to the side.

"I can't move my arm, Dad. It hurts." Blood streamed out of his nose.

"Just hold still a minute," Adam said. He took off his shirt, folded it into a compress, and held it against Lucas's face. "Tip your head back, and it will help stop the bleeding." He felt the length of Lucas's arm, but he couldn't tell if the airbag had broken it. "Hold this against your face. I'm going to find my phone and call the police."

Lucas cried softly and he was shaking. "It hurts. Help me, Dad."

Adam opened the driver's side door, retrieved his phone from the floor, and slowly stepped out onto soft dirt. He grabbed the pint of vodka from under the seat, downed what was left, and tossed the bottle far into the brush. He tucked his prescription bottle of oxy into his boot and steadied himself against the pickup bed. Then he worked his way around the back of the truck, opened the passenger door, and hugged Lucas to him. "It's going to be okay. I promise."

The world spun. Adam let go of Lucas, turned, stumbled, and fell to the ground, retching, throwing up oatmeal and coffee from breakfast and at least a half-pint of vodka. The pool of vomit in the dirt contained some bright red blood, a harbinger of bleeding in his throat. In the bright sunlight, he could also see his shadowy likeness in the sheen on the surface of his vomit. He swallowed hard and gritted his teeth. Suddenly tears burst from his eyes. He looked up at Lucas, who was still crying. He leaned back on his knees, laced his hands on his head, and began twisting and wailing. He shivered uncontrollably. Shame washed over him like an ice-cold waterfall. I could have killed Lucas, he thought. I nearly killed my only son. What's wrong with me? He raised his shaking hands to the sky, palms up, and yelled, "Help me, Lord, please help me."

A police car arrived first. Adam struggled to stand up. He dug his registration from the glove box and his driver's license from his billfold. A seasoned, older officer made his way down the incline and approached. "Well, this is a mess. Do you have your license and registration?"

Adam handed them to the officer. "A cement truck pulled out in front of me, and I stood on the brakes and swerved. My truck went off the road."

"We're you speeding?"

"No, sir."

"Have you been drinking? You smell sour, like week-old vodka."

"No, sir."

"Well, we are going to have to conduct a field sobriety test. You're no doubt impaired."

"I'm too unsteady for a field test."

"Then we'll have to draw some blood, or you can just admit you're impaired."

"I'm not admitting anything. I'm fine."

"I'm going to write you up for a DUI and reckless driving. It's broad daylight, good weather, and the roadway is clear. There is no reason for this unless you are impaired or distracted. Were you texting?"

"No, sir. The phone was on the seat."

"I could cite you for reckless endangerment of a child. He seems okay, but he could be dead."

Adam looked at the ground. "Yes, sir."

He pointed to the arriving ambulance. "The EMT will draw some blood."

"Well, do what you need to do. But the blood test will prove you wrong and the judge will throw out the charges."

Two EMTs scrambled down the embankment and moved Lucas carefully out of the car. They put a sling on his arm and secured it to his chest. "We're going to climb up the hill and carry you with us," one EMT said. They helped Lucas into the back of the ambulance. They checked Adam over and found no apparent injuries except scrapes from the airbag. Adam got into the ambulance and sat down next to Lucas.

"We're going to the hospital and get your arm checked out. It's going to be okay," he told him."Then Adam handed an EMT his truck keys. "Could you please give these to the police officer? He can have the tow truck take my truck to the Ford dealer on Central."

"Will do," he said. "Hold still. I'm going to draw some blood."

Lucas whimpered on their ride to the hospital, and Adam

comforted him with his hand on his shoulder. "It's going to be okay, Lucas. I'll make sure they take good care of you." When the ambulance pulled up to the emergency room door, a nurse met them with a gurney. Lucas was placed on the gurney, and Adam walked beside him as they moved to an exam area. The nurse pulled a curtain around them for privacy. "The doctor will be here in a minute," she said.

Lucas looked up. "I'm afraid, Dad."

"I know, but you'll be fine. You need to be brave, and I'll stay right here with you."

Adam helped Lucas take off his shirt just as the doctor appeared. "Hello, I'm Dr. John Warnock." He flipped through papers on a clipboard. "Single car accident, I see."

"Yes, I got distracted, and my truck slid down an embankment." Adam put his hand on Lucas's shoulder. "This is my son Lucas, and I think the airbag broke his arm."

"I see here that they cited you for a DUI. Are you still impaired?"

"No, it's been an hour, and I haven't had anything to drink."

Dr. Warnock put his hand on Lucas. "Can I take a look at that arm?"

"Okay, but it hurts."

"I'm sure it does. It is either a bad sprain or a broken bone. We'll need an x-ray to know for sure. Do you have any pain anywhere else?"

"My nose."

Dr. Warnock looked at Adam. "That's from the airbag, right?"

"Yes, his nose was bleeding, but we got it stopped."

"How about you, Adam? Any injuries?"

"Not that I know of."

"Good. We'll need to get Lucas to x-ray. I'll call an orderly."

Soon Lucas was on his way to x-ray. Dr. Warnock motioned to Adam. "Let's sit down here for a few minutes."

Adam nodded and sat down. He was sweaty and covered with dirt from the wreck. Dr. Warnock wore a fresh white coat. He was moon-faced and had a broad smile. In his mid-fifties, his face was rugged looking, wrinkled under his eyes, and tanned from the sun. His brown eyes had a luster that conveyed a receptive and compassionate heart, and his blond hair was tousled, giving him a youthful appearance. His manner conveyed a hint of hard-won wisdom.

Dr. Warnock folded his hands in front of him. "We're not busy, so I have some time to listen. Tell me what happened."

Adam pulled up one of his pants legs. "I have chronic pain from burns long ago, so I take pain pills. Sometimes I supplement with alcohol. I was just over the legal limit, but I didn't feel impaired. I guess I'm used to it. Anyway, I got distracted, lost control for a moment, and slid down an embankment. The impact deployed the airbags, and that's how Lucas got hurt."

"I guess your stars are aligned, and God is with you."

"How so?"

"The report says if you'd been going faster, both you and Lucas could have sustained bad injuries; as it is, you were almost cited for child endangerment."

Adam dropped his head into his hands. When he looked up, his eyes teared, and his lips quivered. "I can't believe it. I could have killed my son."

"You've got that right. Today could be a crossroad for you, Adam. It may be time for a new approach to your pain control. You can't quit drinking, right?"

Adam nodded.

"Do you have to drink to feel normal?"

Adam took a deep breath and nodded again.

"And you're taking more and more OxyContin. Your prescription profile calls for one ten mg in the morning and another at bedtime. So, I guess that you're taking three or four a day. Plus the alcohol?"

"Seems about right."

"Adam, this can only get worse."

"I know. We recently lost our daughter Ava. She was five months old, a SIDS baby." Adam swallowed hard, choaking back tears. "Our lives turned upside down. My marriage is in shambles. Maria, my wife, thinks I'm responsible for our daughter's death—you could have done something, she says. You might know her. She's a nurse here. She told me to move out.

I hope it is just a trial separation, but we're not together emotionally, that's for sure."

"This is a tough time for you."

"You think? Maybe you don't know tough." Adam sighed, regretting his sarcasm.

"I don't mean to treat it lightly," said the doctor, " but believe me, I do know a lot about tough, and it sounds like something has to change."

"You're right about that." Adam lowered his voice. "I might be an addict," he managed to mumble. "Can you help me?"

Dr. Warnock smiled, and his face flushed under his tan. "You've come to the right place. Adam, I'm a drug addict. I'm in a physician's diversion program, and I've been clean for four years."

Adam raised his eyebrows and stared at Dr. Warnock, finally dropping his eyes to the doctor's right leg. "You seem to be carrying a lot of pain. Right now, your pain feels worse than mine."

"That's true. Do you sense my pain?"

"Yes, I feel it here." Adam tapped his heart.

"You feel it?"

"Since I was twelve, for some reason, I feel the pain of other people along with my own."

"All the time?"

"If I go with it, it's all the time. I can tamp it down, though, if it's too much. Yours is not too much, but it is strong. It is a throbbing pain, right?"

"Yes, I have a prosthetic foot and ankle." Dr. Warnock raised his pant leg. "I lost my foot and ankle in Afghanistan, near Kabul. I was an army doc for four years. One fine day we drove over an IED, and my foot was right on top of it. Had to be amputated."

"Does it hurt all the time?"

"Yes. They call it phantom-limb pain. My foot hurts and doesn't even exist."

"How do you handle it?"

"I have a protocol for controlling it, but let's get back to you. I'm an addiction specialist. I'll do my best to help you if you want help."

Adam took a deep breath. "I do."

A nurse stepped inside the curtain and handed Dr. Warnock a radiology report, which he scanned.

"Lucas has a cracked ulna. Fortunately, it's not that bad. We'll put a cast on it, and it should heal in four to six weeks. He's young and healthy."

The nurse wheeled the gurney carrying Lucas back into the exam area.

"Hey," Adam said, "your arm bone is cracked, but not broken. But the doctor says you will need a cast."

"It hurts, Dad."

Dr. Warnock patted Lucas's arm. "I'll have Fina put a cast here, on your lower arm. Of course, you'll have to be careful, but you can still use it some of the time. Oh, I need to introduce you." He held out his hand. "Meet Josefina Romero, the best nurse in the hospital." He grinned.

"My Mom is the best," Lucas said. "But you can be the second best."

Josefina blushed and took Lucas's hand. "Nice to meet you, Lucas." Then she looked at Adam. "I'm sure you don't remember, but I was a new nurse graduate when you and your father came into the burn unit about twenty-five years ago. I was your night nurse for about twelve weeks. You can call me Fina. Everyone else does."

Fina had short, dark hair and an angular face with sharp features. Her lips were full, and her cornflower blue eyes seemed magical, twinkly, as though she met the world with permanent joy. She had smooth, light brown skin and a captivating smile. Her voice was soft and warm, intimate. Adam smelled the hint of gardenias, probably from her shampoo.

He felt his heart soften. "I have a vague memory. You changed my bandages and my burn sheets, right?"

"Yes, some of the time. I took a job at a different hospital about a month after you left. So, I wasn't here when you had your skin grafts. Meeting you when you were a nine-year-old burn victim gave me a new sense of what it means to be a trooper—you certainly were. You had tremendous courage." She leaned over and whispered. "Can't say the same for your father, though. He never stopped complaining and blaming."

Adam winced. "He's a wuss. He hasn't changed. He still blames and complains all the time, even after all these years."

"Well, I need to get busy," Fina said as she gathered casting materials. "We can put a cast on right here, Lucas, and you can go home without being admitted. I'll be careful, but I'll bet you're a trooper just like your dad."

Lucas took a breath. "Okay."

"We prefer going home," Adam said. "I don't care much for hospitals—had my fill."

Dr. Warnock stood up. "Lucas, I need to see you in my office in three days, on June seventh. Adam, I would like for you to make an appointment sometime soon, if you want to know more about my protocol."

Adam stood up and shook Dr. Warnock's hand. "Thanks, doc. I'll call and make appointments for Lucas and me. Sorry about your foot pain."

Dr. Warnock clasped Adam's shoulder and lowered his voice. "Just so you know, if we can start on what you need, I can stand up with you in court and advocate leniency for your DUI. Judges like to see addicts in recovery."

"Thanks, doc. Now I get to take Lucas home and explain this all to my wife. A broken arm for Lucas and a DUI for me won't sit well. First losing Ava's and now this—I don't know if our marriage can stand it."

"Soldier on, trooper. I'll see you soon."

14

Adam appeared thirty minutes early for his appointment on Friday with Dr. Warnock. Maria was still in Santa Fe, and Adam was home taking care of Lucas. He felt empowered that he was at the house. Maybe there was hope for their marriage after all. He hadn't told her about Lucas's broken arm or the accident. He had decided to wait until she came home for fear of ruining Maria's vacation.

Adam took Lucas to see Dr. Warnock after three days. Lucas's arm was better and the pain had become a minor ache treatable with children's Tylenol. While at his office with Lucas, Adam made an appointment for his addiction counseling. After checking in, he thumbed through a science magazine and watched as other patients filtered in. He was fascinated by a stylish woman who walked up to the desk. She had a slight sway in her tight black skirt, just enough to catch attention, he thought, without advertising what was underneath. She carried herself with alluring confidence, about five feet six inches tall and one-hundred thirty pounds. She presented her card to the receptionist. "I'm Lola Jenkins here for my appointment with Dr. Warnock."

"You're a little early, and there's one person ahead of you." She nodded toward Adam. Dr. Warnock typically sees drug reps after hours, but he wrote this appointment in himself, so I gather you're here for a particular reason."

"Yes, he asked me to come by so we could discuss several drugs my company manufactures. Please tell him I have the new research he wanted on naltrexone and also a study from Great Britain on buprenorphine."

"Please have a seat, Ms. Jenkins, and I'll let him know you are waiting."

Although there were several vacant chairs, Lola sat down

next to Adam. "Hello, I'm Lola Jenkins, and I'm a drug rep for Bard Pharmaceuticals. We manufacture and distribute drugs that target pain and addiction." She smiled and shook her strawberry blonde shoulder-length hair. Her cleavage showed below the unbuttoned opening in her crisp, white blouse worn under a light green blazer. She displayed a small turquoise heart on a silver chain at her throat. Her green eyes gleamed as she extended her hand.

Adam took it. "Hello, I'm Adam Young. I'm here to see Dr. Warnock."

"Yes, you're the one ahead of me. Dr. Warnock asked me to come by and bring him literature on some new research on alcohol addiction, or 'alcohol use disorder,' as they say nowadays." She took a deep breath and leaned back slightly so that her breasts became more prominent.

Adam squirmed in his chair. Except for his memories of Maria, he had not been attracted to a woman since he moved out. This woman sent a little shiver up his spine. She smelled exotic, like lilac and vanilla. She turned him on, and something from the past awakened in him—strong desire.

"What kind of work do you do?" Lola asked.

Adam took a breath, raising his chest. "Oh, I'm in construction—I'm a construction manager and inspector, and I do finish work. I'm the last one through a completed home, and I take care of call-backs and repairs as well. My overall job is to keep our customers happy."

"I'll bet you're pretty good at that, keeping customers happy."

Adam smiled with the hint of a leer. "I don't get any complaints."

They were quiet for a moment as Lola smiled and gazed at Adam's square jaw, his muscled arms, and strong shoulders. Then she fixed her green eyes on his face and rested her hand on his thigh. He looked at her hand, then her eyes. "Do you ever do outside work?" she asked, almost a purr.

"Sometimes, on the weekends."

"I have some work at my new home," Lola said. "I just recently moved in, and I'm redecorating. Would you be interested in a small side job?"

Adam grinned. "Sure. I'm versatile. What can I do you for?"

"I have about a day's work that I'm not able to do myself, mostly painting, picture hanging, fireplace repair, and installing new closet doors. I guess those are things you could handle?"

"Seems like it. Do you have all the materials?"

"No, you would have to measure and then gather what you need. I have a charge card you can use." She smiled and moved her hand to his forearm. "Are you out of sight, you know, expensive?"

"I charge thirty dollars an hour if it is cash. If you want a bid proposal and to pay by check, I charge thirty-five an hour to cover taxes. Since it's only one day or so, I suggest cash."

Lola laughed and gently slapped his arm. "Cash is one of my most favorite things. So that should be fine."

Adam cocked his head slightly. A little red flag waved in his mind. "What are your other favorite things?"

"Let's wait until you come over to measure, and we can talk about that then."

Adam looked at her ring finger. "I gather you are single?"

"Yes, and you?"

"My wife and I are separated, and she says she's filing for a divorce."

"So, you're available?"

Adam paused. "I hadn't thought about it, but I might be, for someone like you."

"Like me?"

"Yes, just like you. I'm partial to beautiful women. I've never met anyone with strawberry blond hair and green eyes. I mean that as a compliment."

She grinned. "Well, guess what. I'm partial to handsome, well-built men with brown eyes, so that we may have a match. When can you come over?"

"I could come this Saturday, but I'll be taking care of my six-year-old son this weekend, so I would need to bring my son with me. Or, I can come by myself next Saturday. He'll be with friends for a birthday party and a sleep over."

"How about next Saturday? We can talk about things, and I can show you around without distractions. Here's my card. I'll write my address on the back." She took out a pen, made a note on the card, and handed it to him. "Say about ten am?"

"Okay, I'll be there."

A medical assistant came into the waiting room holding a folder. "Mr.Young?"

"Yes, right here."

Adam stood up and followed her. She led him into an exam room, where she checked his blood pressure and blood oxygen level.".

"Adam," Dr. Warnock said, striding in, "it is great to see you again. How is Lucas doing?"

"He's fine. There's a small bruise on his cheek from the airbag, but he wears it like a badge. He tells his friends that he was in a car wreck but that he's okay now."

"How about you?"

"I'm doing alright, but I'm scared, doc. That wreck was my fault, and I almost killed my son. That's got me all twisted up."

"You know the police report said you were impaired, right?"

"Yes, I know. My court hearing is in two weeks for a DUI and reckless driving."

"I said I would help you in court. We can document a prescription for your OxyContin for leg pain. But you were also drunk. Are you ready for some help?"

Adam gazed into Dr. Warnock's eyes. He saw old pain, old but steady, about a level three or four. "I hope I'm ready," he said.

"Recall that pain and substance abuse are my specialties," the doctor said. "I want to disclose to you again that I am in a medical diversion program. Four years ago, I had a drug problem. It was bad, about a four hundred dollar a day habit. I've been clean for forty-nine months and twelve days now, but who's counting?"

"Do you think you can help me?

"You're history is complicated. I read your file, and Fina filled me in some. You met her in the ER. Remember Fina?"

"I remember the pain, but not the people. Fina looked familiar, though."

"Yes, I can well imagine. The pain must have been excruciating.

Your skin graft and surgery records indicate over a dozen operations to keep up with your growth, and the last two surgeons wrote that you would likely have scar pain the rest of your life. Lots of nerve damage from your burns."

"The pain never stops. I get some relief from OxyContin if I take ten milligrams three or four times a day, much better than the hydrocodone I took for years. The compounded lidocaine lotion helps me get to sleep."

"And you self-medicate with alcohol?"

"Yes, alcohol dulls the pain. But, added to the OxyContin, I can go to work through the pain."

"Do you worry that you can't stop the alcohol?"

"Yes, especially now. Like I told you, I have to drink to feel normal."

"I understand." He lifted his pants leg and revealed his prosthetic ankle and foot. "Remember? This artificial ankle remains my cross to bear. My foot still hurts. I thought I could get things going with cocaine, but when I mixed pain killers and alcohol, my pain took control of me."

"What did you do?"

"After I got busted at a clinic where I worked, I started searching for alternatives for pain management. If I didn't quit alcohol and cocaine, I would lose my physician's license for the rest of my life. So, I've been doing research ever since, and that's why I chose pain control and addiction as my specialty."

"But you are still in pain."

Dr. Warnock hesitated, lowering his pant leg. "Yes, some. But other things are going on that contribute. I lost my wife, and she took all our savings. I miss her every day, but fortunately, Josefina came into my life, and we've become good friends."

"Well, as you know, I am at a loss about what to do," said Adam. "Staying out of jail would be a good first step. Do you think I'll have to do jail time because of the DUI?"

"I'm going to appear in court with you. If we tell the judge that you are under medical treatment and share your history, we can likely get you probation and community service. This is your first DUI, right?"

"Yes, my first."

"We're going to have to act cautiously. This is a tough problem,

Adam. Both OxyContin and alcohol are addictive, yet you seem to need them for your pain. I'm not quite sure, but my initial recommendation is that we stay with the prescriptions—OxyContin and lidocaine—and we work on releasing you from the grips of alcohol. Do you want to quit?"

"Yes, I want to be a good father to my son, and I would like to get back together with my wife. But I can't not drink. Otherwise, I get crazy and angry."

"Have you ever been to Alcoholics Anonymous?"

Adam shrugged. "Yes, a couple of times. Didn't do much for me."

"What if we found a way to dissociate the alcohol from your pain and for you to have an occasional drink?"

"That would be a miracle, doc."

"I'm partial to a drug called naltrexone. I've had success with others. With the right dosage and motivation, it reduces your craving for alcohol, separating alcohol from the reactions on your brain's pleasure centers, and especially removing the desire to drink. So, we can tell the judge we're working on your alcoholism."

"I'm game, but what about my pain? Would you increase the OxyContin?"

"No, I want to try something else. Have you ever taken CBD?"

"No, what is it?"

"CBD oil comes from the hemp plant. It doesn't have any THC, so it doesn't produce a high, but once the drug builds up in your system, it helps control pain. It is non-prescription. Would you be willing to try it along with the naltrexone?"

"Sure. This shit has got to stop. Alcohol will eventually kill me, or I'll lose my family."

"One more thing. I also want you to try cannabis for sleep. I'll fill out an application for a dispensary card so you can buy it. I suggest about thirty to forty milligrams to help you sleep. Our goal is to control your pain without OxyContin or alcohol, and this just might work."

"Is it okay to continue with the lidocaine lotion?"

"Sure. You can use as much of that as you want."

"Can you please write down what I'm supposed to do?"

"Okay. Take fifty milligrams of CBD once in the morning and before dinner. Then use your lidocaine as much as you'd like, and just before bed, take forty mg of a THC—an edible gummy, and three milligrams of melatonin. You should be able to sleep with that approach."

"What about my OxyContin?"

"I want you to wean yourself off that slowly. Cut your dose to ten milligrams mg twice a day and come back in ten days for another appointment. I want to see how you're doing. We shouldn't start the naltrexone until you've been off OxyContin for a while, at least seven days. There are adverse effects taking naltrexone with opiates in your system."

"Where do I get the other stuff?"

"Hold on. I'll be right back." Dr. Warnock returned with a small white paper bag. "There's enough CBD for you to take it twice a day for ten days, and there's enough THC for your forty-milligram dose at night for sleep. Try to cut down on your drinking, and when you come back, I'll see about starting naltrexone, providing you're clean from opiates. We'll wait until then to attack the demon alcohol. Address your pain first, then your addiction to alcohol."

"I'll try my best, doc. Sounds like good advice from another addict. We'll see how it goes."

"Okay, please tell the receptionist to schedule you for ten days from today. But, Adam, like I said, for me to start you on the naltrexone, you can't have opiates in your system. I you can't stop the OxyContin on your own, you will need to detox for at least a week in the hospital."

"That'll be tough. I'm supposed to take care of Lucas. I take him to school and pick him up, and then we have dinner together."

"Can you make other arrangements?"

"I don't know. I'll have to think about it and discuss it with Maria."

"Well, the sooner, the better."

Adam made his new appointment, signed some forms, went to his truck, and knocked back a couple of shots of vodka from the pint under his seat. He glared at the bottle and shook it. "Demon rum, you're a mean sonofabitch," he said to the bottle. "You need to leave me alone." He screwed on the cap and slid it back under the seat. A week in the hospital? How could he find a week? Someone has to take care of Lucas. Maria has to go to work. He needed to go back to work. Maybe he could stop the OxyContin altogether and detox at home. Ryan could help with that.

15

Adam and Lucas were eating some double chocolate chip ice cream after dinner on Sunday when Maria came in from her vacation in Santa Fe.

"Hey, Mom," Lucas said, running up to her. "I have a broken arm, and I got a cast. See?" Lucas held up his arm. "I got a bloody nose, but it's okay now. We were in a wreck."

Maria frowned, put her hands on her hips, and glared at Adam. "What happened?"

"I got distracted, and we slid off the road and down an embankment. It was the airbag that broke his arm. We've been to the hospital, and we're both okay. Lucas saw the doctor for a follow up on Wednesday and he's doing well."

Maria held out her arms to Lucas. "Come here for a hug." She wrapped him in her arms and rocked back and forth. "I'm sorry you got hurt," Nacho whined and then pushed his nose in between Maria and Lucas, as though he expected to be part of the hug. Instead, Lucas scratched behind his ear.

"Hey, Mom, want to sign my cast?"

"Sure. Let me get a marker. Do you care what color?"

"Red. I'd like you to sign in red."

Maria found a marker. "Okay, sit at the table and put your arm out straight." She wrote, 'Get well soon. You are my favorite son. Love you, Mom.'"

Lucas laughed. "I'm your only son."

"I know, but you are still my favorite."

Lucas turned on the TV and became absorbed. "Mom, in a little while, can you help me take a bath? I can't get my cast wet."

"Sure. Get your pajamas out of the dryer and run the water. I'll be there in ten minutes."

Adam stood up and walked toward the door. "I guess I'd better be going. The doctor said Lucas can have a children's Tylenol if he complains of pain."

"We need to talk, Adam."

"About what?"

"I can't even depend on you to take care of Lucas. I'll bet you were drunk," she said, crossing her arms.

"I didn't think so, but I got cited for DUI and reckless driving anyway."

Maria glared at Adam. "You didn't think so? Were you thinking at all?"

"My blood alcohol was a little above the limit, but not much."

"Had you taken your OxyContin?"

"Yes, my pain was down to a three or four."

Maria shook her head. "I'll bet they took away your license."

"No, but I have a court date in two weeks. My doctor, Dr. John Warnock, is a pain specialist and works with addicts. I told him I had a problem with alcohol. He's going to help me."

"You told him you have a problem? You've never admitted it before. Why now?"

"The wreck scared me, you know, deep down, especially after losing Ava."

"Well, duh, you could've both been killed. Then where would I be—a dead daughter, a dead son, and a dead husband. Are you blind *and* dumb?"

"I'm going to work on it, Maria. This time I promise I'll see it through."

"Your promises are empty and don't mean a thing." I can't let Lucas ride with you, and you can't be here if you're drinking, and that seems like all the time."

"I'm sick at heart. I love you, and I want our family to be together."

"I'm not up to it, Adam. I need time by myself." She held up her hand, showing the sapphire ring. "I'll find transportation for Lucas to get to school, and we'll make our own dinners. You need to stay away. You're a hopeless drunk."

"No, Maria. Nothing is ever hopeless, and I need to be with Lucas."

"Sorry. Not if you're drinking."

"Dr. Warnock doesn't want to start the medication until I've been off of OxyContin for seven days, so he wants me in the hospital for a seven-day detox from opiates. So maybe I'll go soon. I want to follow through on this. Let's find a way to keep our family together. Dr. Warnock has given me hope that I can whip this problem and find new ways to deal with my pain."

"I'll believe it when I see it; not until. In the meantime, stay away."

"I'll talk with Ryan about helping. He understands what I'm going through."

"Sure. You talk with Ryan, and I'll talk with Carolyn about her friends who I know will help. Just go on about your business, Adam. We don't need you around here."

Adam slammed his fist on the kitchen counter, hard enough to shake the cabinets. Maria jumped and raised her eyebrows.

"Get out—now."

Adam shouted down the hall, "Good night, Lucas. See you in the morning."

"Nite, Dad."

Adam stuffed his hands in his pockets and stomped out of the house, head down and knees shaking.

16

Adam appeared at Lola's house at ten am on Saturday. She was dressed in black yoga pants, a loose green t-shirt, and no bra. "Hello Adam, I wasn't sure you would show up."

He reached up and adjusted his Dallas Cowboy hat. "Well, I need the work, and you've been on my mind. Not much chance that I would forget."

"Come in and let me show you around."

She started in the living room, pointing to a large box. "I bought a new forty-two-inch TV and a mounting bracket for the wall. Can you install it?"

"Sure, no problem."

"This fireplace. It has gas logs, but I've never been able to get it to work. Do you think you can fix it?"

"Probably. I might need some new parts."

"Sure. You can use my card at Lowe's or Home Depot to get whatever you need."

"Sounds like a plan."

"Follow me to the master bedroom, and I'll show you a couple of other things. First, my sliding closet doors are cheap hollow core, and I want them replaced with sliding mirror doors. Can you do that?"

"I can install new tracks and the doors, and if Lowes has the doors, they can deliver. That way, if there's any damage, they're responsible."

"One more thing. I want mirror tile on the ceiling. It should be a rectangular configuration and the same size as the bed."

Adam looked at the ceiling and then the king-size bed. He tilted his head and smiled.

"One other thing," she said. "Can you replace that overhead light with a soft flood light?"

"Sure. Would you like it to shine on the bed?"

"Well, yes, silly." She put one hand to her chest and smiled. "Otherwise, it would be hard to see things in the mirror in the dark."

"Is that it, or do you have more?"

"That's my list, but I might think of other things you can do later."

"I can start on some of this right now. Shall I get my tools?"

"Yes, I was hoping you could get started right away."

"I'll need a small deposit for gas money, say one-hundred dollars."

"Let me get my purse," Lola said. She handed him five twenties.

Adam installed the TV wall bracket first, attached the TV, plugged it in, and made sure he could move through the channels on her cable subscription. He turned to the fireplace. After spending an hour taking everything apart, he discovered that the igniter for the gas logs was not working, so he replaced it with an extra igniter from his spare parts box. Then, after checking the gas supply for leaks, he started the fireplace with the remote control.

Lola appeared with two mugs of coffee. "You're making good progress—better than I expected. So, let's take a coffee break."

Adam and Lola sat on stools at the kitchen bar. Adam sipped his coffee and then turned to her. "Have you ever been married?"

"No. I don't seem to be very good at long-term relationships. I love having boyfriends, though."

"Boyfriends? More than one?"

"Yes, I'm what you call a parallel dater—I like to date more than one man at the same time."

"How does that work out for you?"

"The key is finding men who are okay with being occasional lovers and not exclusive. Unfortunately, most men, unless they're married, don't seem able to handle it." She eyed him with eyebrows raised, smiling.

"I'd have to think about that," Adam said.

"You said you're separated, headed for a divorce?"

"Yes, things seem to be changing."

Lola finished her coffee and put her mug in the sink. She took her keys off the hook on the side of a cabinet. "I've got to go to my yoga practice and then to the grocery store. You can stay here and work while I'm gone."

"I'm finished with the TV and the fireplace, so the bedroom is next. I can pick up the mirror tiles from Lowes and order the closet doors while I'm there."

"Good plan. Here's an extra key for you to use. I'll see you back here later. We can order a pizza for dinner."

Lola grabbed her purse and strolled to the door. Adam noticed that she wasn't wearing panties under her sheer yoga pants. He wondered if she always went commando. Then he smelled gardenias, and he shivered with lust, desire that was different, raw—like a strange force leading him into a dark cave.

Adam had moved the bed and was up on a ladder, installing the mirror tile on the ceiling, when Lola returned. "I'm in the bedroom," he called.

"Ooh, that's going to be nice," Lola said, regarding the two of them in the mirror. "Why don't you stop for the day, and you can order a pizza while I take a shower?"

Adam folded up his ladder, put his tools away, moved the mirror tile boxes into the closet, and pulled the bed back into place. After placing the ladder and his tools in his truck, he returned, washed his hands at the sink, and ordered a large cheese and green chili pizza from an Italian restaurant. He took a beer from the refrigerator, sat on the couch, and turned on the news. That asshole Trump was at it again, lying about his past and success as a businessman. Disgusted, he changed the channel. Soon the doorbell rang. He paid for the pizza and took a couple of plates and glasses from the cabinet. He heard the shower turn off, and within a few minutes, Lola came into the kitchen wearing a fluffy, white terrycloth bathrobe. She brushed her wet hair back and smiled. "Looks like you have dinner ready. Okay with you if I eat in my bathrobe?"

"Of course. What would you like to drink?"

"There's a bottle of chardonnay in the cabinet above the dishwasher. Let's start with that."

Adam brought the bottle to the kitchen bar and poured two glasses. "How about a toast?"

"Okay, what would you like to toast?"

"How about a toast to new friendships?"

"Great. So, you've decided you can handle a new friendship?"

"I'll have to take it slow, but I think I can, especially with someone like you."

Lola laughed and then leaned over and kissed him, lingering a bit with her soft lips.

"You taste like chardonnay," Adam said.

She finished her glass of wine, swirling it around in her mouth. "Try this," she said as she kissed him again. This time she moved her tongue over his and then nibbled on his lower lip.

"Let's watch the new TV," she said.

They moved to the living room and sat on the couch. Adam was at one end, and Lola scooted to the other, leaving a space between them. Then she tapped some white powder out of a small glassine envelope onto the glass coffee table. She used a sharp letter opener to arrange the powder into two rows and handed Adam a rolled-up five-dollar bill. She smiled as her robe fell open. "Here you go. This will perk things up."

Adam hesitated. "I haven't done any coke for a long time. I don't think it's good for me."

"Don't worry," Lola said. "I'll take good care of you."

Adam leaned down and snorted the line with a deep breath. He squeezed his eyes shut and held his breath. "Wow. That lifts you right up." He grinned.

Lola took the five-dollar bill and did the remaining line, rubbed her nose, and moved back to the end of the couch. She picked up the remote and started surfing through the channels. Finally, she stopped at a porn channel. "Do you like porn?"

"I don't watch it often."

"Well, I enjoy it, especially while pleasuring myself." She fished in her bathrobe pocket and pulled out a vibrator. "Do you mind?"

Adam turned bright red, rubbed his face, and pushed his fingers through his hair. "This is all new to me. Aren't you embarrassed?"

"Not at all. Having you watch spices things up."

"Should I touch you or anything?"

Lola smiled. "Not yet. You've probably figured out by now that sensual pleasures are important to me. I think pleasure is my lifeblood, my way of feeling alive. Centuries ago, if I had lived in Italy, I would be called a sybarite—someone who lives in the city of Sybaris and pursues endless sensual pleasure, day after day. People who don't understand might say I am a sex addict, but I'm not. I think I'm more like an enthusiast of pleasure, a connoisseur of the sensual, a modern-day sybarite."

Adam laughed. "You are the first sybarite I've ever met." He felt his face tingling and the back of his neck flush. "Seems a little awkward."

"Just relax and be with your body. Your body knows what to do."

Lola turned up the volume on the TV so she could hear the moans and watched a man perform oral sex on a woman. She opened her robe and turned her legs toward Adam, knees up and spread apart. She was glistening in the light as she applied her vibrator, alternating her gaze from the TV to Adam and back to the TV. He stared at her with his mouth open, rubbing his gums with his tongue. She was a true strawberry blond.

"Do you like to watch?"

Adam scratched the side of his head. " I'm watching, so I guess so." This is incredible, Adam thought as he watched the TV and then gazed at Lola and then at the vibrator and then looked into her eyes. She seemed to like prolonged eye contact, and the smiling connection provided fuel for the sordid thoughts racing through his imagination. She was way out there like no other woman he had ever met and an exhibitionist to boot. What was next?

"You can talk if you want," Lola said. "I can multi-task."

Adam gulped and clasped his hands together in his lap.

"Your body should be reacting by now," she said. "Watching a woman masturbate excites almost every man I've met."

Adam turned red as he felt himself swelling. "Right on. You can include me."

"Don't feel anxious, Adam. This will be all for tonight. You want to take it slow, right?"

Adam nodded and leaned back. Lola moved her vibrator up and down for a long time until she closed her eyes, threw her head back on a pillow, bit her lower lip, and shivered as she climaxed.

Adam stood up, pulling and arranging his pants. "I guess I'd better be going."

Lola left her robe open and stood up as she turned off the TV. "Can you come back next Saturday and finish up the work in the bedroom?" She crossed her arms and smiled as though the last half-hour had been an everyday event.

"I'll call you to make sure the mirror doors have arrived—Lowes said they should be here Thursday between three and five pm. Will you be home, or should I meet them?"

"I should be here. Yes, call to make sure, but I'll look for you next Saturday."

§

Adam returned the following Saturday. It took all day, but he finished installing the mirror tile, the floodlight, the new track, and the new mirrored doors on the closet. He could see himself in the closet mirror and the ceiling tiles from the bed. It was a foray into a new sensuality for him, and he thought he would just let go and see where it led. He felt steady pangs of guilt when he thought of Maria. But, after all, she had thrown him out of the house. He was a man with needs, and Lola was a woman who understood pleasure.

It was dark when Lola came home. Adam had eaten an omelet was watching the rerun of a football game. "I've finished all the work," he said, standing up. "Check it out."

He took Lola's hand and led her to the bedroom. She looked around and laughed. "This is perfect," she said, eyes mischievous. "Did it give you any ideas?"

"I did have a few fantasies."

"I had dinner with a doctor, and I see you made some eggs. Are you hungry?"

"No, I'm fine. Just waiting for you."

"Good." She started walking toward the bathroom, peeling off her clothes. "Come on, let's take a shower."

In the generous-sized shower stall, she lathered him from shoulders to toes, lingering at his thighs. "This is lovely," she said. "You are a fine specimen of a man."

Fully aroused, he washed her, front and back, breasts and hips, then rinsed her. He turned off the water and they wrapped themselves in white towels.

"Come on," she said. "Let's check out those new mirrors." She lit a couple of candles, turned on the overhead floodlight, and pulled him down into the bed. For nearly two hours, they frolicked, massaged, kissed, and wrapped themselves into a half dozen positions, each of which they could see in the mirrors. Lola loved the mirrors and kept one eye open, watching herself as she had orgasms. Adam's lust was fully alive, and he was only subliminally aware of the discomfort in his legs. He laughed to himself. Maybe he'd tell Dr. Warnock about this new pain management technique.

§

From that Saturday on, Lola invited Adam to share their pleasure every other Saturday, a frequency that was acceptable to Adam. They had become fuck buddies. No commitment, just fun.

One Saturday night in late June, Adam and Lola sat naked on the couch watching porn and caressing each other. Adam felt something pushing on his side, reached under a pillow, and pulled out a baseball cap. It was a red MAGA hat from the Trump campaign.

"Wow, Lola, I didn't realize you were a Trump supporter. This is your hat, right?"

"Yes, I support Trump. He's my guy."

"Why in the world would you do that?"

"He's strong, he's a successful businessman, and he has promised to drain the swamp in Washington. I think he's what we need for the country. He seems like a man for all people."

Adam pulled his hand away from between her thighs.

"Is there a problem?" she asked.

"No, I'm just surprised." These Trumpers all spout the same party line. Sounds like Doug, Adam thought.

"Well, come on with me. Let's move to the bedroom."

Even with the soft light, the mirrors, their nakedness, and her gentle stroking, Adam could not respond because of his abject confusion. Lola's magnificent body and her steady attention did not make a difference. Whenever he closed his eyes, the red hat filled his mind, and he felt as though the MAGA hat controlled him, sending forth waves of nausea. My body and her red hat don't work well together, he thought. Trump's orange face loomed up with the red hat, and Adam had to push back on his urge to vomit. He rolled away. "I'm sorry, Lola, but I seem to be off my game tonight."

"Just relax," she said. "You need to get out of your head. I know what I want and how to get it." She got up, turned on some soft jazz, turned off all the lights, and came back to bed with new resolve to extract the pleasure she had come to enjoy from Adam. After a while, aided by silky body lotion, he responded enough for the evening to progress as needed for Lola, the self-proclaimed sybarite. "I knew it would be okay," she said, smiling. "You're my man of the hour, and sybarites never give up."

Adam did not show up two weeks later as planned. He didn't call or text. He didn't respond to her calls. He could not move beyond Trump's orange hair and the nausea when he thought of Lola wearing her red MAGA hat.

In early July, Adam found a letter from Lola stuck under his windshield wiper. She had dabbed it with her gardenia perfume, and the paper was heavy and expensive. She had written with a blue fountain pen, and her cursive was artful. "Please come over Saturday night. I have a surprise for you that you will never, ever forget. Come at exactly eight o'clock. Let yourself in with your key. I will be in the room at the end of the hall." She had included a photo of her and Adam having sex. Lola had heavy-lidded eyes and smiled at the camera with her legs up and knees by her shoulders. Adam's naked back and hips were all that was visible. It could've been any man, but Adam could see his wedding ring on his hand on a pillow. Where was the camera? She must have had it hidden somehow.

He couldn't help wondering if she had other photos showing his face. He found himself growing angry that she would photograph or videotape their encounters without asking or telling him. Did she have a collection?

Back at work, Adam agonized all week and drank too much, hiding his drinking from Rocky and Jim and Ryan. His legs hurt, and he overdid his OxyContin dosage. Although Dr. Warnock's protocol seemed to be helping, he had put off any contact with him and plans for his detox. He was staying at Ryan's, avoiding what he knew, deep down, what had to be next—submitting to the opiate withdrawal that Dr. Warnock required. The CBD, THC, and melatonin helped him sleep, yet he felt dazed, confused, and drawn by the sights, smells, and pleasure of the weeks before. His lust would scream at him in the night, and his mind would tamp him down in the day. Twice, just before dark, he felt a cloud of shame come at him from the horizon. Eager to stay preoccupied, he worked hard, but it made no difference. The draw was powerful, and on Saturday night, he found himself parked in Lola's driveway, driven there by his uncontrollable desire. He was drunk, but he could navigate. He sat in his truck for a few minutes, wondering if he should leave. Then, through his rearview mirror, he saw a black unmarked van parked across the street. Someone was in the driver's seat wearing a red baseball cap backward, peering out the driver's side window with binoculars. Now, who the hell is that? He pulled the bill of his gray baseball cap down over his eyes and got out of the truck.

Adam let himself in at precisely eight o'clock and shuffled down the hall. He could hear music. He opened the door to a once-in-a-lifetime scene. A dozen spice-scented candles burned, and Lola stood naked with an alluring smile on her face. He squinted as though he might see someone else through his impaired mind. She had her hands on the back of her hips, and her skin glistened with body oil and candlelight. She was wearing her red MAGA hat, and her strawberry blond hair shimmered in the soft light. She pushed out her loins toward him, slightly spreading her legs and moving back and forth. "Hey, Adam. Wanna grab my pussy?"

"What the hell?" he said.

"Do you wanna grab my pussy? Surprise. I shaved it just for you."

Adam swallowed, pushed back nausea, and breathed out lust. Speechless, his mind was awash with fleeting images, cartoons of what might be next. There she was, right before him, offering herself unabashedly, and he stood frozen in time. He sniffed and rubbed his nose. The scents of potpourri, cloves, and vanilla floated from the candles in the warm air. The soft music seemed to come from everywhere, and Lola's green eyes flashed at him with yearning.

In his mind, he kept hearing Trump trash talk about women. Angry, he couldn't take his eyes off the red MAGA hat perched jauntily on her head, and yet, the lure of her body drove him on. The swirling mix of anger and lust in his heart seemed strange, and his body was rigid.

Lola drew close, unbuttoned his shirt, and then undid his belt and jeans. He stood still in the candlelight as his pants dropped to his feet. He stepped out of them. Then his underwear. She kissed him with her full lips and tongue, pushed her warm breasts against his bare chest, and caressed his body below. He responded with gusto, but then, without warning, his flag unfurled in the doldrums of his imagination—Trump's lying face and red hat brought him down way beyond flaccid, like swimming in icy water. He pointed his finger at her MAGA hat. "That hat bothers me. Is there a camera? Are you taking pictures?"

"Oh, come on, Adam. Relax, it's only a hat. Fucking me beats politics any day, and no, I'm not taking pictures."

He reached over, grabbed the bill of the MAGA hat, threw it into a dark corner, took a deep breath, squeezed his eyes closed, and imagined Maria in her sheer, white nightgown, backlit by moonlight, smelling of lavender and cinnamon, smooth brown skin yielding to his touch.

Lola dropped to her knees. "Here, let me help you with that," she said.

Pushing back his nausea once again, he stroked her hair as she continued. The scented candles, her nakedness, her eagerness, her soft hair, and Adam's imagination worked together to bring him once again to full throttle. Lola pulled him over to the bed, pushed him down on his back, and mounted him, riding him bareback, hands on his chest, like a cowgirl in barrel race on the straightaway. And Adam, there in the dark, arched himself against Lola's moistened skin, kept his eyes closed and imagined he was inside Maria. What ensued was a desperate thrusting that conveyed fear that this could be the last time, and that fear created an edge where they both danced until they were exhausted. Then, without speaking, Adam got up, dressed, and then leaned over and kissed Lola. She returned the kiss with eagerness. He stroked her hair. "Goodbye, Lola."

"See you soon?"

"Probably not."

"It won't be long, Adam, and you'll be hungry for me again." She took his hand and put it on her breast. "All you have to do is text or call."

Adam climbed into his truck and knocked back three swallows of brandy. He smelled Lola on his hand, rubbed his lips, and took another swallow. The same black van was still parked across the street, motor running. Adam took another ten-mg OxyContin, started the engine, and drove away. The black van followed. Was he losing his mind? He cried and pounded his hand on the steering wheel. He suddenly noticed he was woozy, so he pulled off the road and parked in a dark corner of a Walmart parking lot. He buried his face in his hands and let out a mournful wail, soon replaced by deep breaths. Then under him—almost, it seemed, with a loud gurgle—a large drain opened, his hope and courage swirling down into a dark sewer, a sewer that ran fast, as though a dam had broken upstream. He knew it. He was losing his mind. Two more gulps of brandy, and then he passed out on the passenger seat. The black van circled him a couple of times and then drove away.

17

Sunday, the following day, Francisco Duran parked his black van in Lola's driveway and rang the doorbell.

"Oh, Francisco," Lola said. "Come on in."

They sat at the kitchen table, and Lola poured coffee.

Francisco put a baggie half full of white powder on the table. "Here's your supply. Do you have new photographs?"

"No, not today. My last friend is the low-hanging fruit, but he's a broken-down alcoholic. I don't think he'd even be good for fifty dollars." She handed Francisco a copy of the photo she had sent to Adam. "This is all I have, and it only shows his back."

"Not good enough. I need pictures of faces and genitals. I've got the arrival and departure photos I took from my van, but you have to do the rest. Let's go check things out and make sure everything is working." He walked to the bedroom, pulled a chair over to the ceiling floodlight, and stood on the chair. Francisco pushed on a slight separation between the ceiling and the light, activating a pressure switch, and a small door dropped down, revealing a video camera aimed at the bed. He checked the camera's memory chip and the charge on the batteries, then returned the camera to the bracket that held it.

"The camera is good to go," he said, climbing down. He gestured to the headboard. "And your remote control is right there by your alarm clock. Videos are better, and you can start and stop the camera easily. We'll use video clips first, and then we'll print the juicy still shots and make eight-by-tens."

Lola clamped her hands on her hips and frowned. "We're supposed to be partners, and I feel like you're pimping me out. Let me do my job, and you do your part."

"I need more photos." Francisco's eyes narrowed. "That coke is not cheap, and you're up to two hundred dollars a day. So don't piss me off. I can always find another whore."

"You can't find women who can hustle rich guys and know how to handle things. You need an intelligent, beautiful woman who's connected. I'm a professional escort, not a whore."

"We're falling behind whether you're a professional or not."

"Okay, okay. I'm working a couple of well-heeled doctors. I have an appointment on Monday with a plastic surgeon. He makes a fortune fixing boobs and butts. He thinks I'm repping new pharmaceutical products, but I'll have him in bed before you can say tummy tuck. Come by next Sunday, and I'll have a video for you."

Francisco approached Lola, his face menacing. He clutched Lola's throat with one hand and grabbed the back of her head with the other. He squeezed hard as Lola's eyes widened, and she turned red. He bent her head forward and squeezed hard with the other hand. He put his mouth to her ear. "Listen, I answer to people too. This is a good scam. Don't fuck things up, or you'll get hurt, and not just by me. Do you get it?"

Lola nodded, tears dripping. He released his grip, and she gasped for air. She heard Francisco let himself out the door and followed, peeking out the window until she heard the van drive away. A cold wave of fear crashed over her, and trembling, she leaned against the wall. This was not the Francisco she knew. What did he mean by he wasn't the only one who would hurt her? She found a pint of chocolate almond ice cream in the freezer, sat down at the table, and ate the whole thing.

§

On Monday, Lola appeared in Dr. Eric Johnson's office for her appointment. She had brought a couple of studies on Bard Pharmaceutical gabapentin and liquid codeine. Dr. Johnson used mild pain control for his implant patients, and Lola was eager to switch him to Bard products. She wore her light green pants suit and a crisp white blouse. The pants were tight, and she had unbuttoned the top three buttons of her blouse, showing ample cleavage. Her shoulder-length strawberry blonde hair curled under, framing her face, and a green silk scarf set off her eyes.

"Come on in my office," Dr. Johnson said. "Tell me about the Bard studies on pain control."

Lola sat by his desk, bent over, withdrew several folders from her briefcase. Out of the corner of her eye, she could see Dr. Johnson watch her cleavage jiggle. So far, so good. She went over the design of the studies, charts, and results. The Bard gabapentin was slightly superior to other brands. The liquid codeine was not significantly better than others, but patients said it had a good taste.

"Well, I can certainly give the gabapentin a try. I'll specify the Bard brand on my next prescription, and we'll see how it goes."

Lola reached into her briefcase, flashing her cleavage again. "I have some patient coupons. They discount the first prescription by fifty percent. Here's a handful you can keep on your desk."

"Thank you."

Dr. Johnson was a handsome man. He was about fifty, clean-shaven, with silver-gray hair, a rectangular face, bright eyes, and a broad smile showing perfect, white teeth.

"Ms. Jenkins. May I call you Lola?"

Lola smiled. "Sure. May I call you Eric?"

"Fine with me." He made intense eye contact. "I gather you've noticed we both have green eyes."

"Yes, I noticed that first thing, and your broad shoulders. Do you work out?"

"Three times a week at the gym. I go in the evenings after work."

"Don't you have to get home? I suspect someone has your dinner ready."

"Well, that someone is me, and dinner is frozen pizza. I'm single."

"You know what? I should prepare a home-cooked meal for you. Do you like beef stroganoff with mushrooms?"

"Yes, I love stroganoff."

"Are you free on Wednesday evening?"

"Yes, I'm available."

"Shall we make it a date? Say, six-thirty?"

"Gosh, I guess so."

Lola wrote her home address on the back of her business card and handed it to him. "This will be fun. I love to cook."

"Can I bring anything?"

"A nice Chardonnay would be great."

He stood up and extended his hand. Lola took it, and he raised his eyebrows and smiled. "I'll see you at six-thirty—bearing gifts."

Lola walked out of his office to her car, her mind busy. Okay, Francisco, this will be a good one. He looks luscious, so I get to enjoy it, and we'll get a good video. I know he knocks down four-hundred grand a year, plus speaking engagements. He'll be able to pay for a long time. I'll bet he's already fantasizing. Better shave the netherworld again.

§

Lola was stirring noodles into boiling water when the doorbell rang. Strips of beef were browning in avocado oil and flour. The kitchen smelled buttery. Under her apron, she wore a loose white dress with a high bodice. Her hair was gathered into a ponytail and tied with a green ribbon, and her shoes were black flats. Her make-up was modest, barely noticeable, and her legs were bare. The only thing she wore under her dress was dusting powder that smelled like fresh honey.

After checking to see the black van was parked across the street, she opened the door to the bright shiny face of Dr. Eric Johnson. "Hello, and come in."

"Here's the Chardonnay. I hope it is a brand that you enjoy."

Lola took the bottle and glanced at the label. "It's perfect, Eric. Thank you. Come in the kitchen, and we can visit while I finish the beef stroganoff. Then we can move to the dining room."

She poured wine for each of them, and Eric sat at the kitchen table. Adjacent, in the dining room, Lola had set the table with her good china, cloth napkins, a fresh flower centerpiece, and tapered candles in tall, silver candlesticks.

"Lola, I want to thank you for the invitation. I haven't had a home-cooked dinner in months."

"Oh, this is only the beginning," she said, making eye contact.

"Is there dessert?"

Lola smiled and locked her eyes on his. "Yes, I've got a dessert ready that you will never forget." She took her time removing her apron, noticing Eric's subtle admiring glances as he surveyed her body.

While chatting about drugs and work-related activities, Lola prepared two plates and put them on the dining room table along with a green salad in a Nambe serving bowl.

"Bring your wine. We're ready to eat."

Eric sat down after helping Lola with her chair. "Should I offer grace?"

"How lovely. I didn't know you are religious."

"Yes. My mother took me to a Methodist church while I was growing up, and I've been offering health education classes at church, mostly breast cancer awareness. Our pastor has become a good friend." He smiled and winked. "That may be because I'm generous with my annual pledge. I thank God every day for the abundance in my life. I think our spiritual health comes from being grateful for what we have."

"Eric, I agree with you. I'm grateful that we met and that you are here and for what may come from this." Lola folded her hands and bowed her head. "So go ahead. Please say grace."

"Thank you, Lord, for good home-cooked food and new friendships. Amen."

"Amen" Lola raised her head. "That was short."

"Yup, short and sweet and to the point."

"I've been wondering. How did you get interested in plastic surgery?"

"I think it started when I was a teenager. My social studies teacher got breast cancer and had a partial mastectomy. She was away for a while, but she appeared normal and attractive when she returned. My mother told me that a plastic surgeon had reconstructed a new breast to replace the removed one. The surgery lifted her spirits, made her look normal, and instilled a sense of pride in her appearance. I was so happy for her. I wondered if someday I could make someone feel that good by changing their appearance. Then in medical school, one thing led to the next."

"That's a noble and thoughtful motive, Eric. Helping people look good brings a lot of joy into the world. I'll bet your patients are fond of you because you care about their appearance."

"I've had a few complaints, but not many. Most women are proud of their implants."

Lola put the back of her hands under her bodice and pushed her breasts up. "Maybe someday, but I don't need help yet."

Eric grinned. "In my professional opinion, you are correct."

Lola gathered the dishes and brought them to the sink. "I'll tend to these later. Let's move to the living room and relax a little. Sit there on the couch, while I turn on the TV."

18

On Friday, Lola and Francisco sat together in Eric Johnson's waiting room. At precisely eleven am, the medical assistant said, "Ms. Jenkins, Dr. Johnson will see you now."

"I have my employer with me, and he'll be accompanying me to my appointment."

"Very well."

Eric raised his eyebrows in surprise to see Lola's companion.

"This is my employer, Francisco Duran," Lola said. "He's here to share some important information."

"Are you with Bard Pharmaceuticals too, Mr. Duran?"

"No, he's my employer for a different venture. Our visit is not about drugs."

"Please sit down. What information do you have?"

At Francisco's nod, Lola took three manilla envelopes from her briefcase. One was marked "My Mother," one was marked "My Church," and the third one was labeled "My Files." She slid them across the desk to Eric. He opened the first one and slid out the contents, twelve eight-by-ten glossy photographs. The first two, dated and time-stamped, showed him entering and exiting Lola's house. He paged through the other ten photos with eyes popping and his mouth open. His face turned red, he shuffled in his chair, and then stood up and gestured toward Francisco and Lola with fists balled. "You sonsofbitches"

"Easy does it," Francisco said. "We are going to become friends before this is over."

Dr. Johnson glared at Lola, biting his lower lip. "It's over right now.

Take your whore and get the hell out of here. I can't believe you would do this, Lola."

"Whoa. We've got to talk about things," said Francisco. "I have duplicates. This first set goes to your mother, and I'll deliver the second one to your pastor, unless…."

"Unless what?"

"Let's say a down payment of five-thousand dollars and a-thousand a month after that."

Eric glared at Lola. "You blackmailing whore. Is there a moral bone in your body?"

"A woman has to make a living," she said with a shrug. "And I've got a habit to feed."

Francisco stood up. "Five-thousand right now, and I won't beat you bloody. If I have to wait, then I'll hurt you bad." He grabbed the doctor by his tie, yanked him forward across his desk, and snapped open his switchblade, all in one smooth motion.

Eric pulled back and put up his hands. "Okay, no need for that. I've got money." He sat down at his desk. "Whom do I make the check out to?"

"No checks. You need to go to the bank right now and get cash. Large bills."

"I can't just leave in the middle of the day."

"Sure you can. Tell your receptionist you have to run an errand. We'll drive you."

They got in the black van and drove to the bank. Eric went in while Lola and Francisco waited in the parking lot. He soon came out and handed Francisco a bank envelope. "Count it. Five-thousand dollars in hundred-dollar bills."

"No need to count it," Francisco said. "I trust you."

They dropped him off back at his office.

Eric leaped out of the van, leaned down to the open window and said to Lola, "I don't want to see you again, and I expect you to give me all the photos."

"Not so fast," said Francisco. "I'll tuck the photos away unless we need them. I'll be by on the first of the month for your first payment. After that, everything will be cool as long as you pay. Your mother, pastor, and church folks will get a real surprise if you don't. Plus, I have a video file especially edited for your employer and internet ready. I shouldn't have to tell you how that will change your life, at the very least you'll have to leave Albuquerque in disgrace." Francisco paused, narrowing his eyes. "If you fuck with me, doctor, you'll need a plastic surgeon to fix the scars on your face after I cut you up. It will happen when you least expect it. Do you understand?"

"Yes, I get it." Eric glared at Lola and shook his head. "I pity you. You put your body out there for money and blackmail. You're a beautiful woman with a well-paying legitimate job. You don't need to do this. Are you so shallow that you have no respect for yourself or others?"

Lola put on her red MAGA hat and pulled her ponytail through the back. "Money buys a lot of respect, Eric. Don't be such a wuss. This is a cruel world, and I'm not a loser."

"Yes, but you don't have to prostitute yourself. You could have a decent future."

"That's enough," Francisco said. "Lola is my rainmaker, and we don't need your smart mouth giving her ideas. See you on the first."

§

The black van drove away, and Eric shuffled back to his office. He looked through the three manila envelopes and then locked them away in his file cabinet. He wrote down the van license number on a sticky note, and then he called his receptionist and asked her to cancel his remaining appointments for the day.

"I have a horrible headache," he said. "I'm going home to rest, and I'll call you later about the schedule tomorrow."

When he got home, he called his friend Antonio Romero. Antonio, now a lead detective, had been with the police force for over ten years. Eric had helped Antonio's wife, Melinda, with breast reconstruction and had allowed Antonio to pay a reduced fee over time. Melinda had been ill for several years, and they had used all of their savings for medical bills. "Let me know if I can ever help you with anything," a grateful Antonio had said after the surgery.

"Hey, Antonio, this is Eric Johnson. I think I need your help."

"You think?"

"I'm sure I need your help. Can we meet somewhere?"

"How about coffee at the Starbucks by your office, say six pm?"

"Okay. Could you look up a license plate in the meantime?"

"Sure. What's the number?"

§

Eric ordered coffee for two, then joined Antonio on soft chairs in the corner.

"Okay, what's this all about?" asked the detective.

"Did you get the license registration?"

"Yes, the van is registered to a limited liability corporation called Great Investments, LLC. The president is named Smith, and they list a post office box in Dallas as an address."

"That's not much help."

"Sorry, that's all I could find."

"No need to be sorry. I had an encounter with someone named Francisco Duran, and I thought maybe his name and address would pop up."

"What was your encounter?"

"Antonio, I got myself into a jam."

"How so?"

"With a woman, Lola Jenkins. It turned out I was a mark for a scam and didn't realize it. She was something else, and I got carried away. It makes me shiver to think about it. But her accomplice, Francisco Duran, was pimping her out. They took videos and made still photos."

"Compromising?"

"Oh, yes, and then some."

"She was a professional?"

"Yeah, and all the photos are explicit; I am now eligible for the porn photo Oscars.

"That bad, huh?"

"You can see my face and my body and her body and our antics in every photo. They knew what they were doing, and now I'm being blackmailed."

"Did you pay them?"

"I gave them five-thousand dollars in cash as a down payment, and they also want a thousand dollars a month to keep the photos under wraps."

"Did you go to a hotel?"

"No, we went to her house. She has mirrors on the ceiling over her bed and mirrored closet doors. She liked watching us and watching herself, I think. She enjoys sex, or she's a good actress."

"You have her address, right?"

"Right."

"That may have been a fatal mistake on their part. She should have gone to a hotel."

"How so?"

"Usually, people are habitual with their scams. They repeat the process. They will find another mark, and she'll take him to her house. This is a head start. We know the scene of the crime. I can put a detective on it, and he can do a stakeout. In the meantime, we'll look for the black van."

"I think Francisco took the photos of me going in her house and coming out of her house. Your detective can look for a parked van and a man with a camera."

"Okay. Let's meet here on Saturday, and I'll bring you up to date. Did he seem violent? Was he armed?"

"He flashed a knife and said he would cut my face if I didn't pay. I'd say that's violent."

Antonio nodded. "We have a clear case of extortion and blackmail. These people belong in jail. I'll ask my detective friend, Carter Wilson, to open a file and do the stakeout. He'll call you, and you can go over the details again with him. Maybe you'll remember other things."

"Did I tell you that I'm scared?"

Antonio smiled. "Yes, I figured as much."

"There's something else. I tried my first cocaine while I was there. Lola said something about feeding her habit."

"Well, that goes to motive. Francisco may be Lola's dealer and has her under his thumb."

"He made it abundantly clear that he was in charge, but I think he works for somebody."

"Okay, I'll have a black-and-white cruise by your house a couple of times during the night. As long as he thinks you'll pay him, he'll stay away, but we might as well be vigilant. Maybe we can catch them when you make your next payment. We'll see how it goes. In the meantime, don't worry, I've got your back."

§

Eric carried on his typical routine for the rest of July. He went to work early for his hospital rounds, and then he saw people in his office the rest of the day. He was home by seven pm, cooked a simple dinner, and watched TV or read his medical journals. He left the curtain open on his bedroom window so he could see the traffic going by. He felt reassured whenever he saw a black and white police car pass slowly by, driven by two uniformed officers. One would. shine his spotlight on the doctor's front door and along the front of his house. Grateful for their presence, he was able to sleep, knowing they would be by several times during the night.

On the Saturday before the first of the month, Eric met with Antonio and Carter Wilson at a restaurant near his house. This next payment would be due Tuesday. After they ordered omelets, and Carter flipped through the small notebook he kept in his shirt pocket.

"Here it is. The black van was parked outside Lola's house last Monday evening. About seven pm, a man in his fifties drove up in a green Subaru Outback. The vehicle belonged to Joseph Hamilton, an anesthesiologist at the Lovelace orthopedic clinic. He went in at about seven o'clock and came out at ten-thirty. The driver of the van took pictures. A large burly man with a shaved head and neck tattoos sat in the passenger seat. He wore a black sweatshirt. They drove away shortly after Joseph Hamilton left in his Subaru."

"I guess he's their next mark," Eric said. "Because of her drug rep job, she has access to men in the medical field."

"Doctors have money," Antonio said, "and they are often overworked and lonely. Easy prey for a sexy, beautiful woman."

"I want to nail this bastard," Carter said. "Let's set up a sting."

"I'm game," said Eric.

Antonio took a sip of his coffee. "I'm guessing Francisco will want to drive you to the bank to get the cash, right?"

"I don't know. He probably expects I'll have it for him at the office."

"You can act confused, you know, expecting a repeat of last time," Carter said.

"Sure. I can say I thought he wanted to drive me to the bank so he would watch my every move. Last time he said he had an appointment at eleven am."

"Okay, then, let's work with that," Carter said. "We'll have a couple of unmarked cars in the bank parking lot and a SWAT team standing by across the street. When you come out of the bank, and just before you get in the van, we'll grab him. The money and your photos are the evidence for blackmail. You brought the photos, right?"

"Here's the envelope. These are my file copies."

Carter paged through the photos. "Jesus Christ, Dr. Johnson, you are all over the place and photogenic as well. And that's Lola Jenkins in all her glory. How did they get these pictures?"

"Lola has mirrors and a floodlight on her bedroom ceiling, and I suspect the camera is in the ceiling space near the light."

"Well, we can expect that Joseph Hamilton is in for a surprise," Antonio said. "I think I'll go by his house and tell him what he's fallen into."

"That'll give him a chance to get ready," Eric said. "Tell him he can call me if he'd like. Francisco and Lola may show up in his office. That's what happened to me."

"Carter will go by and see Dr. Hamilton. He'll need coaching."

"I can do that later," Carter said. Here's the plan. We'll set up at the bank at eleven am Monday. You should be there a little after eleven-thirty. There are likely two men, and I doubt Lola will be with them. She has served her purpose."

§

On Tuesday morning, Eric sat at his desk, writing notes, when the receptionist bussed to say that Francisco had arrived.

He stood up as Francisco came through the door, closing it behind him.

"Hey, doctor, it is the first of the month. Do you have a payment for me?"

"Eric feigned embarrassment. "I have it—but not here. I assumed you would want to drive me to the bank again."

"Francisco's eyes flashed with anger. "That was just for the first time. From now on, have it ready."

"I will," Eric said earnestly. "Today, we'll need to go to the bank and get the cash. Sorry, I'm new to this game."

Francisco snorted, but led him to the parking lot, where a large man sat in the passenger seat of the black van, cleaning his fingernails with a combat knife. Francisco shoved Eric into the back seat. They drove around the block of couple of times to ensure no one was following, then made their way to the bank. Francisco parked in a space near the exit.

"Okay, Johnson. Same as last time. Hundred-dollar bills."

Eric went into the bank and returned within a few minutes. He walked up to the driver's side of the van and held out the bank envelope. "Here's your money. I called a cab to get back to the office." He moved out of the way toward the back of the van.

Four plainclothes policemen ran to the vehicle, two on each side, and drew their guns. "Police! Out, out, get out now," Carter ordered Francisco. "You are under arrest."

Francisco raised his hands as Carter jerked open the door. Francisco floored the accelerator, and with tires squealing, jumped the curb and fishtailed down the street, horn blaring. The thug in the passenger seat leaned out the window and emptied his pistol at the two officers on his side. "Gun, gun," they shouted. Two men from the SWAT team jumped out of their vehicle and stormed the black van, shooting at the tires. One of the officers took a bullet in the leg and crawled behind a parked car.

Carter jumped into the unmarked car Antonio was driving, and the two detectives chased the black van. The large man reloaded, leaned out the window again, and started shooting at Carter and Antonio. Two bullets hit the windshield and were buried in the seat between them, a near miss. "That bastard is a good shooter," Carter said. "I'm dropping back, and we'll notify dispatch for additional backup."

Francisco drove recklessly, swiping parked cars, running red lights, and turning up alleyways and side streets. He sped up after coming out of an alley, turned sharply, and then drove into an open warehouse door. The door closed quickly. Antonio drove out of the same alleyway and stopped at the street. They looked right and left. There was no sign of Francisco. "I think we lost the bastard," Carter said. "We'll put out an APB on their vehicle, but chances are they'll hole up somewhere until the dust settles. It was a good plan, but he had nothing to lose, so they took a big chance—and it paid off. They got away."

"At least we can pick up Lola Jenkins," Antonio said. "And we need to find the cameras."

"She's into cocaine and had a significant supply. That's probable cause for a search warrant. I'll call a judge and get one. We should have it by this evening if I put a rush on it."

The judge granted the search warrant quickly, and Carter and Antonio parked in front of Lola's house at six pm. Lights were on in the kitchen. They knocked at the door, and Lola answered, dressed in jeans and a white T-shirt. "Hello, officers. How can I help you? Would you like to come in?"

"Yes," said Carter. "We have a search warrant, and we're looking for drugs."

"Sure, come in and look around. There are no drugs here except for my prescriptions."

Carter and Antonio donned rubber gloves and began to search. Lola followed them around, insisting there was nothing to find. Antonio searched the drawers and medicine cabinet in her bathroom. On a hunch, he dumped out half a dozen sanitary pads from the box, and a baggie full of white powder fell out. "Hey, check this out. It looks like enough to arrest her with an intent to distribute. She may be a dealer. I guess we'll find out." He wet his finger, touched the powder, and then tasted it. "It's cocaine, all right."

Lola raised her eyebrows and took a deep breath. Fear gripped her. In her mind, she watched her future crumble in front of her. A ten-year career could come to an end. Maybe they would let her work while pursuing a drug diversion program. Perhaps she would be fired. Could she end up in jail? Lola had heard that possession with an intent to distribute could be a three to five-year sentence in the state women's prison. She put her hand on her mouth. In twenty-four hours, she would be in a bad way. Where would she score? Her fear shape shifted as her hands shook, her stomach cramped, and tears filled her eyes. Deep down, she felt an icy sense of dread, and it took all of her strength to control her tears and to push down the screams that stuck in her throat.

"That's not mine," she said. "I don't know where that came from."

Carter snapped some photos of the box, the baggie full of cocaine, and the cabinet where he'd found the box. "You can argue about that later, but we have enough here for an arrest."

"I need to call a lawyer," she said.

"You can do that when we get to the station."

Antonio dumped out Lola's purse on the dining room table and rifled through everything. There were no drugs. He paged through her checkbook looking for clues about how she paid for her drug habit. He jotted down notes about a couple of other checks and dropped the checkbook into an evidence bag.

Carter took out his handcuffs and turned to Lola. "Hands behind your back, please. You are under arrest for possession and the intent to distribute. Anything you say can be held against you. You have the right to an attorney, and if you can't afford an attorney, one will be appointed for you. Do you understand your rights?" Lola nodded, and he fastened the handcuffs. "Please come with me to the car."

At the station, Lola was fingerprinted, booked, and detained in a holding cell to await her arraignment.

"This should put a stop to the scam for a while," Antonio said. "Now, all we have to do is find Francisco Duran and whoever he's working for."

"We should warn Dr. Johnson," Carter said. "He's at risk, and we'll need to cover his house with twenty-four-hour unmarked surveillance.

I wouldn't put it past that asshole Francisco to seek revenge. If we want to make the blackmail stick with Lola, we have to find another mark to testify. Two witnesses are ten times better than one."

"I'm sure Joseph Hamilton will testify to his tryst with Lola, but he hasn't been approached for money yet," Antonio said. "There was no sign of the Hamilton photographs. Francisco probably has them. However, I looked through her checkbook. There were carbon copies of each check, and there were a couple of checks made out for cash, but they were small. She probably trades work for drugs or uses cash. There were a couple of checks made out to Adam Young for 'repairs, and for 'supplies and materials.' I'm guessing he did some work on her house."

"He should be easy to find," Carter said. "Maybe he heard something or saw something."

"Good catch," Antonio said. "I'll have someone check with the Construction Industries Commission. If he's a legitimate contractor, he'll be licensed, and his address will be on file."

Carter handed the evidence bag and checkbook to Antonio. "Do you think he got caught up in her scam doing construction work? Did she take pictures of him?"

"I don't know. Let's find him and ask him. I'll bet he knows something."

19

Responding to a tip from Albuquerque Constructors, Antonio located Adam Young at the Ryan Wither's apartment. He knocked at the door, and an unshaven well-built man answered. "Hello, officer. How can I help you?"

"Are you Adam Young?"

"Yes, sir."

After identifying himself, Antonio asked, "Do you know a Ms. Lola Jenkins? I believe you did some work for her."

"Yes, but I haven't seen her for a while."

"May I come in? I have a couple of other questions." He noticed a child of about six who was hovering behind Adam, his arm in a cast. "Don't worry. You're not in trouble. I just need some information."

"Sure, come in. Would you like coffee?"

Adam sent Lucas to another room to play, then prepared coffee and sat at the kitchen table with the detective.

"Now, what's this about Lola Jenkins?" he asked.

"We picked her up for cocaine possession, but we think she's involved in a blackmailing scam as well. She hit up a doctor for big dollars after showing him an array of photographs. They were, well, pornographic and explicit. She hid the camera somehow. Did she ever ask you for money?"

"No, in fact, she paid me to do some work at her house."

"How much?"

"Thirty-five dollars an hour. I worked about twenty hours altogether."

"Do you think she's a prostitute?"

"No, but she gets first prize for being an oversexed liar. That woman is something else." He paused, looking toward the room where his boy was playing. "This is all confidential, right?"

"Yes, our conversation is confidential. Did Lola take any pictures of you?"

"I don't think so. Oh, wait—there is one picture. She sent it to me in the mail."

"Can I see it?"

"It's embarrassing. Just a minute, I'll get it." He rose, hen returned with a photo, and handed it to Antonio. "You can see us having sex and her smiling with her knees on her shoulders. But all you can see of me is my back. I wondered if it was me, and then I spotted my wedding ring. It's me all right."

"Did she offer you any drugs?"

"I'm not in any trouble here, right?"

"That's right. I'm just gathering information."

"We shared a couple of lines of coke."

"Did the cocaine belong to her?"

"Yes, she had a baggie more than half full, probably twenty grams or so."

"See if I have this right. You worked on Lola's house, did a couple of lines of coke, and then had sex?"

"Yes, that's about it."

"Did you ever go back?"

"A couple of times, until I discovered that we were not compatible, regardless of the pleasure. We don't share the same political beliefs."

"Oh, how's that?"

"No offense meant, but she's a Trumper and likes to wear her MAGA hat when she's having sex. Turned me off bigly."

Antonio laughed. "Don't worry about offending me. I'm a never-Trumper, and so is my detective partner Carter Wilson. I can see how a red Trump hat could alter the mood."

Antonio gave Adam his business card, then walked with him to the door. "Call me if you remember anything else. By the way, make sure you stay away from her house. She has a partner, and we're trying to find him.

He's a bad man. I'm told he likes to hurt people. His bodyguard likes to hurt folks too."

Adam shook his head, his expression grave. "There's no chance I'll go back there. Lola's trouble, and I don't need more trouble."

20

Francisco and his bodyguard, Joey Grimm, sat on folding chairs in the warehouse as the sun faded in the west. The door to the back room was locked, and there was no light under the door.

"How long are we going to wait?" Joey asked.

"Until you see a light come on under the door. The boss man will come in the back door around nine pm. He likes to work at night."

Francisco paced around the warehouse and Joey stretched out in the van.

At nine-thirty a light came on and the office door opened. Francisco stood before a well-dressed older man with silver-gray hair, broad shoulders, and a black eye patch. "Hey, boss. Here's the payment from Dr. Johnson." He handed over the thousand dollars in the bank envelope. "But we need to find that bastard. He needs to pay for screwing us over. I'm going to cut his face to ribbons."

Reginald Hammer listened as he counted the money, then pocketed it. "You know you were stupid to come here. Are you sure you weren't followed?"

"We made a clean getaway. We've been here for hours. No sign of anyone."

"The police scanner says they're searching the neighborhood," the Hammer said. "You fucked up, shooting a cop. They'll be searching all week."

"We should get out of here, right?" Francisco asked.

"Soon, after midnight. When is he supposed to make his next payment?"

"First of the month."

"Keep your eye on the prize," the Hammer said. "And don't do anything stupid. The cops have already connected you to the photos. If Dr.

Johnson gets hurt, you will be the main suspect. Either way, if they catch you, they will hold you without bail. Even our attorney wouldn't be able to spring you."

"So, what should we do?"

"Change the game."

"How?"

"Let's collect the next payment a few days early. You can text Dr. Johnson with a burner phone and have him meet you with the cash at a secure place. We'll send plenty of muscle to cover you. Tell him the price has gone up to five-thousand a month. Tell him if he goes to the police, you will release some choice photos to his employer."

"That changes the game, all right, and he can afford five-grand."

"You need to lay low for the rest of the month, and so does Joey." He motioned to the bodyguard. "Joey, you should take a trip to Denver and stay gone for a month." He handed him a roll of cash.

"Okay, boss," Joey said. "I'll be gone by morning."

"Francisco, get on a bus and take a vacation—Galveston, out of the way, and we have a safe house there. When you get to Dallas, transfer to a different bus. Use your fake identification."

"Okay, will do"

The Hammer handed him three-thousand dollars. "That should cover expenses."

"What should we do about Lola?" Francisco asked.

"I'll make some calls and let you know."

"Without her coke, she's liable to sing like a canary."

"If she does, you are the only one she knows, and no matter what she says, you won't be worse off. She doesn't know anything more than the police know. We don't need t worry about Lola."

"She might talk about our last mark, Dr. Joseph Hamilton."

"Have you shown him photos yet?"

"No, not yet."

"No laws broken so far."

"She could be picked up on drug charges."

"That would be her problem. Leo Sabatini, my attorney, could offer to help if she keeps her mouth shut. Otherwise, she'll end up doing three to five."

"She could say I was her dealer, but there's no proof. And even if she mentions Joseph Hamilton, it probably won't go anywhere. I've got all the photos, so she doesn't have anything to show him or the police."

"We'll hold off on Hamilton until you are back in town. Take the van out on the mesa and burn it. Joey can take you to the bus station. Give me those photos for safekeeping. I want you gone by sunrise."

Francisco handed the Hammer a thick manilla envelope he'd stashed under the back seat of the van. "Will do. I'll see you in three weeks or so."

He waited until two am, and he drove slowly and on back roads to the mesa. Joey followed in a nondescript white pickup truck. Francisco parked by the edge of an arroyo and doused the van with gasoline, inside and out. He started the fire on the passenger seat and then pushed the van into the arroyo. He hopped up into the pickup, and they drove to the bus station where Francisco bought a ticket to Dallas and boarded a bus for the 5:30 am departure.

§

Lola was surprised when an attorney showed up to enter an appearance for her. Since this was a first-time offense and there was some doubt about her intent to sell, the attorney could post bail and get her released."

"Why did you post my bail?" Lola asked.

"You have a benefactor," Leo Sabatini said.

"Who is that?"

"He's anonymous as of now."

"Why does he care about me?"

"He wants to help you, but he needs your silence in return. You don't know anything about extortion or blackmail. The men you entertained were for your pleasure, and that's it."

"Easy enough. You can tell him my lips are sealed."

"I will, and you should know that nobody crosses him. The consequences are too severe."

"I understand. Can he hook me up with a supplier? I need to score."

"I'll see what we can do."

"I need to score today." She wiped her hand across her mouth. "I'm getting squirrelly."

"Okay, take this burner phone. Someone will call you later today. Don't use the phone for anything else."

"Got it."

"I need to stress—this is not a game, Lola. Once I met a man who figured he could outsmart my client—big mistake. Within two days, the man was cut up in pieces and stuffed in a fifty-five-gallon drum full of hydrochloric acid. By the end of the day, he was slime, and the barrel ended up in the landfill. There are no second chances with my client. Do you understand?"

"I said I get it. Where's Francisco? Will he bring me the coke? He works for your client, right?"

"Francisco is on vacation. I'll have Lorenzo Russo call you. You'll know him by his Italian accent."

Leo handed Lola his business card and dropped her off at her house. There was a four-door gray Chevrolet sedan parked across the street. The driver was looking at Lola with binoculars. "Looks like you have a stakeout going on. I'm your attorney if anyone asks."

§

Leo Sabatini drove to the warehouse, parked inside, and walked to the office.

"I made her bail and told her the rules," he said to the Hammer.

"Think she'll sing?"

"No, I think she's scared, and she's strung out. If we keep her supplied with coke, she'll be quiet as a mouse. I gave her a burner phone and told her Lorenzo Russo would call. She asked me if Francisco works for you. I didn't tell her anything."

The Hammer smiled and adjusted his eye patch. "Francisco had an unfortunate accident."

"How's that?"

"He fell off a fishing boat this morning and drowned."

21

Lola snatched up the burner phone the instant it rang.

"This is Lorenzo Russo. Meet me at Albertson's in the produce section in one hour."

"I'll be there."

At the grocery store, she spotted a short, swarthy man with black hair, standing next to the lettuce beside his shopping cart.

"Lorenzo Russo?"

"Yes. Take this shopping cart. There are a couple of glassine envelopes under the powdered sugar. Put those in your purse and go through the self-checkout. I'll call in a couple of days."

Lola pushed the cart to the dairy section, retrieved the envelopes, added a half-gallon of milk and chocolate ice cream to her shopping cart, and went through the self-checkout. When she got to the car, she shook out some powder on the back of her hand and inhaled a small nose full. Although tempted to do more, she knew better than to linger, and she didn't know when she would get more. The little snort took the edge off, and she drove home in rush-hour traffic without shaking.

At dusk, just as she was about to do another short line of coke, there was a knock at the door. Lola looked through the peephole and then opened the door. "Ashley, my God, what has happened to you?" Her friend had a split lip and a black eye. Her auburn hair was a jumbled mess, but like Lola, she had retained her alluring figure.

"It was Tony," she said. "He got drunk and crazy. Can I come in?"

"Sure. Gee, Ashley, I haven't seen you for months. Where have you been?"

"I was making good money with the escort service, sometimes a thousand dollars a night. Tony got upset about my work and wanted me to stop. I couldn't afford to, so I split from him and went to Boulder. After three months, he found me. Made me come back to Albuquerque with him."

"Made you?"

"He said if I didn't come with him, he would mess me up bad, you know, cut my face so that I couldn't work again."

"That bastard. How long have you been back?"

"A week or so. Things were calm for a few days, and then he started drinking and doing meth. He got crazy and used me as a punching bag. I got away, but. I didn't know where else to go. Can I hide out here for a couple of days?"

"Does anyone know you are here?"

"Just the cab driver, and I've never seen him before. I had him drop me off two blocks down the street and then walked. Tony doesn't know who you are or that I know you."

"That was smart. Let's get you a bath and something to eat. You're a mess."

Lola helped Ashley out of her clothes. Ashley had bruises on her stomach and limped from a deep bruise on her thigh. Lola ran the water and added some bubble bath. She helped Ashley slide down into the warm water.

"Oh, that feels good," Ashley said. "I need to soak for a while."

"I'll heat some chicken noodle soup," Lola said.

When Lola returned, Ashley was almost asleep in the tub.

"Shall we wash your hair?" Lola asked.

"Oh, that would be nice."

Lola pushed the sprayer hose onto the faucet and adjusted the water. Then she wet Ashley's hair and rubbed in coconut and peach shampoo. Soon the bathroom smelled like peaches, and Ashley smiled a little while holding her lip. "This is wonderful, Lola. You sure know how to treat a friend."

"Well, we go way back. What has it been? Ten years?"

"I think it was eleven years ago when we met. Wasn't that job interview astounding? There were fourteen applicants, and Bard Pharmaceuticals hired us both."

"We were quick studies, weren't we? We finished the training early and passed with flying colors."

"I regret now that I quit. The retirement program and the health care benefits were great, but I got burned out after seven years. One night in Santa Fe, I did the escort thing and picked up a thousand dollars. After that, I was off and running. It was easy money. I got called for all-nighters about every week or so, and a full night brought in two thousand."

"I guess you know I'm still with the company," Lola said. "I'm almost at the top of the salary scale."

"Yeah, I'm amazed you've stayed with it. Most drug reps last only five years or so."

"I've met a lot of interesting doctors." Lola raised her eyebrows and grinned. "Sometimes they can be entertaining."

"Do they pay you for your extracurricular activities?"

"In a way. They pay me with their time and attention. Occasionally I have long weekends in Las Vegas, all expenses paid, plus shopping for clothes and jewelry. You might say that I help them with their loneliness, and they help me with what I need."

"Anyone special?"

"I'm, as they say, polyamorous. There are several."

Lola helped Ashley stand up and wrapped her in a towel. She wrapped her hair with another towel and held her steady as she stepped out of the tub. "Let's go to the kitchen. I warmed up the soup, and you need to eat something."

In the kitchen, Lola set out two bowls of chicken noodle soup and a plate of soda crackers. She filled two wine glasses with chardonnay. "Let's toast."

"Okay, you say the toast."

"Let's toast to the good fortune of you landing on my doorstep."

Ashley sighed. "Thanks. I don't know how I can repay your kindness. You are a lifesaver. I'm going to leave Tony once and for all and go somewhere far away. I've been thinking about Seattle or Portland. Those are big cities where I can change my name and get lost."

"You can hang out here for a while until your bruises heal. After that, I've got an extra suitcase, and we're the same size. I've got plenty of extra clothes for work. We can pack a couple of pants-suits, a few blouses, underwear, and black two-inch heels. You wear size seven shoes, right?"

"Yes, Lola, that's so kind. I wish I could stay around and rekindle our friendship. You have a big heart."

"Well, I don't know about that, but I could sure use a friend, too. I've been lonely. Not for men, but for a woman friend I can trust and care about."

Ashley finished eating. Lola gave her a white, terrycloth robe to wear, and they sat in the living room. Lola turned on a movie on HBO, then opened one of the glassine envelopes and shook out powder on a small mirror. She rolled up a twenty-dollar bill and handed it to Ashley. "Here, this should perk you up a little and take your mind off those bruises." They each did a line. Within a few minutes, Ashley yawned and said, "I'm feeling tired. Where can I sleep?"

"Let's share my king-size bed. You'll rest better than on the couch. But, hey, I'm tired as well." She wet her finger and tasted the cocaine. "It tastes all right, but we shouldn't feel this tired. It's as though someone cut the coke with something—maybe fentanyl. I can barely keep my eyes open."

Lola didn't even bother removing her jeans and T-shirt as she joined Ashley in bed. Both were sound asleep within minutes.

A loud explosion rocked the house, and flames crackled through the utility room and rolled down the hallway. Lola opened her eyes to the sound of a roaring fire at the bedroom door. The fire sounded like a train barreling through the house. Thick, dark gray smoke was filling the room. Coughing and barely awake, Lola tumbled out of bed, stepped into her tennis shoes, and began shaking Ashley. "Wake up, Ashley! We've got to get out of here. Her friend was breathing, but still. She didn't open her eyes. "Come on, wake up!"

Ashley finally opened the eye that wasn't swollen, but then turned over and pulled the covers up over her head with a groan. "I need to sleep."

"The house is on fire. We've got to get out."

Ashley sat up and looked around in the darkness. "I can barely move."

"Hurry, you've got to move, now."

Lola ran to the bedroom door and started to open it. The knob was hot. The whole door was hot. She knew if she opened it, flames would rush in. She ran to the window and opened it all the way. Then she went back to the bed, grabbed Ashley by the arm, and pulled her up. "Hold my hand. We're going out the window."

Ashley took a step and tripped on her own feet. Her head hit the footboard of the bed, and she collapsed unconscious onto the floor. Lola tried to pick her up, but Ashley was too heavy. She grabbed her burner phone from the nightstand and dialed 911. "Fire," she said, coughing, and croaked out her address. She returned to Ashley and tried to drag her friend by her feet, but she felt so dizzy that she couldn't move her. Smoke was pouring into the room.

Lola wet a towel in the bathroom, wrapped her face, and tried pulling Ashley up on her feet. Ashley was too heavy. Tears filled Lola's eyes, both from her helplessness and from the smoke. Again, she grabbed Ashley's ankles and tried to pull her across the carpet, her eyes burning in the thick smoke. She let go of Ashley and sobbed. She was too weak and doped up to move her. Blinded from the darkness and the smoke, she felt her way along the wall until she came to the window. She climbed out backward and dropped to the soft ground below. She heard sirens from approaching fire trucks as she vomited, fought for a couple of deep breaths, and passed out.

She awoke to the sounds of gushing firehoses and men shouting. What was happening? In her drug-induced confusion, she crawled across the yard and hid at the base the orange-flowered trumpet vines that covered the wooden fence. There she dropped her face into hands and muffled a scream because she knew. Someone had tried to kill her. Someone had laced her cocaine, and the fire was not a coincidence.

§

Adam's cell phone rang at six am.

"Adam, this is Lola. I need your help."

"Lola? You've got to be kidding. Why would you call me?"

"Because you're dependable, a boy scout, someone who probably won't turn me down."

"What's going on?"

"Can you meet me somewhere? I need transportation and some money for a bus ticket."

"I don't have any money to speak of. You know that."

"I just need a ride and about a hundred dollars. Can you help?"

"Where are you?"

"I'm at an outdoor table at Starbucks by the CVS Pharmacy on Fourth Street."

"Okay, I guess. I'll be there in a half-hour."

Adam pulled up in his pickup, bought coffee inside, and then came out and sat with Lola at the table. She looked as ragged as he had ever seen her, and she reeked of smoke. "Okay, now tell me. What in the hell is this about?"

"I've got to swear you to secrecy. My house burned down, and people think the fire killed me in my sleep."

"What?"

"I heard the firemen talking. There was an explosion—the water heater—and then the house burned. Ashley, a friend of mine, was visiting, and she died in the fire. I got out and hid, and they assumed she was me—burnt beyond recognition, they said." Lola coughed and began trembling.

"Drink the hot coffee," said Adam. "I'll be right back." He sprinted to his truck and returned with a hoodie, which he draped over Lola's shoulders.

She smiled weakly. "Thanks. I think someone cut my coke with fentanyl," she went on. "They figured I wouldn't wake up. No one knew Ashley was there. That's why I've got to disappear. If they find out I'm alive, they'll try again. I'm beside myself. I'm just sick about Ashley. She came to me for help, and she ended up dead."

"Who are they?"

"I guess you've figured it out. We've been running a scam and blackmailing doctors. The whole thing collapsed when Francisco, my dealer, tried to get money from a plastic surgeon, and the police were at the bank to arrest him. He got away, but they shot one cop."

Adam nodded. He already knew about the case from Detective Romero but didn't want Lola to know he'd been questioned. "So, what are you in all of this?" he asked.

"I'm a loose end. I got picked up for possession, but a lawyer got me off, and a guy named Russo brought me some coke. I think Russo cut it with fentanyl so I wouldn't wake up in the fire. It was the only sure way they could keep my mouth shut."

"This is a freaking mess," Adam said. "But here's a hundred bucks. I hope you get some help to get off the coke wherever you are going. Where shall I take you?"

"Can you drive me to the Santa Fe bus station right now?"

"Okay, let's hurry. I don't want anyone to see us together."

They drove to the Santa Fe bus station in silence, and Adam parked.

"I don't want to know where you are going. I don't ever want to see you again. So don't call me."

Lola gave him a sad smile. "As far as everyone knows, I died in the fire. So, I'll disappear, change my name, and start over."

She kissed him and got out of the truck. "Wish me luck."

"Luck."

Adam pulled his hat down, and scrunched himself down low in the seat, as if he were half his size, trying to make himself invisible. He got on the interstate at the St. Francis exit and drove back to Albuquerque without stopping.

Good Lord, Lola, I hope this is goodbye forever.

22

Once again Adam's phone was ringing at an early hour—this time at four am. This had better not be Lola again, he thought, fumbling for his phone. But it was the nurse manager, calling from Edward's care home.

"Mr. Young, I have some sad news. Your father died about an hour ago. Our on-call doctor said he had a pulmonary embolism."

Adam rubbed the sleep from his eyes and put his cell phone on speaker. "Edward died?"

"Yes, I'm sorry to inform you."

Adam felt stunned. His mind raced over years of the past. In the darkness of his bedroom, he thought he should cry or shout or slam his fist against a wall, but all he could feel was a stark absence, a space in the world that once contained Edward but now was empty, a relief of sorts. Now the walls of Edward's life created a vacuum, and soon sunrise and the demands of a new day would fill the space with a whoosh. Edward was dead. Well, good riddance. There is now one less asshole in the world, one less man who spewed anger and criticism at every turn, one less negative force. Yet, deep in Adam's soul, he felt waves of guilt. Was there something he could've done?

"Thank you for letting me know," Adam said. I'll call McLaren's funeral home. They can pick up the body, and I can go by and arrange a service. Can you assemble his personal belongings?"

"Yes, we can do that. Do you want Edward's clothes?"

"No, let's donate his clothes and shoes to the homeless shelter. I'll go through his other things when I come by. Say about nine am?"

"I leave at seven, but I'll inform the day shift that you'll be coming. If you call McClaren's soon, they will pick up the body by noon or so. In the meantime, you can see him when you get here."

"Okay, I'll also ask Lawrence Olson, our financial trustee, to come by and settle the business matters. I know we owe you some money."

"Yes, part of a month. There are no new bills."

"Thanks again. I'll be there soon."

Adam sat on his bed in his underwear, his elbows on his knees. What should he be feeling? Sadness? Regret? The loss of a father? Honestly, all he could feel was a deep relief and the remnants of Edward's pain that ushered Edward out of this world and to his final spiritual home. God would receive and forgive him, even though he didn't deserve it. Regardless, Edward's abuse would no longer be a part of Adam's life. Edward could never again blame Adam for his mother's death or Edward's physical plight. He could put Edward's blaming ritual in the past, where it would dwindle in its power and then disappear. Adam had received a gift. Finally, he could be free of Edward's hatred. He felt as though Edward's death pulled away a blanket of haze so at last he could see the stars and the light from the future.

Adam called McClaren's, went by Edward's care facility to pay his respects, gathered his father's belongings, and then drove to McClaren's to make funeral arrangements. Edward's body had been pasty white, and he seemed to have shrunken to the size of a child. He died with a frown on his face. As in life, so in death, Adam concluded. His father's menacing aura had evaporated in the fresh breeze that came through the window, and the acrid smell of disinfectant mixed with the fresh air. Although staff had washed Edward's body with green soap, he still gave off the stale odor of a dumpster baking in the sun.

Once again, Adam sat at a table with Mr. McClaren, just four months after Ava had died. But, this time, Adam was alone. He'd called Maria to tell her, Maria did not want to participate. She said she would come to a service, but that was all. She had grown to hate Edward because of how he'd treated Adam over the years.

"I'm sorry that your father passed away," Mr. McClaren offered.

Adam shrugged. "I think the years of anger had just chewed him up on the inside. They said it was an embolism, but if there is a disease called anger-itis, then by God, that's what he died from."

McClaren nodded. "An embolism can be sudden, and I'm guessing he didn't have much pain. Did he leave any last wishes for a funeral service?"

"He told me he would like to be buried next to my mother, Margaret. Her gravesite is in the Eternal Hope cemetery on the Paseo. Edward bought an extra site when they buried my mother."

"I'll check it out. We share burial records with most cemeteries."

"I don't want anything too expensive. A simple wooded casket is all. We can publish an obituary and have a short service here in your chapel if that's acceptable."

"Did Edward have a church home?"

"No, he stayed away from churches. Do you have a chaplain you can hire?"

Mr. McClaren wrote some notes on a yellow notepad. "Yes, we have several pastors who can fill in. They usually receive one-hundred-fifty dollars."

"That's fine. I'll need a written estimate for everything—flowers, chaplain, music, use of your chapel, and a wooden casket. Please include everything, including tax."

Adam took a business card from his pocket and handed it to Mr. McClaren. "Here's the information on our Trustee, Lawrence Olson. He will be paying the bill."

"Do you want a viewing?" We can prepare Edward's body and put him in the chapel for friends and relatives to come and see. Viewings are often the afternoon before the funeral service."

"No need for that. Edward didn't have any friends, and I can't think of anyone who would want to see him."

Mr. McClaren stood up. "I'll prepare a detailed quote and send you and your Trustee a copy. Please let him know that we'll need a deposit within the next day or two."

Adam shook hands with Mr. McClaren and turned to leave. "Oh, one more thing. Do you pay for placing his obituary in the papers?"

"Yes, that's all included. Bring me the obit, and we'll take it from there. Is there a hometown newspaper?"

"Edward went to high school and worked for ten years in Denver. He was fifty-eight a month ago, the same age my mother would be if she hadn't died."

"When did your mother pass away?"

"Mom died in nineteen ninety-one. I was nine, and I went to live with my aunt, Jane Sullivan. She's the mother I've known ever since."

"We'll be sure to reserve space in the Denver papers. Is August 5 an acceptable date for the service? That is a Saturday, and it gives us ten days to get things prepared."

"Sounds fine with me," Adam said. "I am an only child, and there's no other family, so I'm in charge. I'll let people know. The attendance will be light. Some folks from the assisted living center may want to attend."

§

The next day, Adam struggled to write an obituary. In his efforts to keep it neutral or positive, he could only squeeze out a couple of paragraphs. He scanned it and emailed it to Mr. McClaren. He called Lawrence Olson to inform him of Edward's death and to discuss funeral costs. The trusts were set up separately after the settlements, so Edward's trust would pay the final expenses. The balance would go to Save the Children, a charity that Adam's mother always favored, and Margaret's sister Jane had made sure the attorney incorporated Margaret's wishes into the trust.

The memorial service was short and bland. About twenty people attended, more than Adam expected. The guest pastor assured everyone that Edward was in a better place—that his painful suffering had ended, and, in many ways, his death was a blessing from God. Adam couldn't quite follow the logic. Edward was dead, and that's a blessing for him? It's more a blessing for me, he thought.

Nevertheless, he chose not to question the pastor. At the gravesite, the pastor read a passage from the Bible about there being many rooms in heaven, and Edward had a room prepared for him. Edward had gone on into eternity. He was now at peace, in his room.

Maria had stood beside Adam for the service. After the gravesite remarks, she took Adam's hand. "I know you have mixed feelings, but I'm sorry your father has passed away," she said. Then, she walked to her car and drove away.

Adam noticed a stranger standing near the grave. He was a man of about sixty with short white hair. He was about six-foot-two, two-hundred-plus pounds, and dressed in a white shirt, dark slacks, shined black shoes, and a blue blazer with an American flag tie tack in the button on his lapel. He displayed a gentle smile and lively golden-brown eyes as he approached Adam. “Hello,” he said, extending his hand. “I’m Russell Kramer. I saw the obituary in the paper, and I wanted to be here.” He was carrying a small bouquet of yellow and white daisies. He stepped past Edward’s grave and placed the bouquet on Margaret’s headstone.

“May I visit with you for a moment?”

“I guess so,” Adam said. “I don’t recall meeting you. Were you Edward’s friend?”

“Hardly. I didn’t know Edward well. I only met him once.”

“So why are you here, Mr. Kramer??”

“Please, call me Russell. There’s a park bench under that tree.” He led Adam to the bench, and the two men sat.

“I’m here because of your mother,” he said.

“Did you know her?”

“Yes, and this is the day we were both waiting for.”

Adam frowned. “You mean Edward’s death? What the hell is that about?”

“I’m here to tell you a secret I’ve kept for thirty-two years.”

“I don’t even know who you are. Sounds crazy.”

“Perhaps. Maybe we’re all a little crazy.”

Adam wasn’t sure he could handle anymore crazy just now. “Okay, say what you have to say.”

“Now that Margaret and Edward are both deceased, I can tell you something that Margaret knew, Edward knew, and I knew.” Russell took a deep breath and wiped his hand across his mouth. “You need to get ready—you know, relax and listen. Don’t say anything.”

“Come on, man, hurry up. I’ll listen, but not for long.”

“It was the Christmas season in nineteen eighty-one. I was married, and my wife was pregnant with twins. Margaret worked part-time in the fragrance and perfume section at Macy’s in the mall. I was shopping for perfume for my wife, and Margaret helped. She picked out a fragrance, sprayed her wrist, and held her arm up to me to smell. Her gesture was alluring, and the aroma was evocative, like a dream, suggesting soft skin and passion. I sniffed and then looked into her eyes. She held my gaze. I could feel the heat from her wrist on my lips as she smiled. I like to think we were both smitten at that moment."

Adam cocked his head. "Smitten? Then what happened?"

"We had an affair. I have never felt passion so deep or so intense. Margaret felt the same. We continued until February, and then I had to step away because my wife was suspicious, and she was nearly ready for the twins to be born. I felt guilty and ashamed of my behavior. But Adam, Margaret became pregnant, and I am your biological father."

Adam paused for a beat. "No shit?"

"It's the truth, Adam."

"Holy Christ, it's been thirty-four years. Why are you telling me this now?"

"I promised Margaret I wouldn't ever say anything while she was alive. Edward realized she was eight weeks pregnant, but Margaret assured him of her love and devotion, and they were married before the end of the month."

"Edward knew?

"Yes, Margaret told him. She also said the affair was over."

"So, Edward knew she was pregnant with another man's child and married her anyway? That's not the Edward I knew. He was an asshole."

"Margaret told me that Edward was kind, thoughtful, and a good provider. She told him the truth, but he wanted to marry her anyway. He was a stand-up guy. Margaret knew I couldn't leave my wife and family, and she saw the marriage to Edward as a way out of her current plight."

"A stand-up guy? I don't see that. He treated me like crap after Mom died in the accident. We're not talking about the same person."

"I read about the accident, and I was here for Margaret's funeral. No one knew me, and I left right after the graveside prayers. I think Edward had been a loving parent until then, but I saw that he blamed you for Margaret's death, and now he would have to raise you alone. Still. Edward had promised Margaret he would never tell anyone our secret. And even though he soured and treated you poorly, I think you were better off with Edward as your father."

"Better off?"

Russell hung his head. "I got in trouble soon after you were born. I served two years in federal prison. I'm a felon, Adam."

This gets crazier and crazier. "What did you do?"

"Back then, I was a financial planner, and I embezzled some money from a client. My twin girls were born in March, and I was not doing well—I found a lot of solace in a bottomless bottle of brandy. Unfortunately, we needed the funds for ordinary everyday living expenses, so when the client found out, I lost my license and pled guilty to financial irregularities."

Jeez, the apple doesn't fall far from the tree, Adam thought. That might explain my alcoholism. "And now?"

"When I got out, my wife took me back, and I worked in the life insurance industry. I had sobered up in prison. She figured I had learned my lesson, and I guess she was right."

Russell dug in his pocket and showed Adam his medallion. "Check it out. I'm thirty years clean and sober."

Adam took the coin and held it up to the light. It bore the words "Unity, Service, Recovery," as well as Roman numeral thirty, XXX."

"Did you go to AA?"

"Yes, and I still attend at least one meeting a week."

"After thirty years, you still attend meetings?"

"Yes, it keeps me honest and humble, and I usually sponsor one or two newcomers."

Adam gazed up at the blue sky with a single white cloud overhead. It looked like a huge gorilla with its arms open, until the cloud paled and broke up in the breeze. "How did you get sober?"

Russell gave Adam a knowing look, as if he saw through to the reason for Adam's question. Then he laughed. "Well, prison helped since they enforced abstinence, and there were AA meetings twice a week. I knew I only had one chance to be a father to my twin girls, and I had to be clean and sober to do that. So, I was motivated to change, and I was willing to surrender to the truth—I was an alcoholic. I've been relatively successful with insurance, and my girls are now your age. But unfortunately, neither are married, and I have no grandchildren."

"So, I have two half-sisters?"

"Yes. Maggie and Melody."

"Sonofabitch. Do my sisters know about me?"

"No, not yet, but I hope to come clean on about my entire history and somehow make a family from the wreckage of my past. My girls are wonderful women, and I hope they will warm up to you after they hear the story."

Adam's lips quivered as he swallowed hard, covered his face with his hands, and began to weep. He pounded the bench with an open palm, then stood up. He put his tear-streaked face up close to Russell's face. Adam gritted his teeth and grabbed the front of Russell's shirt with both hands, pulling him closer. He spoke sharply through pursed lips. "You bastard. I put up with Edward's bullshit for twenty-five years, and he wasn't even my father? Where were you when I needed you? This can't be true." He pushed Russell back onto the bench and turned his back.

"Oh yes, this is true," Russell said. "I understand you're angry, but, hey, I'm here now seeking your forgiveness and trying to create a new future." He drew a yellowed envelope from his inside blazer pocket. Adam saw his name on the envelope, written in flowing cursive. "Here's a letter from your mother. I haven't read it, but she said that someday if she was deceased and Edward had passed on, I should give it to you. So here."

Adam grabbed the envelope. "I need to leave now. A few people are coming to our house to offer condolences. I can't leave Maria alone to manage things."

"Can we catch up later?" Russell asked.

"I don't know. Maybe. Call my cell phone in the morning."

"Okay, I've got the number."

"How?"

"McClaren's gave it to me because I told them I needed to talk with you about the service."

Adam trudged to his truck. He stooped as he walked, feeling as if he was carrying a heavy backpack full of rocks. At the driver's side door, he squinted, looked up, and then gazed back at the cemetery. Even though the sun was bright, Adam saw a thin mist covering the graveyard. His mother's and Edward's headstones stood up through the fog and seemed to glow like neon lights. Adam felt confused and distant, as though all the gravesites might disappear into the clouds. Maybe Russell was a figment. He sat in his truck for a while and drank before starting the engine and driving to his house.

After he had helped Maria clean up and thanked their guests, he said goodbye to Maria, drove to a quiet place in the Placitas hills, took a deep breath and a long swallow of vodka, and opened the letter.

Christmas Day, 1981

My Dearest Adam,

Since you're reading this letter, that means I've died, Edward has passed on, and you've met Russell Kramer. Although Edward was my devoted husband and friend, he is not your father. Your biological father is Russell. I am not proud of my behavior, but Russell and I fell in love over Christmas in 1981, and we spent every moment we could find being together. I was engaged to Edward, Russell was married, and his wife was pregnant with twins. We could not imagine making our relationship work, so, painfully, we decided to part ways and resumed our regular lives. I was sad, but your birth brought me new joy, and Edward did everything he could to make our married life happy.

I am sorry that you've spent however many years it's been not knowing. I beg you to forgive me and to remember that I have loved you every day. Russell Kramer is a fine man, and you can count on his integrity and honesty. He will make a good friend and ally if you allow it. You are indeed the joy of my life. You have brought me great happiness and a sense of fulfillment. Your birth was the meaning of my existence—always remember, you are loved. I will forever be grateful I am your mother. I love you all the way to the stars—Mother

Adam read the letter three times before folding it up and gently sliding it back in the envelope. He swallowed hard and then wept, his stomach in knots. He opened the truck door and vomited on the ground.

He wiped his face with a red bandana and drank a swallow of vodka. Then he looked up at fluffy white clouds that billowed over the mountains as they shapeshifted through his tears. One of the clouds formed the likeness of a little boy running. A nearby cloud looked like a woman with her arms open, beckoning as if to say, "Come to me." As he wiped his tears with the back of his hand, the winds aloft dissipated the shapes into formless wisps and streaks. Gray, menacing storm clouds moved in, wrapped themselves around the upper half of the mountains, and brought crackles of lightning to the peaks. In a nearby cottonwood tree, intense beams of sunlight sparkled and then faded away from the brilliant yellow and green quaking leaves. From the west, rays of bright sunlight lit up the rocks and trees with a warm watermelon color, spread out over the dark clouds like a layer of golden frosting, and then slipped away into the gloaming.

For Adam, time seemed to have stopped, and everything was happening at once. He shook his head back and forth, feeling it was too much for his mind to absorb. Then he smacked the side of his head with the heel of his right hand. Come on, Adam, get with it. Rumbles of thunder announced rain would soon be on the way and bring moisture to the dusty land.

Adam's hands shook as he placed the envelope in the glove compartment and then drove to Ryan's house for the night. On the way, he knocked back the rest of his pint of vodka. He parked his truck, went directly to his room, slipped out of his clothes, fell into bed, and slept until daylight. He dreamed he was lost in Uncle Cliff's amusement park and fell from the top arch of a roller coaster ride. Thirty-two feet per second squared, he thought. This is going to hurt. He awoke to the ring of his cell phone at seven am. It was Russell.

"You awake?"

"Yeah."

"I was hoping to meet you for coffee, but something has come up at home. I've got to head back to Denver this morning."

"Okay. Another time."

"I'm going to tell my wife about you, Adam. I think after thirty-four years, she will be reasonable. I'll tell her I want to spend some time with you. I think we can work it out."

"How about Maggie and, uh, Melody?"

"Them too. I may get everyone together at dinner or something like that. I'm still thinking about how to break the news."

"Well, good luck. Maybe I'll see you later."

"Adam?" said Russell.

"Yeah?"

Check with your doctor. It may be time for you to take some action."

"Maybe you're right. Bye."

23

Adam settled into a chair in Dr. Warnock's exam room.

"I think I'm ready for that opiate detox," he said. "A lot of crazy stuff is going on. I'm not sure I can handle it all."

"What's the most troubling?"

Adam threw up his hands. "It's all troubling. I lost my baby daughter; my wife and I are separated; I've had problems at work; my father, Edward, died, and then, three days ago, a man named Russell Kramer showed up at Edward's funeral and said he was my real father. He gave me this letter. I guess my mother wrote it a couple of months after I was born." He showed Dr. Warnock the letter. "Said he had saved it for over thirty years."

Dr. Warnock took a few minutes to read the letter. Then he scooted his chair closer to Adam. "Wow. Sounds like you've moved into the twilight zone. Most people couldn't handle half of what you're going through. First, let me offer my condolences for your loss of Edward."

"Thank you for that, but you can save it for someone who deserves it."

"It sounds like you are in the eye of a storm. What did you say to him, your real father?"

"I got angry. I mean, where was he when I needed him? Why did I have to put up with Edward for so long?"

"Is he still here in Albuquerque?"

"No, he went back home to Denver. He said he was going to tell his wife and daughters about me. Turns out I have two twin half-sisters. Russell wants to seek forgiveness and have an extended family. Fat chance of that."

"That seems admirable, but I hear you. Where was he for thirty-four years?"

"My mother made him swear that he would keep the secret until both she and Edward had died. So even if he wanted me to know, I think his promise to my mother was the driving force."

"What are you going to do?"

"Russell is an alcoholic and has thirty years of sobriety. Even though I was pissed off, he is somewhat inspiring. He served two years in federal prison, got sober behind bars, and still attends AA meetings. He seemed to see I was struggling, even though I didn't drink in front of him. He suggested it might be time for me to take some action—and I understood what he meant. I can't keep going like this. I'm exhausted, and I don't want to lose anyone else. So: detox."

"That's great, Adam. I agree that it's time. And I am not surprised to learn that you have an alcoholic parent. I'm sure you know that there's a likely genetic component to alcoholism. We checked on your health insurance, and you have coverage for up to thirty days of rehabilitation from substance abuse. Since detox is part of the rehab protocols, they will cover your hospital stay with a fifty-dollar co-pay for each day. I think you will need seven days. What about your friends and family?"

"I've talked with Maria, my employer, and my friend Ryan. Everyone's supportive. Maria is taking a couple of vacation days so she can shepherd Lucas to and from school for the first part of the week, and then Ryan has agreed to pick up Lucas at home, take him to school, bring him home and make dinner until I'm out of the hospital."

"Ryan sounds like a good friend. And your employer?"

"Rocky and Jim Olander are both encouraging. I didn't realize it, but I'm more valuable to them than I thought. They want me back in good shape. They said I'm talented and important to them. They even said I could use vacation time, and they will pay the co-pays."

"That's got to feel good."

"I was surprised, but it made me feel hopeful."

"Let's review the approach I'd like to take. This will be a little unorthodox, a combination of established science and alternative treatments. First, you'll need seven days of detox to get the opioids out of your system. Also, we need to manage your use of alcohol. We can put you on a regimen as soon as you're relatively clean from OxyContin and alcohol. Adam, it helps a lot that you want to do this."

Adam sighed. "I'm stuck and confused. I can't go back, I can't move ahead, and I can't stand it where I am. I've got to do something. This shit's got to stop."

"You know you're a medical challenge, not like most other addicts."

"What do you mean?"

"Well, you have chronic pain that we need to control. You have anxiety that you calm with alcohol, and outright abstinence will not work. So, our challenge is to manage an addict so he can use minor amounts of what he's addicted to. Ironically, we will need to control your addictions, pain, and anxiety with drugs. We'll have to be creative, that's for sure."

"Do you have a plan? It's hard to build things or repair things without a plan."

Dr. Warnock laughed. "I hear the contractor speaking here. But yes, there's a treatment plan. Initially, we'll use an anti-anxiety medication called Librium to ward of the seizures that can come from alcohol withdrawal. That will also help with weaning down the OxyContin. You'll start with an IV for fluids and Librium hourly for six or eight hours or as needed. Also, I think I'll start you on a hundred milligrams of CBD three times a day for your pain, and we'll rub your legs with lidocaine gel every hour. I'll keep a close eye on how you're doing and adjust your dosage if necessary."

"Then what?"

"Our goal is to reduce your OxyContin to nothing at the end of a week. The CBD and lidocaine will be a regular part of your life, and we'll add a naltrexone injection at the end of the week and every four weeks thereafter. We'll slowly taper you off the Librium. It can be a nasty addiction, and we don't want to add to your problem. Then you can use a small dose of OxyContin, say five milligrams twice a day. I want you to attend AA meetings to learn about the twelve-step program. You may want to meet other addicts, make new friends, and see how their twelve-step work helps them stay sober. After your initial detox, I want to see you in the office for therapy every two weeks for a while."

"Sounds like an elaborate plan."

"Adam, this will not be a piece of cake. You'll hurt, shake, vomit, and maybe hallucinate. You'll wish you could stop the detox, and until we get you knocked back, you might get belligerent. Some folks even get violent. Fina said she would check on you during the night and call me if you need sleep medication. As we taper off the Librium, we'll add cannabis edibles to help you sleep and ease your pain. I'll get you a medical marijuana card, and we'll stock up on some forty milligram gummies. Usually, that's enough for sleep."

"I tried the samples you gave me. I slept better, usually through the night."

"Good to know that the gummies helped."

"You've spent a lot of time thinking about this. Why?" Adam asked.

Dr. Warnock smiled. "I've already told you; I've been there. I understand addiction, I'm eager to help other addicts, and, unlike some other physicians, I believe you can use addictive substances to deal with underlying issues—in your cases, the chronic pain in your legs and the anxiety that pain produces."

"I must say, I'm stunned by your concern. I'm not used to someone understanding, let alone caring."

"Without getting melodramatic, I want you to know that I think you are worth saving and that you have many good years to offer to your family. You're a good man, Adam, and I'm looking forward to working with you. Can you check into the hospital on tomorrow morning? They have a couple of beds in the rehab section. Otherwise, they won't have a vacancy until September. By the way, you know it's a locked ward, right? Once you sign yourself in and agree to detox and treatment, you won't be able to leave. Your signature is your commitment."

Adam blanched but nodded. "I suspected as much. All right, then, So, I'll be at the hospital admissions office tomorrow morning at eight."

"It is normal to be afraid, Adam. Unfortunately, fear is a constant companion of addicts."

"You've got that right."

"I'll be there at eight to help with the admission process. It wouldn't hurt to have a couple of shots of vodka before you get to the hospital. That will make the first twenty-four hours easier."

§

Adam signed the last of the paperwork and took a deep breath as a burly male nurse escorted him to the rehab wing on the hospital's fourth floor. The double doors closed with a whoosh and a clang. He heard the lock snap shut as the nurse ushered him into his private room.

"Here are your hospital clothes," he said, handing Adam a gown and some slippers with rubber soles. "You need to wear the slippers whenever you get out of bed, and it is okay to wear your underwear underneath your gown. Do you know how to pray?"

"I guess so."

"That's good. This will be a difficult week, and people say that praying helps."

The nurse hung up Adam's clothes in the closet as he put on his gown. "There's a new toothbrush in the bathroom and a pillow to put on the floor."

"A pillow?"

The nurse smiled kindly. "Most people say a pillow is a good cushion for your knees on the cold tile floor when your head is in the commode."

"For when I throw up, right?"

"Yes. There's a small bucket by your bed as well. Use it when you can't make it to the commode."

"I can hardly wait."

"Here's your remote for the TV. I'll put it on your nightstand next to your pitcher of ice water. Your urinal is next to the bucket."

"Are we having fun yet?"

The nurse grinned. "Not yet, but soon. Remember, this will just be a temporary visit to hell. It'll be worth it later—a good thing to remember when you are hugging the bucket. Now please lie down on the bed so I can get an IV started and hook up your oxygen. If your respiration gets too low, we may have to put on a heart monitor. You're going to need fluids, and the IV is a good way to administer drugs."

Adam got into bed, and the nurse started an IV on his left arm. "Later, when you stand up or need to walk, you can roll the IV stand along with you. You'll be getting Librium every hour for the next eight hours; then, we'll reduce the dose as needed. That will keep you from having seizures from alcohol withdrawal—but plan on being zonked out. Don't expect to get up and walk around. You will be heavily sedated, and believe me, that is best in the beginning. Here's your call button. You should call for help when you need to use the bathroom. I don't want you walking by yourself for a couple of days."

Adam watched as the nurse used a syringe to put Librium in the IV tube. He felt tingly and sleepy and nauseous. Within ten or fifteen minutes, he was semi-conscious. He clicked on the remote and stopped at a channel where Judge Judy was admonishing a tenant for not paying a utility bill. As usual, the landlord had added it to the rent, but the tenant said the water tasted terrible and he was not going to pay for it. As Adam fell into a slumber, judge Judy told the tenant to either step up and pay the bill or move out.

24

Adam stirred as he felt gentle hands on his leg. The clock on the wall wiggled and changed shape, but the hands announced two am. Fina held a large jar of lidocaine and was slathering slathered handfuls on his ankles, shins, calves, and knees. The lidocaine felt fantastic, and instead of the sharp shards of pain that generally raced up and down his legs, he felt a cool, dull throbbing.

"Are you awake?" Fina asked.

"More or less."

"How do you feel?"

"Druggy, floppy."

"How about your legs?"

"What you're doing helps."

"What is your pain scale?"

"It's coming and going. On a real scale, I'm about two-hundred pounds."

"I mean, do your legs hurt?"

"I don't see them flying away."

"We've cut your OxyContin down a bit, Adam. I'm trying to determine how much pain you have. Can you tell me? You could hold up three fingers or four fingers, for example."

Adam grinned and held up his middle finger.

"Please, Adam. Is your pain a three, a four, a five? I need to enter it in your chart as we cut back on your OxyContin."

"Three, four, close the door. Let's say four, but I've got to go to the bathroom." He knew he was being goofy but chalked it up to the Librium.

"Let me help you up. Okay, I'm putting your slippers on. Now stand up. Hold on to the IV stand, and we'll walk slowly."

They made their way to the bathroom. Adam bent over and threw up in the toilet. He kept vomiting until he had only dry heaves. His eyes watered as Fina washed his face with a wet washcloth. "That's good, Adam. We want to get all that poison out of your system by Wednesday."

When Adam awoke again, it was daylight, and a cheerful, full-figured woman with red hair had brought him a tray with hot tea and one piece of toast. "You may want to sip on the tea, and the toast will help settle your stomach. This is optional. You may not feel like eating anything at all. I put out a glass of ice water if you want to sip."

"Who the hell are you?" Adam asked. "And what day is this?"

"I'm Marjorie from the kitchen, and today is Tuesday. I'll be bringing your meals, such as they are, all this week. It's nice to meet you, Adam. I wish you luck with this ordeal. Tomorrow we might try some lime Jell-O."

"I'm not hungry."

"Well, at least take a couple of sips of water. You need fluids."

Adam's hands shook so badly that he needed both hands to hold the water cup. Some spilled down the front of his gown.

As Marjorie left, Dr. Warnock walked in. "Adam, how are you doing?"

"I'm shaking, I feel as if ants are crawling on me, and I need to throw up."

"Sorry for your discomfort." He looked at the clock. "It's almost time for your Librium. I'll give it to you early. It will help you sleep. We're cutting back the dose." He produced a syringe of Librium and dispensed it into the IV tube. Adam felt his eyelids droop. "Thanks, Doc. Sleeping is good."

"You've made it through the night and almost through the second day. We need to stay with it. Do your legs hurt?"

Adam smiled. "Some. About three or four, shut the door, your sister is a famous whore."

Dr. Warnock put his hand on Adam's knee and laughed. "So, we're okay for now. Right?"

"As long as I can sleep."

"I'll check on you later."

When Adam awoke, the sun had set, and dusk settled on the trees and parking lot outside his window. He felt nauseous. He swung his feet to the floor, pushed his toes into the slippers, and headed to the bathroom, pulling his IV stand with him. The wheels squeaked, Adam lost his balance, and he and the IV stand fell to the floor. He crawled into the bathroom, dragging the IV stand, and retched over the commode, but nothing came up. His stomach was sore from so much vomiting. Wobbly and unstable, he stood, leaned against the sink, and splashed some water on his face. Then, shuffled back toward his bed, the IV stand clattering behind him on the floor, he saw a wave of shadows encircle him, squeeze around his stomach and chest like a shroud wrapped too tight. He was trapped. There was no escape. The doors were locked. In a near panic, he took a final step to the bed and flopped down, dragging the IV stand across the floor by his IV tube, pulling the needle out of his arm. The noise brought a nurse. "What happened here?"

"Bathroom, IV stand tipped over."

"This is only your second day. Remember, you're supposed to hit the call button and get help going to the bathroom."

"Whatever, but I'm sick."

The nurse picked up the IV stand, hung up a new fluid bag, and started an IV in his other arm. "I'm going to put extra tape on this, so it's harder to pull out. Also, it's time for your Librium, so I'll add that now. We've tapered down to fifty milligrams every two hours."

Adam shut his eyes. "Whatever."

"Sorry, this all feels so bad. But, after the first couple of nights, it will get better, especially when you can eat something. Are you hungry?"

"Hell, no. Leave me alone."

Marjorie appeared in the morning with a glass of orange juice and a piece of toast. Adam drank a few sips of the orange juice and ate one bite of the toast.

"Well, that's progress," Marjorie said.

Adam twisted, bent over, and threw up the orange juice and toast into the bucket by his bed. He wiped his mouth with a tissue.

"Sorry," he said. "It tasted good going down. Coming up, not so much."

"We'll try again later," Marjorie said. "Shall we try applesauce for dinner?"

"Sure. I've always liked applesauce. Maybe I can keep a little down."

Adam tried to read, watch TV, sketch out plans for a house, and write a letter to Maria. He couldn't focus for more than five minutes. He felt as though his mind was swirling around in his head and wouldn't stop long enough for him to finish anything. Then, a phalanx of foot-long scorpions moved across the wall and toward the door. He threw a pillow at them. "Get the hell out of here. This is a hospital." Several of the scorpions laughed at him and waved their tails. Several giant cockroaches crawled across the wall from the closet and waved their antennae at the scorpions, chirping. Finally, the door to his room opened, and all the bugs skittered out as Dr. Warnock walked through the doorway. "Hey, how's it going today?"

"Weird, shaky. Seeing dancing cockroaches."

Warnock nodded as if that was normal. "How's the pain in your legs?"

"Seems like a four or a five."

He looked at Adam's chart. "You've already had Librium, but it looks like you can have a ten milligram OxyContin as your morning dose. Would you like to take it?"

"Yes, and maybe some more lidocaine."

"Okay, I'll tell the nurse. Do you think you can make it through the week? This is day three. Only four more to go."

Adam gritted his teeth. "Think so, Doc. Think so."

"Tomorrow, we'll cut back some more on your Librium and see how you do. Then, if you feel okay, we can get you a walker, and you can walk the halls for some exercise."

"Not yet though. When I stand, my legs throb, and the pain ramps up."

"We'll see what tomorrow brings. I'm proud of you, Adam. You volunteered for this, and you've committed yourself. That's rare among addicts. I'll check in on you later. Don't worry. It gets better every day."

"Thanks. It's nap time." Adam put a pillow over his face and fell asleep. Then, as dusk appeared in the window, he opened his eyes.

"Brought you some lime Jell-O," Marjorie said. "There's a little piece of angel food cake with a honey glaze. Thought you might like something sweet. We often withhold sugar of any kind, but Dr. Warnock didn't think that was necessary with you."

Adam sat up as Marjorie arranged his tray.

"This is the first time I've felt hungry. I guess that's a good sign."

She handed him a spoon. "Hey, Adam, check it out. Your hand is only shaking a little."

Adam smiled and held out his other hand. "The left one seems steady, too."

"You're almost halfway through your detox. You still have challenges, but you are on a downhill slope on your way out of here. I'm proud of you."

Adam had not noticed before, but as he took a bite of Jell-O, he saw that Marjorie was shapely under her green scrubs. Her smile was fetching, and her light green eyes conveyed mysterious compassion, as though she thrived on helping others and, perhaps, laughing and having fun when she was turned loose. She reminded him of Maria. He felt a passing tingle in his loins, a feeling of attraction he had not experienced until now. Was he waking up? Was he becoming more conscious?

"I'll be back for your tray in a little while. Try to eat everything. That's mint tea in the teacup. It will settle your stomach and help you sleep." She turned and walked toward the door. Her hips looked like an upside-down dancing heart. He got busy, ate everything on his tray, and drank all the mint tea.

Marjorie came back within a short time and gathered up his tray. "Well, aren't you a good boy," she said, winking. "Did you eat everything just for me?"

"I want you to be pleased with me," Adam said. His face flushed.

"This is what I like to see. Finally, you seem to be getting your energy back, and, thankfully, you are not impaired." Her eyes twinkled. "It almost seems like you're flirting with me."

"Maybe I am."

Marjorie took his tray and headed out of his room. "I'll see you for breakfast. Maybe we'll try a poached egg on toast tomorrow."

"Thank you. Marjorie, you are a bright light in a dark time."

As the moonlight from a full moon came through the window, the door opened, and Dr. Warnock appeared. "Hello, Adam. You have a visitor, but I wanted to check with you first. Are you up for seeing Russell Kramer?"

Adam jolted up in surprise. "My father?"

"Yes, sometimes we let the immediate family into the rehab ward. He said he won't stay long."

"Okay, I can handle it."

Dr. Warnock stepped out and returned with Russell a few steps behind him.

"Adam, I heard you were in the hospital, so I came to visit."

"Thank you. Seems like a lot of effort."

"You're important to me, Adam."

"Have you told your wife about me yet?"

"Honestly? No. She thinks I'm on a business trip. There hasn't been a good time to tell her about you."

"What about Maggie and Melody?"

"Haven't told them yet either."

"How did you know I was here?"

"I called the company where you work, and they suggested I call your friend Ryan, who knew who I was and referred me to Dr. Warnock." He nodded at the doctor. "The doctor thought it would be fine for me to visit. First, I want to encourage you. I know how hard alcoholism can be, and I've got your back if you need anything. You are on a tough road, but you're not alone."

"Thanks for that." Adam motioned toward Dr. Warnock. "Fortunately, I have an outstanding doctor who also knows the drill. He has experience with addicts."

"Yes, it seems you're in good hands." Russell took a small box out of his jacket pocket. "Adam, I brought you a burner phone that has a couple of hours prepaid. I programmed in my own burner phone number. It's on speed dial. Just press five. That way, we can talk privately."

Adam accepted the phone, moved by the man's thoughtfulness.

"Okay, thanks. I do hope I won't be your secret much longer. I don't like you hiding the truth."

"It shouldn't be much longer. Maggie and Melody are coming over for dinner next weekend, and I plan on telling everyone then. We'll all be on our best behavior at the dinner table, so it should be a civil discussion. I'll let you know how it goes."

Dr. Warnock studied Adam's chart. "Do you mind if I talk about your treatment in front of your father?"

"That's fine."

"I'm cutting your Librium to a hundred milligrams every six hours, and I cut your pain pill to five milligrams morning and evening. To help compensate, we will increase your CBD dosage, and I'll ask for an extra lidocaine treatment during the night. I will be monitoring your pain every six hours."

"When should I start walking?"

"Let's try this. After breakfast tomorrow, you'll have your pain pill and get lidocaine on your legs, so the pain should be manageable. I'll ask one of our physical therapists to walk along with you then and stabilize your walker."

"Okay, I think I can do that. I'm not shaking as much. But my mind feels like a gerbil on a wheel. I can't put two thoughts together."

"That's expected," Dr. Warnock said. "But by the end of the week, you should be able to write a letter about your experience here."

"A letter?"

"Think of it as a personal journal. First, I'll ask you to write notes about where you've been, what you learned, and how you will shape your future. Then, you keep it as a reminder, and we use it in your therapy."

"I'm getting sleepy. Russell, thanks for coming. Doc, thanks for your care."

Adam dozed off.

At two am, Fina woke him up. "I'm going to work on your legs for a while, so I'm taking your covers off."

"Oh, hello, Fina. I'm glad it's you."

"You have to admit it's a little weird. I helped you with skin grafts more than twenty years ago, and here I am, putting lidocaine on the same skin."

"I guess that's why you are so good at it. You understand."

On Thursday morning, Marjorie arrived with an egg on toast as promised. Adam ate everything and finished a glass of orange juice.

"Do you feel any nausea?" Marjorie asked.

"No, I'm fine."

"We are going to add famotidine to keep your stomach settled. It's a simple antacid." She put a small white pill on his tray. "You should take one now."

"Okay, will do. Marjorie, can I tell you something?"

"Sure."

"You look beautiful today."

"Thanks, Adam, but you are flirting again. Don't you have a wife?"

"Yes, but we are separated."

"Oh, I'm sorry to hear that. I'll be back at lunchtime. I'm afraid Jell-O and toast are on the menu again. You can also have a slice of chocolate cake."

"Good. I've been craving sweets—and alcohol."

"We take care of the sweets. You take care of the alcohol. I'll see you at noon."

The physical therapist arrived at nine am, helped Adam stand with his walker, and they walked about fifty yards to the nurse's station and back to his bed.

"You just covered the distance of a football field," the physical therapist said. "Good job. I'll be back tomorrow and every morning until you go home."

Adam fell asleep and then awoke when Marjorie arrived with his tray—Jell-O, toast, chocolate cake, and hot mint tea. "Here you go, Adam. I've got to run. See you in a little while."

"Marjorie, I have a question."

"Yes?"

"Are you ever on the menu?"

"Now you're being silly. Eat your toast."

After he ate, Adam dozed off again. He slept until six pm or so when Dr. Warnock came in. "I think you are doing remarkably well, Adam. Just a few more days, and then I'll get you out of here. In the meantime, we'll stabilize your meds. You can take fifty milligrams of Librium every day, five milligrams of OxyContin morning and night, a hundred-fifty milligrams of CBD morning and night, lidocaine as needed for your legs, and I'll add forty milligrams of a THC gummy at nine pm. Then, on your last day, I'll give you an injection of naltrexone, and we'll talk about managing your reactions. The naltrexone will take away your cravings for alcohol, and you'll need an injection every four weeks. So, there you have it. That's my protocol for you. I'll need to see you every two weeks for three months for therapy, and I recommend that you attend AA meetings at least once a week. I'll get you started with a Saturday noon meeting here at the hospital."

That night, Adam saw some rats running on the floor and a few scorpions and cockroaches on the ceiling. After chewing up the THC gummy, the rats and scorpions went away, and he slept through the night. The pain in his legs did not wake him up.

He walked up and down the hallway on Friday, and Saturday. Each day he got stronger, took his meds as scheduled, talked with staff, and by Sunday, Dr. Warnock dropped the Librium to fifty milligrams a day for the next week, and then he would drop it altogether. "You certainly don't need to get addicted to benzodiazepines," Dr. Warnock said. "Librium is addictive and hard to stop, so we should do it right away. We can increase the CBD if your pain gets above a three or four.

On Sunday afternoon, Adam walked the halls for over an hour. He smiled and waved as he passed the nurses' station and received smiles and applause in return. He headed back to his room. Then beside him—almost, it seemed, like a loyal golden retriever walking at heel—a warm presence touched his left leg, and the pain in his calf diminished by half. Was it the CBD? Would it last? This was hopeful.

On Sunday night, the end of Adam's week, Dr. Warnock, Fina, Marjorie, the physical therapist, the floor nurses, and Russell Kramer gathered in Adam's room to celebrate with cake and ice cream. When Adam cut the cake, they all clapped and cheered.

“We wish you well,” said Fina grinning. “I’m hoping you can stay away from the demon rum. We don’t need a slip.”

“As your father, I’m proud of your accomplishment,” Russell said.

“I’ll bring your last breakfast here in the morning,” Marjorie said. “Waffles with maple syrup, bacon, two eggs, milk, and orange juice. Then you can get dressed and leave.”

Dr. Warnock moved in close to Adam and hugged him. “You’ve got a great start on your new life. I’ll see you in about a week. Your appointment is Saturday at eleven am here in my hospital office, and I’ll take you to the AA meeting at noon. Also, I have a surprise for you, but we’ll wait until then.”

25

It was a close call. Maria shivered when she thought about it. Her feelings confused her—fear and guilt at the same time, a mishmash of emotions and pain that surrounded her rapid heartbeat. But at least they stopped it in time, or nearly in time.

Ryan and Lucas had been eating dinner when she came home. She had worked the day shift and stayed late charting and preparing for tomorrow.

"Hi, Mom," Lucas said. "Uncle Ryan bought us Happy Meals on the way home. Would you like some fries?"

"Thanks, Lucas, but I think I'll pass. I had a quick bite in the cafeteria."

Ryan smiled and popped some French fries in his mouth. "I hope this is okay," he said. Lucas said he likes Happy Meals."

"Sure. I appreciate you picking him up and getting dinner. A Happy Meal now and then won't hurt this growing boy." She leaned over and kissed Lucas on top of his head.

After dinner, Lucas plopped down in front of the TV while Maria and Ryan drank chai tea and visited.

"I had normal callbacks most of the day," Ryan told her. I missed having Adam along, so I spent the morning training a new employee. He has a lot of construction experience, and it will be good to have a substitute when Adam is not available."

"I hope he's doing okay," Maria said. "I was tempted to drop in and see him on the rehab ward, but his doctor urged me to stay away for fear of derailing things—I gather that his detox will take all his energy and fortitude."

"It can be brutal," Ryan said. "He's been an addict for a long time, so he's in for a whirlwind of pain."

"I thought about our getting back together, but I'm just too angry to try. Of course, I'm hopeful for Adam's recovery. I can't muster much hope for our reconciliation, though." Maria twisted the LifeGem on her finger. Her other fingers felt bare where she's put away her wedding ring and engagement ring.

Ryan stood up to leave and nodded toward Lucas, asleep on the couch. "Should I take him into bed, or is it too early?"

"Would you carry him to bed, please? I'll tuck him in. He wakes up soon after daylight, and he needs his sleep. Nacho has started sleeping beside his bed. They seem to comfort each other."

"Sure."

Maria watched as Ryan gathered up Lucas, helped him take off his clothes, put on his pajamas, and pulled up his covers. Nacho turned four circles and settled next to the bed. She withdrew to the kitchen, listening as Ryan softly said, "Good night, Lucas. I'll come by in the morning and take you to school."

When Ryan returned to the kitchen, he saw that Maria had started crying. "Are you okay?" he asked.

"I'll be fine." She returned to Lucas's bedroom, kissed him, arranged his covers, rubbed his back for a while, and then came back to the kitchen. "You know," she said, "whenever I get home from work, I am dead tired and forlorn. I can't seem to get through this. I imagine Ava is still here, but I know she's not. I feel like there's a dark hole where my heart should be. The pain never stops."

Ryan stood up and opened his arms. Maria melted into his hug and took some deep breaths. For a moment, she felt warm and comfortable. "I'm grateful that you care, Ryan. I'm going to take a shower. You can let yourself out, right? Finish your tea if you'd like."

Maria stood under the shower until the hot water was all gone. She dried herself off, dusted herself with body powder, and put on her panties and her light blue terrycloth bathrobe. Overcome with waves of sadness she and sat on the commode for a moment, weeping quietly.

Would this suffering ever end?

When She came out of the bathroom, Ryan was still sitting at the kitchen table.

"Are you sure you'll be okay here by yourself?" he asked.

"I've had a good cry, so I should be okay. I'm so tired. I'm sure I'll fall asleep right away. Thanks again for being here. We'll see you tomorrow."

Ryan stood up. "Come over here," he said, opening his arms again. Maria came to him and settled in against his chest. Ryan reached down, slung one arm under her knees, and lifted her as easily as if she were a child. Maria put her arms around his neck as he carried her to her bed. "Here you go," he said. "I'll stay here with you and rub your back until you fall asleep."

Despite a pang of doubt, Maria nodded. "I guess that's okay."

Streaks of gray dawn filtered through the window when Maria awakened. She was on her left side, and her mind was in a bewildering fog—gray streaks like the dawn. She was naked except for her panties. Ryan's huge arm lay over her side, and his hand cupped her breast. She could hear his steady, quiet breathing. Spooning her, he felt warm and comforting, from the back of her knees to the top of her shoulders. Maria backed into him a little, murmuring nonsense, sleepy sounds. After a few moments, she moved again and felt his aroused state poking on her from behind, between her thighs. She awoke fully, jumped up, grabbed her pajamas from her dresser drawer, and put them on. She was buttoning the top up when Ryan awoke and sat up. He wore only his boxer shorts.

"Oh, boy, I guess I fell asleep. This is awkward."

"Why were my clothes off?" Maria asked.

"Your robe got twisted around you, and I thought you would be more comfortable sleeping without it."

"Why are your clothes off?"

Ryan pulled on his pants and his green polo shirt.

"Can you answer me? Why are your clothes off?"

"I'm not sure," Ryan said. "Must have happened when I was asleep." He gave a sheepish grin. "A man can always hope, right?"

Maria felt herself down there. "Did we...did we do anything?"

"No, of course not. Not that I wouldn't want to, but we just fell asleep. That's all."

"You were holding my breast."

"A little like a moth to a flame. You are like gravity, Maria. You draw men to you."

"So, this is all my fault?"

Ryan flushed. No one is at fault. It's just that—you may be the most beautiful woman I've ever seen. I can't hide it any longer, Maria. I want to be with you—all the time."

"Yes, but that would be cheating. You're a good friend, Ryan, but even if I wanted to, I couldn't do that."

"But your marriage is on the rocks, and you're separated. Headed for a divorce, right?"

"That's true, but Adam is trying. I give him credit for that. And besides, we're just friends."

"Maria, you're more than a friend to me, and you need comforting. Being with you would be a dream come true. You are a fine person, valuable in every respect, a prize for any man. I would take good care of you and Lucas. He seems to like me, and I love you."

"Come on, Ryan. You love me?"

"I have for a long time. You're a wonderful woman. Give me a chance."

Maria crossed her arms. "This is awkward. I don't know what to say."

"Well, does it feel good to you to be loved by a healthy man with no addictions?"

"I think everyone wants to be loved. It is a little embarrassing to hear you say that to me."

"Don't be embarrassed. This could be a life-changing time for you, Maria. Maybe a new door has opened."

Maria backed toward the bathroom. "I'm a married woman and I've just lost a child. I can't even think about this now, Ryan. Please, just go to the kitchen and make some breakfast for Lucas. Tell him that you came over a little early so you could make him French toast or something. I'm grateful for your help, but I need to be alone."

"Isolation is not good," Ryan said. "The best way to grieve is to talk with another person. I'm here for you."

"Well, maybe so, but I need to be alone for now, and I for sure don't need anyone holding my breast. Adam doesn't need any more grief either, especially when he's trying to get sober. You're his best friend—what would he think?"

"This is not something he needs to know about."

Maria retreated to the bathroom, listening to the sounds of Ryan making breakfast. When she smelled food, she emerged and sat down at the kitchen table with Lucas.

"Hey, little man, come over here and sit in my lap."

Lucas smiled and climbed up into her lap. "We're having French toast," he said.

"Yes, I heard. Ryan, thanks for breakfast."

Ryan put French toast on their plates and got the maple syrup from the cabinet. "Syrup okay? I'll get the strawberry jam if you'd prefer."

"This is fine," Lucas said. He broke off a piece of crust and slipped it to Nacho, under the table.

Maria grabbed a piece of French toast and headed for the bedroom. "I'm almost late for work. I need to be there by seven."

"Okay, I'll rinse off the dishes. We'll leave for school in a half-hour or so."

Maria turned and called over her shoulder. "Thank you, Ryan. You'll pick him up after school, right?"

"Yes, we should be here by four-thirty, and I'll get a pizza for dinner."

Maria dressed in her green scrubs and tied her hair back in a ponytail, then she walked through the kitchen with her car keys in hand. "Thanks again, Ryan. I'll be checking with Carolyn to see if she can help with transportation for Lucas. It seems like it's too much for you with work and all."

"No, it's not too much, but you should do whatever you'd like."

"See you later, Lucas."

"Bye, Mom. We'll get pepperoni and green chili and save some for you."

"Sounds good. Love you, my little man."

"Love you too, Mom."

26

Maria mused while she was driving to work. Ryan seemed to be a good man—moral, upstanding, a hard worker, rugged and handsome. Might not be too bad after all. She pulled her scrub shirt open a little and sniffed. She could still smell the slight odor of Ryan's Old Spice. She remembered he was gentle and decisive. She had a dim awareness of his hand cupping her breast; she could have pulled it away but did not. I guess I liked it. Guess I like him, and he says he loves me, that I'm a real prize for any man. Could that be true? His body was softer than Adam's, and, when spooning, he'd embraced her with warmth and a feeling of safety. I keep saying I want to be alone, but maybe not all the time. Perhaps it would be good to have a companion to come home to—a companion who is clean, sober, and dedicated to my wellbeing.

Ryan's truck was in the driveway when she got home at five pm. Ryan and Lucas were sitting at the kitchen table when she came in.

"Hi, Mom," Lucas said. "We saved some pizza for you."

Ryan stood up and pulled out a chair for her. "Come on, sit down, and I'll make you some tea."

Maria smiled and sat down. "Thank you. This is nice."

"Guess what, Mom."

"What?"

"Ryan is going to take us for ice cream later. He said he would get us Klondike bars or whatever we want."

"Well, if we go to Baskin-Robbins, I want mocha almond fudge," Maria said. "I have a chocolate craving."

"I'll take you to wherever you'd like," Ryan said.

"Lucas, if you don't mind, I'll ask Ryan to come back here after we get ice cream and help me move some furniture."

"Fine with me," Lucas said. "I like having Ryan here." Nacho moved close to Ryan and put his nose on Ryan's knee, hoping for attention. "Plus, Nacho likes having him here, too."

Ryan rubbed Nacho between his shoulders. "I'd be pleased to help, Maria."

"Could we play Go Fish?" Lucas asked.

Maria nodded as Ryan glanced at her. "Your mom and I think there will be time for a short game before your bedtime."

Lucas grinned. "Okay, I'll set things up before we go for ice cream."

What's with moving furniture? I didn't even think about it until just now. What's going on with me? I feel light and almost weightless, as though something I don't understand is controlling me. She wrung her hands together, caressing her LifeGem ring.

Fully sated with pizza and ice cream, the three settled down to play Go Fish. Lucas won.

"Good game," Ryan said. "Now I think it's time for bed. Do you want help with your pajamas?"

"No, I can get ready by myself. After I brush my teeth, you can tuck me in if you'd like."

Maria hung in the doorway as Ryan fluffed up Lucas' pillow and pulled the covers up under his chin. "How's that?"

"Thanks, Uncle Ryan. Good night."

Maria stepped over Nacho, sat on the edge of Lucas's bed, and ruffled his hair. "Good night, my little man. Sleep tight."

"Nite, Mom."

Ryan and Maria sat down in the kitchen. "Lucas seems to like you."

"Yes, and I like him too. I've always wanted to have a son, even if he's a stepson. I missed a lot in my childhood, and so I can imagine all the needs of a young boy."

"You have a rich fantasy life, Ryan."

"Oh, you don't know the half of it." He blushed but was grinning. "So, what furniture do I want to move?"

What do I want to move? I'd better think of something. Oh, I know. "I want to rearrange my bedroom. Come on, I'll show you."

"Okay, I'm ready, willing, and able."

She led him to the bedroom. "I want to move the dresser and mirror to where the bed is and the reading chair and table to the corner by the window. Then we can move the bed to where the dresser was."

"I get the picture. I can do this by myself, no problem."

"No, I want to help." Maria scooted the chair and table the window while Ryan moved the dresser. Then she pulled the quilt and sheets off the bed, and Ryan stood the mattress and box springs up against the wall while they moved the bed frame. He replaced the box springs, mattress, and headboard and waited on the other side while Maria shook out the bottom sheet.

"This is fun," Ryan said. "To be making the bed with you."

"I don't know about fun, but it's unusual, that's for sure."

"This is our first time."

"First time? For what?"

Ryan smiled. "This is our first time of making a bed together. Should I make you some tea?"

So now what.

"That would be nice."

Ryan heated the water while Maria dug out a new box of chai from the cupboard.

"What if I stayed over again tonight?" Ryan asked lightly.

"That's probably not a good idea."

Not a good idea. Maybe it is a good idea. My mind is jumping all over the place. How do I feel about Ryan? I look in the mirror and see a woman who wants to be alone and doesn't want to be alone at the same time. Maria had an odd thought. Maybe Ryan could hold me and leave me alone at the same time? How can I want two opposite things? It would feel good to have Ryan hold me while I fall asleep. I could wear my flannel pajamas and panties. What could it hurt? He would have to get up before Lucas wakes up. Why am I even thinking about this?

"I would be sure to get up and dressed before Lucas wakes up." Ryan added.

"That would be an absolute requirement." Now, why did I say that?

"Can do. I could rub your back until you fall asleep. Would you like that?"

"Maybe another time."

"Adam is in the hospital. Anyone who drives by and sees my truck knows that I'm helping you with Lucas. This seems like a good time." Ryan put his hand on hers. "Whatever you want. That's all that's going to happen. I promise."

"You promise?"

"Yes, what happens is only what you want."

Maria took a long shower and washed her hair. She dried off and smoothed on lilac body powder. After she brushed her hair, ran the hairdryer, and brushed her teeth, she tied her hair back in a ponytail and put on a new pair of flannel pajamas that no one could mistake as sexy. She added her blue terrycloth robe for good measure and walked to the kitchen table.

Ryan looked up. "Wow, you clean up real nice. Your fragrance is captivating—makes me want to get married or something."

"Or something?"

"Let's just say you're beautiful and a dream come true. You're an outstanding medical professional and a gorgeous woman as well. Smart mind, body to die for."

"You certainly are full of yourself tonight. Are you always this elaborate with your compliments?"

"No, I usually don't compliment people, especially women, because I don't want to come off as insincere. You, however, are another matter, and I believe you know I mean it. I wouldn't tell you I love you unless it's true."

"I do believe you, Ryan, but I don't know what to do about it."

"There's nothing to do about it except believe me and see where it goes from here."

"Don't get your hopes up. My heart shut down when Ava died. I feel love for Lucas, but I don't feel much else except sadness."

"You're talking about it, you're active at work, you appear to be clean, dressed, and in your right mind. You smile occasionally—all signs that you're making progress and on a healing path. I think you've come a long way in a short time."

"Thanks, Ryan. Those things are hard to see from in here."

"Everyone needs validation, and you, of all people, deserve it. I admire who you are, Maria. The world needs more women like you."

Maria felt her neck and face flush. "That's kind. Thank you."

"Are you ready for your backrub?"

I guess this is decision time. If we move into the bedroom, get in bed, and he lifts my pajama top and rubs my back, well, haven't we crossed a line or something? Maybe not. I can insist that the back rub is the limit of Ryan's touching. Besides, it will help me relax and sleep better.

"Okay, Ryan, but I'm going to hold you to your promise. Nothing but a backrub and then we go to sleep."

"That's fine. We will only do what you want."

Maria brought Ryan a bottle of lotion. "This is my lilac and cinnamon body lotion. It should be good for a backrub."

She pulled the covers down and got into bed. She felt a little shaken when Ryan undressed down to his candy-striped boxer shorts. "You didn't say anything about you getting undressed."

"For heaven's sake, I can't sleep in my clothes. Just imagine I'm in my bathing suit."

Maria hid her face in a pillow and stretched her arms over her head, eyes closed. Ryan lifted the back of her pajama top and spread lotion up and down her spine and to the sides of her rib cage. She could feel every movement. His hands were gentle, strong, and seemed to have a life of their own. Wherever she felt a desire for touch in a particular place, well, there his hands were. They were reading her mind or the skin on her back—she didn't know which. It was as though she had sunk into a soft cloud, and angels were dancing on my back. Incredible. No one had touched her since Ava died. Maybe Ryan knew that. It didn't matter because his smooth, long strokes were making up for whatever she had missed.

She put the LifeGem up to her lips and pushed against his hands like a cat rubbing against his leg. He moved the pressure of both hands to her lower back, at the top of her tailbone. Without warning, her hips and thighs tingled and relaxed. Ryan must have found pressure points that were all twisted up. If her butt cheeks could have talked, they would have said, 'this is how we want to be.' She didn't move or object when Ryan pulled her pajama bottoms down below her cheeks and began kneading her with the heels of his hands. The tingling increased. She felt warmth moving up her back and around her stomach. She sensed that her skin was flushed.

"This feels like heaven, Ryan. Your hands are skilled."

"Years ago, before I got into construction, I learned some massage therapy. I thought I might go into sports medicine."

"You are full of surprises. I feel like I can't move—it's a good feeling—may fall asleep soon."

"Good plan."

Maria hovered on the soft edge of sleep when Ryan stopped. He left her top up, pulled her pajama bottoms down and off, turned her on her left side, and spooned his whole body against her. She didn't resist because he was so warm and comforting. What could it hurt? Two grown adults seeking a little comfort from each other. Besides, Ryan admired her. She felt his love in the warmth of his two-hundred and fifty pounds and the wafting smell of Old Spice. She must have drifted off.

Through layers of sleep, she became aware of his hand between her thighs, a hand and fingers that probed and touched like feathers. Without thinking, she pushed her hips back and lifted one knee a little. He rubbed in the right place until she was quivering, and then she felt him push himself along. She was wet. Where in the world did that come from? She pretended she was sound asleep as he inserted himself and pushed. His movements were rhythmical and steady, slow, and strong. He left his hand in place, so she was covered completely and filled with warmth and adoration. She turned her head and whispered, "Do you have any protection?"

"Not to worry, my love. I had a vasectomy five years ago."

Though still not sure why, she just let it happen. Then, the next night, she let it happen again. She supposed she enjoyed being cherished, but Ryan was more of an athlete than a lover. She couldn't see this arrangement continuing. It had to be just one of those things soon forgotten. His vasectomy was a Godsend…if Ryan was truthful.

After she changed the sheets and vacuumed the bedroom on Saturday morning, Maria told Ryan that he could no longer stay over. He nodded. "Here, let me help with those things," he said. He gathered up the laundry and took the sheets, pajamas, and underwear to the washer. Maria felt squeamish and a little embarrassed that he was sorting her clothes. It seemed that he lingered as he added detergent and softener and started the cold water, light load.

"You know that Adam is scheduled to be discharged from the hospital on Monday, and he will no doubt want to return to his duties helping me with Lucas," Maria said.

"It's only been a week. Are you going to let him?"

"We'll need to talk about that, but I could sure use his help if he's sane and sober."

"You have me if I'm needed. You know that."

Maria could only nod, more confused than ever.

27

Adam checked out of the hospital after lunch on Monday. He felt great—clear-headed and essentially without pain. He promised Dr. Warnock that he would stay on the protocol and keep records of his medications, his pain level, and the number of hours he slept each night. He had completed a journal with his sobriety goals and personal comments about his commitment to recovery. He saw today as the beginning of a new chapter in his life. When he called Maria, she agreed to him picking up Lucas, provided he was sober and, as she said, in his right mind.

Adam surprised Lucas at the school pick-up driveway.

Lucas ran up to him, grinning. "Hey, Dad," he said. "I got excited when I saw your truck."

"Yeah, I talked with your mom, and she's willing for us to get back on schedule," Adam gave Lucas a bear hug. "Let's go home, play a game of Chutes and Ladders, and get dinner ready. I think your mom will be home by six."

Lucas slid across the seat, so he was next to Adam. "I missed you, Dad."

"I missed you, too. Did Ryan get you to school on time?"

"Mom took me and picked me up on Monday and Tuesday, and then Ryan took over for Wednesday, Thursday, and Friday. He was on time, and he made us French toast for breakfast."

"He made breakfast for you and Mom?" Adam asked.

"He came over early. He was cooking when I woke up. He has a cool truck."

"Yes, it's newer, and Ryan takes good care of it. It's a Ford F-one-fifty."

"I like yours, too."

"What shall we make for dinner? I was thinking about meatloaf and mashed potatoes. How does that sound?"

Adam pulled into the supermarket parking lot. "Come on with me."

They picked up two pounds of ground beef, a bottle of catsup, a bottle of bar-b-que sauce, five pounds of new potatoes, and a pound of butter. Lucas gathered up six cans of dog food for Nacho. Adam winked at Lucas and put a box of six Klondike bars in the basket. Lucas shook his head. "Mom only gets one at a time. She says having them at home is too tempting."

"Maybe so, but if you eat one after dinner, and Mom and I each have one, that just leaves three. So, I think we can handle the temptation."

Home in their familiar kitchen, Adam felt a wave of happiness as Lucas washed and peeled four potatoes while he mixed catsup, bar-b-que sauce, salt and pepper, and a little brown sugar into the ground beef and shaped it into a meatloaf pan. Then he set a pot of water on the stove. "Okay, Lucas, let's cut those potatoes into small pieces and cook them in the boiling water." He moved a step stool in front of the cooktop. "Here's a wooden spoon. You need to stir them every few minutes, so they don't stick to the bottom." Adam slid the meatloaf in the oven and set it to 400 degrees.

"The potatoes should be soft enough to mash in about thirty minutes. The meatloaf will take about forty minutes," he told Lucas.

"Okay, I'll keep stirring."

"About every five minutes is probably enough."

Adam took a small bowl from the cabinet and shook out brown sugar from the package. Then he mixed in catsup, bar-be-que sauce, and a little honey. "We'll take the meatloaf out of the oven a little early, spread this paste over the top, and cook it for another five minutes or so."

"Mom's home. I hear her car," Lucas said.

§

Adam was smoothing his hair and smiling as Maria walked in the door. Lucas ran to her for a hug, and she stood still with her mouth open, and eyebrows raised. Adam seemed taller than she remembered, and he had an aura of youthfulness and good health. He was clean-shaven, his eyes sparkled, and the gray bags under his eyes had disappeared. His gaze was intense, and he took in the presence of Maria like a thirsty man coming upon a pitcher of water.

He gave a low, soft whistle. "Maria, you are even more beautiful than I remembered. It is so good to see you."

"You look good yourself, Adam. I guess detox agrees with you."

"I'm through with a life of addiction. I still feel kind of raw; but Dr. Warnock and I are managing my leg pain and anxiety with a protocol that keeps me alert and productive."

Maria walked closer to Adam. He opened his arms, and though she was not sure why, she melted into them and accepted a long hug. She wrapped her arms around him and nestled her face into the hollow of his neck. "You smell good."

"Just soap and water and a little cologne from Fina. I think she said it was Dolce and Gabbana, or something like that."

Maria felt a stab of jealousy and frowned. "Who's Fina?"

"Josefina Romero is a nurse manager on the detox ward. She and Dr. Warnock, my doctor, are engaged. Hey, get this. She was at the hospital over twenty years ago when I had skin grafts in the burn unit. She remembered me. Can you believe that? I guess what goes around comes around."

"Did she say anything? I think it's unusual for a nurse to give a patient cologne."

"Yes, I thought so too, but when I was discharged on Monday morning, Fina handed me a little box with the cologne bottle and said, "'Here you go, Adam. New fragrance, new life.'"

"She said she thought my wife would like it."

Maria laughed. "I don't know what to say, Adam, but you do smell good—I hesitate to say, sexy. Right now, you remind me of when we first met. It's great to see you healthy, sober, and, well, present to Lucas and me. It feels like you are fully here." She paused." But I still don't trust you."

Adam pulled Maria back into another hug and whispered in her ear. "Whatever you suspect might be my failings with Ava, my doctor says

I need to ask for your forgiveness and do whatever I can to be a good husband, even though we're separated."

Maria stepped back and looked up at him. "I've been working on forgiveness, Adam, but I'm not there yet." A shiver ran up her back as she took a deep breath. She pressed the LifeGem ring to her lips. She knew Ava was in there, but, sadly, the gem felt cold in her mouth.

Lucas piped up. "Hey, Mom, we're having meatloaf and mashed potatoes. I'm helping with the potatoes." He stepped up on the stool and stirred the boiling water.

"Sounds great. I'll go change out of my work clothes and then set the table."

Soon she returned dressed in her flannel pajamas and her light blue terrycloth bathrobe. She wore fuzzy slippers topped with little rabbits, and her hair was loose around her face and neck. She quickly arranged three place settings, put some water on for tea, and sat down. "The table is ready."

"You are gorgeous," Adam said. "More beautiful than ever."

She blushed and felt his sincerity wash over her. She felt acknowledged and regarded, even though his compliments were about her appearance.

He took out the meatloaf, spread the brown sugar paste on top, and put it back in the oven. Then he drained the potatoes and dumped them in the mixing bowl. "Hey, Lucas, want to turn on the mixer?"

"Sure." He started the mixer on a slow setting as it swirled through the potatoes. Adam added half a stick of butter, a little milk, and some salt and pepper. Soon the potatoes were mashed. "Looks good. You can put the bowl on the table, Lucas. I'll cut some slices of the meatloaf."

Dinner was delightful. Adam talked about his detox, the people he'd met, his doctor, the nurses who helped him, and then he told Maria and Lucas about Russell Kramer.

"This is an incredible turn of events, Adam," Maria said. "I can't believe that all this time, you've been dealing with a stepfather instead of your birth father. That's got to feel weird, confusing. It makes me confused, too." She shook her head and ran her hand through her hair. "Maybe it explains some of Edward's meanness toward you. I guess we'll never know. But I can't help but wonder if things would have been different for us if we'd known before we got married. It's almost too much to take in, let alone understand."

"Yes, confusing but hopeful. Russell will tell his wife and the twins about me this weekend. Can't imagine their reaction. He wants us to be friends."

"I don't know what to say. A new father in your life, and new stepsisters."

"It's strange and a surprise, but I'm going to see where it goes."

"Your anxiety seems to have calmed, Adam. Do you feel more at peace?"

"I do. I've had time to think about everything, about what I genuinely want out of life."

"Well—and I'm just guessing here—I imagine that your anger at Edward is melting away some?"

"Seems to be. I don't feel like a volcano ready to erupt anymore."

Maria pulled Lucas up onto her lap. "Thanks for helping your dad with dinner. It was great. I guess you know you have a new grandfather."

"You mean Grandpa Edward was not my grandfather?"

"He was what you call a step-grandfather. He was Adam's stepfather. That's because he married Adam's mother."

"Is my new grandpa the man named Russell Kramer?"

"Yes. I think he will come and visit soon, right Adam?"

"I'll invite him. I know he would like that. Hey, Lucas, are you up for a quick game of Go Fish?"

"Sure," Lucas said. "We can play Chutes and Ladders later." He got the playing cards from the bookshelf as Maria cleared the table. She was feeling little waves of comfort, like when they were first married. She still felt nervous and wary. But she was struck by what a good dad Adam was to Lucas. Couldn't ask for better.

After the card game, Maria hugged Lucas. "Time to get into your pajamas and brush teeth."

"Okay, Mom. Is Dad going to stay here tonight?"

Maria looked at Adam. He smiled, raised his eyebrows, and folded his hands in his lap.

"Well, I know he will take you to school in the morning and pick you up. I sure do like the dinners you guys prepare."

Lucas moved over to Adam and hugged him. "Nite, Dad. I miss you when you're not here. I'll see you in the morning." Lucas left to change into his pajamas and brush his teeth, then returned to the kitchen. "Can you guys tuck me in?"

Maria smiled at Adam, and they walked with Lucas to his bedroom. Then they both helped him with the covers and his pillow. "Goodnight, my little man," Maria said. "Goodnight Nacho." He wagged his tail and thumped it on the floor.

"Good night, Mom. Good night, Dad."

They returned to the table.

"What do you think about my staying over tonight?"

"Okay, I'll get some sheets and a blanket for the couch. You can sleep there."

Adam heated water for tea, found some chai teabags, and prepared two cups with saucers. Saucers? She couldn't remember him ever putting a saucer under a cup.

They drank their tea and spent an hour traveling down memory lane—their wedding, Lucas's birth, moving into their mobile home, Adam working with the building company, the falling out with Doug, Carolyn's friendship, their love for Ava. Adam quietly wished for Maria's forgiveness. He did not deny that perhaps he could have done more, but at the time, and with the resources at hand, and his condition, he had done all he could. Maria acknowledged to herself that what he said was probably true.

§

Maria sipped her tea, then frowned and touched her hand to her chin.

"Are you okay?" Adam asked. "You seem distracted."

"I had a distasteful incident today at work. I can't seem to get it out of my mind."

"A bad accident?"

"No, more like a bad father."

"How so?"

"A little girl. You know me, Adam. I'm committed to healing people, and sometimes I get confronted by problems beyond my control. I have a strong sense of justice for mothers and children."

"I know. That's one of the reasons I love you—your compassion."

"I got tested today. You know I hate it when children are objects, when they are seen as owned and not people with hopes and feelings. Children are not objects of desire, and they're certainly not candidates for beauty contests.

"Working the ER, I see far too many vain mothers and abusive fathers—maybe it's because so many show up in the emergency room. I can't get over the disdain I feel for the father of a little three-year old girl I helped today."

"What happened?"

"It was shameful. The girl was on a gurney crying. Her father was standing there with a goofy smile. I asked him what happened."

"My daughter is my pride and joy," he said, "and I think she broke her arm."

"Is her mother here with you?" I asked.

"No, she's at work. I'm the designated babysitter."

"It was like he was showing off. He stood her up on the exam table and held her hands out. The girl flinched. Broken arms hurt. Then he said, "Isn't she a living doll? When I dress her like this in her pink dress, pink socks, pink lacy underpants, and a pink hair ribbon, she reminds me of cotton candy, melts-in-your-mouth sweet." He spoke sharply to the child. "Stop crying, honey."

"How did she hurt her arm?" I asked him.

"Oh, she slipped on a toy rabbit and tumbled down the stairs."

"Right. Can you believe it Adam? A toy rabbit and a pink fetish, reminds him of cotton candy. Geeze, she's three-years old and her arm is broken, and this deadbeat dad is caught up in his own fantasies. The guy was weird, a first-class jerk."

"Do you think she tripped on the rabbit?"

"The x-ray showed a radial fracture as if her arm had been pulled and twisted. I talked with the doctor about a potential abuse report, but he said there wasn't enough evidence."

"You think her dad broke her arm?"

"I couldn't tell for sure, but he was too jovial and excited about her pink underpants for me to believe anything he said."

"Gosh, I'm sorry you have to put up with people like that."

"What's the matter with people, Adam? Do you think everyone gets pulled to the darkness—is evil always with us?"

"I think everyone has the capacity to do nasty things, but if we love enough and often, we don't act on the impulses. Don't we both believe that love and compassion overcome evil?"

"Fortunately, we both believe that."

"We can't control people. We should do what we can and leave the results up to God."

"I agree, but right now I just want to forget about him, but I worry about his daughter. Girls should not be taught that they are living dolls. They need to be loved, not displayed like a prize. Meeting men like him makes me grateful for men like you. You're a good man, Adam."

§

She made up Adam's bed on the couch while he took a shower. He came out of the bathroom in his boxer shorts and sat on the sofa. He grinned. "Hey, will you please tuck me in?"

Maria laughed, fluffed up his pillow, and pulled his covers up to his chin.

"Would you kiss me goodnight?"

She stood frozen for a moment, then leaned down to peck him on the cheek. He put his hand behind her neck and pulled her down for a full kiss on the lips. She didn't resist and discovered herself flicking her tongue in his mouth, tasting his fresh toothpaste. She shivered, put her hands on the sides of his face, and kissed him some more. She felt her heartbeat quicken. Had the old flame just been ignited? Did her body know more than her mind? In many ways, Adam was an attractive man, and kissing him had always made her heartstrings sing. She didn't know what was happening. Her anger seemed to be in abeyance, and her body needed comforting—that's how she felt right then.

"Wait for a while until I shower and brush my teeth and then move into our bedroom."

"Are you sure, Maria? If I move into our bed, I'm not going to be able to keep my hands off you."

"I figured."

"So, you're serious?"

"See you in a half-hour."

She came out of the bathroom covered with only a towel. Adam had lit a candle on the dresser and was waiting under the covers. When she joined him, he wrapped his arms around her gently. He was naked. She tossed the towel on the floor and kissed him, and she felt overpowered by warmth and lust.

"I love you, Maria, and I'm on the road to recovery. I want this marriage to work more than anything."

"You know, Adam, underneath it all, I love you, too."

They made love far into the night until we were both worn out. She felt a deep comfort that he knew what she liked—in fact, their coupling was luxurious beyond words. Neither of them said anything about protection, and their sleep came quickly.

And so, for sure, there's that, she thought as she drifted off to dreamland.

28

Adam was already in the kitchen making poached eggs on toast with avocado—Maria's favorite—when she came in, yawning, stretching, and smiling. Adam hugged her and kissed her neck. "Breakfast will be ready in a few minutes. Could you wake up Lucas?"

Lucas stumbled into the kitchen, rubbing his eyes. "You don't have to wake me up, Mom. I heard Dad making breakfast." Nacho padded along behind him.

They sat down with their plates and orange juice.

"I'm glad you stayed here last night," Lucas said. "I feel safe when you're here."

"I love staying here," Adam said, smiling at Maria. "There's no place I'd rather be."

Maria wiped her mouth with a napkin. "I like it, too, but you should sleep at Ryan's like you've been doing."

"Will do, but I would like to stay over occasionally if that's okay with you."

Maria smiled and crossed her arms. "This breakfast was wonderful, Adam. Thank you."

"How does occasionally sound?"

Maria stood up. "I've got to get dressed for work. Occasionally is probably all I can handle right now. I've got stuff to work through."

"I understand," Adam said. "See you for dinner."

After taking Lucas to school, Adam went to Ryan's house and decided to do some laundry. Ryan was at work and wouldn't be back until later. Adam was eager to share his detox experience with his friend and talk with him about his recovery plan. Ryan will be proud, he thought.

He gathered his clothes from the bedroom and loaded the washer, then opened the dryer door to remove whatever was there so he could dry his things. He pushed a basket up to the dryer door and started pulling out the dry clothes—Ryan's jeans, t-shirts, underwear, socks, and polo shirts. He reached into the back and dragged out a handful of assorted small items. There were a couple of dish towels and—Whoa, what's this? He held up a pair of hip hugger blue panties. He touched them to his nose and smelled the faint remnants of lavender and cinnamon. They were Maria's size six. What the hell was Ryan doing with Maria's blue panties? What the hell? Had he sneaked them out of Maria's dresser or laundry basket? Did he slip them off Maria, do the deed, and then stuff them in his pocket as a souvenir?

Adam's mind churned. His demons arose from the darkness and pushed into his mind. His anxiety ramped up until it was overwhelming, and he began to shake with fear and anger. He closed his eyes. A gorilla appeared and insisted they dance.

Adam stuffed Maria's blue panties into his pocket, drove to the grocery store, and bought a fifth of vodka. He parked in a secluded place in a park and proceeded to get stinking drunk. He awoke in a couple of hours with his face in his own vomit. This was too much, way too much for an addict to handle just after detox. Heavy shame. That's what he was, a shameful failure, just like Edward had said he was.

He drove around the various job sites until he found Ryan's truck. He pulled in behind it and waited. Ryan came out of a house, and Adam got out of his vehicle and stood blocking Ryan's truck door.

"Hey, Adam," Ryan said. "It's great to see you. I guess you are out of detox, right? Sorry to say, but you look awful."

Adam glared at Ryan. "You sonofabitch."

"Hey, what's going on?"

"You tell me." Adam pulled Maria's blue panties from his pocket and waved them in Ryan's face. "Maria's panties were in your dryer, asshole. How did you get them?"

Adam felt a sharp spike of psychic pain erupt from Ryan's mind. Then he watched Ryan decide to lie. "Now, don't jump to conclusions, Adam. I had a date, and we came back to the house after dinner. We got a little carried away. My date left her panties, and I put them through the wash."

"They're Maria's size. They look like Maria's, and they smell like her scent. I bought them as a Christmas present last year."

"You sound paranoid. I helped Lucas with transportation and dinners, but that's all. I did what I said I would do. I didn't take Maria's panties."

"You're a liar," Adam said. "I don't know how you got them, but I hope you took them from her dresser or from the dirty clothes." Adam poked his finger at Ryan's chest. "You'd better not have hit on her."

"C'mon, Adam. That's a mean accusation. You're drunk and covered with vomit. You need to get cleaned up, and we can talk later when I get home."

"I won't be there. I can't trust you anymore."

Adam got in his truck and peeled off, tires screaming. He found a cheap motel on Central Avenue, dumped his stuff on the bed, and called Dr. Warnock's office. The receptionist said she would ask Dr. Warnock to call Adam when he had a break. In the meantime he took a shower, and the phone was ringing when he got out.

"Hey, Adam. What's going on?"

"I'm in a bad way and feel like getting drunk—again."

"Again? Okay, can you meet me in the Emergency Room?"

"I'm on the way."

Adam parked his truck and shuffled to the ER, where Dr. Warnock was waiting.

"Adam, good to see you," Warnock said. "Why are you in such a bad way? Are you in pain?"

"My asshole best friend Ryan is hitting on my wife. I found her blue panties in his laundry." Adam showed them to Dr. Warnock.

"Are you sure those are Maria's?"

"Her size, her favorite color—still smell of lavender.

"But are you sure?"

"Well, not absolutely sure. Ryan said they belong to a woman he dated."

"Adam, you sound a little paranoid. How has Maria been treating you?"

"She welcomed me, and I think she might forgive me. I stayed over last night. We slept together."

"Doesn't sound like she's got her eye on someone else."

"Yeah, she didn't act like it. We both want things to go back to normal, whatever that is, but she doesn't want me to live with her yet. I'm helping with transportation with Lucas."

Dr. Warnock examined Adam and took his vital signs. "You seem to be doing okay physically, but other than Ryan, how are you doing mentally?"

"I got drunk when I found Maria's panties. Didn't know what else to do. I wanted to kill Ryan."

"Everyone has a slip now and then, especially when they don't have strategies for dealing with emotional setbacks. We were able to get your body detoxed—but your mind and emotions still have a way to go. That's what the AA meetings are for."

Adam nodded, feeling miserable.

"So, I gather you moved out of Ryan's apartment?"

"I moved out right away."

"Where are you staying now?"

"In a cheap motel on Central."

"Do you feel like drinking?"

"I'm not craving alcohol, exactly, but I need the effects, you know, change how I feel."

"I think we need to change that, and you need daily monitoring—a sponsor."

"Sponsor?"

"Someone to hold you accountable."

"You mean like you?"

"That's what I was thinking. I have a small guest house behind my house. You could stay there for a while, and we could visit in the evenings."

"That would be great. Thanks."

"Here's my address, Adam. You can move in this evening. I should be home by six. Fina stays with me, so don't be surprised when you see her. She has your best interest at heart, too. So, we are likely to double-team you and keep you on the straight and narrow."

Adam laughed. "I think I can handle it." Then he grew somber again. "I can't thank you enough, Doc. I surely don't want to waste all that work of detox."

29

Adam picked up Lucas, and they had a hamburger and pineapple pizza for dinner. Maria came home about five-thirty.

"Hey, Mom," Lucas said. "We saved you two slices of pizza. Dad got my favorite."

Maria smiled. "Well, pineapple is not my favorite, but since you requested it, I guess I can eat some. Good idea, Adam."

Lucas scampered into the living room with Nacho, and Adam lingered.

"I need to leave right away. I moved out of Ryan's apartment, and Dr. Warnock invited me to move into his guesthouse."

Maria cocked her head. "You moved out of Ryan's apartment?"

"He's not the friend I thought he was."

"How so?"

"He lied to me, and I think he might be a pervert." Adam stared at Maria. "He keeps women's underwear in his dresser."

"That sounds weird. I'm surprised."

Adam continued to make eye contact. "Me, too. He even had blue panties exactly like yours. My guess is that he keeps underwear as a souvenir. Maybe he even fondles them, you know, to remember."

Maria winced. "Wow, that is weird. Moving out sounds like a good decision, Adam. You don't need to be around people like that. You have more than enough to manage. I had no idea Ryan is like that."

"Better watch yourself if he comes around. I don't want him hitting on you. After all, we are still married."

"Since you are back on duty with Lucas and dinner, I don't see why he would come over anyway."

Adam walked to the living room and put his hand on Lucas's shoulder. "Lucas, I'll see you tomorrow morning. Love you."

"I love you, too, Dad. Bye."

Adam scratched Nacho behind the ears. "Guard the house, Nacho. These are my favorite people."

§

Dr. Warnock and Fina helped Adam move his few things into the guest house. Fina started a pot of coffee.

"Let's sit down and have some coffee," Dr. Warnock said. "I want to talk with you about a treatment idea."

They settled at the kitchen table. Fina poured coffee and joined them.

Dr. Warnock folded his hands on the table and looked at Adam. "I've been involved in research on pain for a long time, and I found something I think is worthy of scientific pursuit. We keep looking for drugs to control pain, but what if a state of mind could control it? Then, what if the challenge was to get into that state of mind?"

Adam sipped his coffee. "You mean like meditation, things like that?"

"I know meditation can help, but it seems a bit transitory. No, I mean a state of mind that involves your whole being, a state of mind that becomes a habit, a part of your personality."

"A state of mind?"

"I've been reading about people who overcome profound difficulties, and I've noticed that all of the folks who overcome pain and setbacks have something in common—they want, with their entire being, to put their pain in the background and move through their problems and come out healthy. Others have a victim mentality and even small challenges drive them to dysfunctional outcomes."

"You mean dysfunctional like addicts, drunks?"

"Right. They become victims and blame others for their plight, when, in reality, they are often the eye of their own storms. They become angry, resentful, and mean. They turn to alcohol and drugs. They abuse people they profess to love."

Sounds like Edward, Adam thought. And me? The last thing I want is to be anything like Edward. "In one of the AA meetings at the hospital, someone said you can't recover unless you absolutely want to—and want to recover for yourself and no one else. Is that what you mean?"

Warnock nodded. "I want to focus on the wanting part. 'Wanting' is a mystery, but it must come from somewhere. Maybe it comes from giving up and surrendering to God or a higher power. That's a common and profound belief. But what if there is more to it?"

"How so?"

"I think people who overcome problems have to have ambition. Not necessarily for a career or money. I mean they have a desire to achieve a particular end. For some addicts, it may require surrendering together with desire. Can you surrender and desire something at the same time? I believe you can."

Adam rubbed his aching right calf. "What does that have to do with pain?"

"Here's where the idea takes shape. Maybe if you have ambition, a strong desire, for a particular outcome, and also surrender in the face of whatever is stopping you, then your pain becomes less because your mind is filled with what you desire. That becomes your state of mind, and it tends to crowd out our feelings of pain."

"How would we know?"

"We know because we learn from our pain. Our pain teaches us that pain is in our way."

"Example?"

"Other than your recovery and family, what do you want more than anything else?"

"Hmm, I keep telling Lucas that I want to have my own construction business and be my own boss."

Fina tapped Adam's arm and smiled. "More than anything else?"

"Yes."

"And what is in your way?" she asked.

"Well, clearly, my pain and my addictions and my empty bank account."

"Do you have ambition?"

"I think so, but I don't have the means or the time."

"What if you had both?"

Adam shook his head in bewilderment. "I don't know."

Dr. Warner leaned toward Adam and took both his hands. "Adam, we would like to help you start your own business and to hire you for your first project."

Adam gazed down at their clasped hands, stunned. "Why would you do that?"

"Because we care for you, and because it's time for me to start giving back."

"What he's not saying," Fina said, "is that he's having a challenge with his own recovery and helping you will also help him. Right, John?"

"Busted. Yeah, that's right. I'm not entirely altruistic."

Adam sat back in his chair. His eyes watered. He opened his mouth to say something but choked up and couldn't speak.

"I have come to believe," Dr. Warnock said, "that if you truly have ambition, if you have a deep desire, and if you can surrender all else, then you can move ahead and leave at least some of your pain behind."

"Do you honestly think so?" Adam asked, wiping his eyes with a napkin.

"It's worked for me. I don't know why it wouldn't work for you. When I set my mind on helping folks with pain and addiction—when my ambition became what I believe is a true state of mind—my phantom limb pain dropped from a five or six to a two or three. It faded in the face of my ambition. My mind favored my purpose over my pain."

"So, how does that apply to me?"

"First, I want you to let Fina set up your construction business, and help you with licenses, tax ID numbers, a suitable truck, business cards, and other stuff. She's talented with things like that. She'll help you with a start-up budget for the cash you'll need and a repayment schedule. In the meantime, you draw up some plans for a two-bedroom cabin."

Adam raised his eyebrows. "You want me to build a cabin?"

"Yes. We own five acres a half-mile past the end of the main road in Placitas, and we would like to have a cabin as a getaway. I can take you out there this weekend, and you can recommend a building site. But that's not all."

"What else?"

"I want you to build a cabin for you and your family on the same land. The two cabins could share a well and a driveway and still be separated by the trees. Fina and I would pay for your work by giving you the second cabin. You would own it free and clear—we would pay for the whole project."

"Dr. Warnock, you know that doesn't work out. I'd be way overpaid."

"I don't care about that. I care about your sobriety, family, and ambition."

"That's unbelievable. That would change my whole life."

"That's my hope. There is no downside here. We have the means, and you have the talent and the ambition to succeed with your own company. Your sobriety will heal your family."

"When?"

"How about we start in a day or two with paperwork? You can give your employer two weeks' notice, and we'll help with money along the way. Of course, you will have to pay us back for whatever we advance and put into your new company, but the cabin will be your prize, the fruit of your ambition and efforts."

"How do you know you can trust me?"

"We don't know for sure, but you seem to believe that you need to recover for yourself, not anyone else."

Adam rubbed his hands together. "But what if Maria doesn't want me back? What if I fail?"

"If you focus on recovering for yourself, then you won't fail. We'll walk alongside you. Your seven-day detox was just a start—getting the opioids out of your system so we could start the naltrexone—not a miracle. This is your journey. You must do the spiritual and psychological work yourself. We can't do that for you."

Adam took a deep breath. "I'm scared I can't do it—can't muster the strength."

Warnock nodded. "I hear you, but even if things don't work out with Maria, you still have a son, and you can still bring Lucas to the cabin and have a life together—you'll be clean and sober and in your right mind. You'll have your own company."

Adam tossed and turned most of the night. The excitement from the coming sunrise filled his mind and crowded out his sleep.

30

Tony Giano and Lorenzo Russo sat in the back booth in a diner on Central Avenue. Tony was a large, mean man with dark eyes, dark hair, a chiseled square face, and a long, jagged scar that ran from his chin to his earlobe. He clenched his rough, scarred hands. They may have seen better days, but a right cross from Tony would still put any opponent on the floor with a broken jaw.

He had already explained to Russo that he had come to Albuquerque from San Diego, searching for Ashley, his escort service meal ticket and girlfriend. The last time she he had escaped, she'd gotten as far as Boulder and eluded him for three months. She'd split with three kilos of pure cocaine worth about thirty-five thousand per kilo, a hundred-grand altogether. When he caught up with her, he recovered two kilos she had in her car, beat the crap out of her, and threatened to maim her permanently if she ran away again. "I'll cut your face. Your escort days will be over." he had said.

Ashley had been the source of considerable income along with his drug dealing. His main travel route was from San Diego to Las Vegas and Albuquerque. Tony's trips were lucrative, often distributing twenty or thirty kilos of coke among customers in all three cities. Reginald Hammer often told Tony he was one of his most effective dealers and that he favored his discretion and income over his other dealers.

Russo was shaking his head. "No one has seen Ashley. When you first called, The Hammer put out an underground search among all the escort services, but there's no sign of her anywhere. She just disappeared. Maybe she didn't come to Albuquerque."

Tony glowered. "Oh, she came here all right. I found a ticket agent at the Greyhound bus station in Boulder who remembered selling her a ticket to Albuquerque. Remembered her black eye."

"She's street smart," Russo countered. "Maybe she got off the bus in Denver, Colorado Springs, or Santa Fe. For that matter, maybe she bought another ticket and went on to Las Cruces or back to San Diego."

"Maybe so. I'll put out some feelers."

"Did she have any friends here in Albuquerque?"

"I think she knew a few other women in escort services," Russo said.

"You got any names?"

"I saw her a couple of years ago with a woman named Lola. I think she was a drug rep. But I heard Lola died when her house burned down a month or so ago."

"Yeah, I heard about that," Tony answered. "Shame. Anyone else?"

"Customers, johns?"

"Nah."

"Did this Lola have friends here who might remember seeing Ashley?"

Russo shrugged. "She was busted for possession with the intent to sell by a couple of local detectives. The Hammer bailed her out."

"Maybe they saw Ashley somewhere with Lola."

"Maybe. You sure you want to talk with a detective?"

"No, not me, but I know a woman who can, Pamela Overstreet. She's a corrections officer at the prison in Santa Fe. She owes me a favor, and I'm sure she'd talk with a detective about a missing person. Do you have a name?"

"I have a vague memory of a cop named Romero."

"Okay, I'll check it out. I need to find Ashley. She sold a kilo of my coke, and by God, she's going to pay."

Tony reached Pamela Overstreet by phone after she'd talked with Detective Romero.

"She was out on bail when her house caught fire," the corrections officer told him. "Romero said she was involved in a blackmail scam with sex photos, but when she was killed, the whole thing went away."

"Did he mention any names?" Tony asked.

"There were a couple of doctors involved in the scam, but they were clueless except for the photos. Romero has stayed in touch with the doctors, so I would shy away from them."

"Anyone else?"

"They talked with a guy who did some work on her house. His name is Adam Young. They decided he was an innocent bystander caught in the fray and didn't know anything."

"Do you know how I can find this Adam Young guy?

"He works for Albuquerque Constructors. Maybe you could find him there, but he wasn't a mark. Probably not much help."

"Thanks. Keep your ears to the ground. I've got to find that bitch Ashley."

"Will do. And Tony, stay on the downlow. There's a push on drug dealers in Albuquerque."

"Okay, thanks. See you around."

§

At about three pm, Adam drove into the construction yard in his pickup and unloaded materials. A guy got out of a nearby parked car and walked into the yard.

"Hey, are you Adam Young?"

Adam turned around. Wow, this guy is ugly. Looks like one mean sonofabitch. "Yeah, that's me. What's up?"

"I've got a question. Did you know Lola Jenkins?"

Uh oh. What's she got herself into now? Adam wondered. "I did a couple of days' work for her some time ago," he told the guy. "I saw in the newspaper that she died in a house fire last month."

"Did you ever meet any of her friends? I'm looking for my wife, Ashley. She's gone missing, and I'm worried."

"Never did meet any of her friends," Adam said. "It's too bad, the fire and all. Seemed like a nice lady. I think she worked for a drug company."

"This is Ashley. Do you know her?" He showed Adam a photo of a lovely blonde about Lola's age.

"Sorry. I'm pretty sure I'd remember if I'd ever seen her."

The guy gave Adam a business card that read: Tony Giano, Real Estate Sales, and listed a 303-area code and a Denver address. "Please give me a call if you think of anything. I'm desperate to find my wife."

"Okay, will do. I wish you luck in your search. I hope she turns up soon."

Tony drove away. Adam took a breath, got in his truck, and headed to Warnock's guest house. Wonder what that was all about, he thought. I'd hate to meet that guy in a dark alley. He looks like he just got out of prison. Then it struck him. Ashley. That must be Lola's friend who got killed in the fire.

31

Adam answered his cell phone. "Hi, Adam, it's Lola. How have you been?"

"Lola, you shouldn't be calling me."

"I understand someone is looking for me."

"This guy came around looking for Ashley. Said she was his wife and had gone missing."

"Did you say anything about the fire?"

"Yes, said you had died."

"I need to talk with you, Adam. You're one of the only people I trust. I just need fifteen minutes to tell you what's happened. I'm not the same."

"You need to lose my phone number."

"Please, Adam, meet me in the Walmart parking lot on Eubank at about six-thirty tonight. It will be dark. I'm a redhead now, and my hair is short. I'll be in a white Ford van. Call me Lila."

"Look, Lola—Lila. I'm in a good spiritual place now. I just finished detox, and my world has changed. I don't want to be anywhere near you. I can't stray into your world. Your photos and blackmail make me sick to my stomach. So don't call again."

"But Adam, I'm not that way anymore, I swear."

"Bye, Lila."

One day later, Adam answered his cell phone. The caller ID said the caller was unknown.

"Adam, it's Lila. Please don't hang up. This is a different burner phone. Please meet me. Fifteen minutes, that's all. This is not about sex or blackmail, or MAGA nonsense. I've turned my life around, and I need your help. This is about the right thing to do."

"You sound serious, Lila."

"Serious as a heart attack. How about the Walmart parking lot at eight?"

"Okay, fifteen minutes, but that's all."

"I'll be in coveralls and a baseball cap, and my bodyguard will be with me. He has a white Ford van that says, 'Precision Restoration and Painting.'"

"You have a bodyguard?"

"Yes, because of the work I do. I'll explain when I see you."

At eight pm, Adam drove to the far side of the parking lot and pulled up next to a white van. The driver, an imposing refrigerator-sized man, got out of the van and slid into the passenger seat of Adam's truck. The man's head was shaved. His gray, deep-set eyes squinted half shut under dark eyebrows. He had a dark beard, weighed about 240 pounds, and was thin-lipped. His gray, deep-set eyes squinted half shut under dark eyebrows. He carried a .45 caliber Wilson Combat pistol on his hip. He held out his ham-fisted hand. "I'm Blaze Wildrunner. I'm from the Taos Pueblo, and I'm here searching for my niece Inez. Lila's helping."

"Did she run away?"

"She disappeared three weeks ago, while shopping in the grocery store. She's twelve years old and was dressed in jeans and a denim shirt. Two people in the store saw her struggling, being pulled into a black van by two men. The van had a California license. They abducted Inez. I'm sure they traffic in young women."

Adam looked around. There were no other cars. "How did you end up as Lila's bodyguard?"

"A friend of mine saw the black van in Albuquerque. So, I came to search for Inez."

"And Lila?"

"I heard there was a house I needed to find. The people there might know something about Inez—they might have seen her. It was called Hope House. Lila works there. She cooks, cleans, and helps take in abused women, children, and runaways. She's often out in the city, and she needed protection from the abusers, so I volunteered to be her bodyguard if she would help me find Inez—you know, use her contacts to see if we can locate her."

"So 'Precision Restoration and Painting' is a cover?"

"Yeah. Let's get back in my van, and Lila can tell you more about Hope House."

Adam and Blaze Wildrunner moved into the back seat of the van. Lila was in the passenger seat. Adam almost didn't recognize her. Her hair was a soft red, almost auburn, and cut short. She wore paint-spattered white overalls, and the shirt underneath was buttoned up to the top. Adam shook his head and smiled. "I barely recognize you, but your green eyes give you away. I take it you are no longer a sybarite taking pictures and blackmailing doctors?"

Lila squeezed her eyes shut and shook her head. "Adam, I've been soul-searching since Ashley was burned to death. I didn't like the woman I had become. I know my cocaine habit made me rationalize my behavior. I've felt deep guilt and remorse that I didn't say anything about Ashley to anyone. I just let everyone believe that her body was me. I lived, and she became nothing. I needed to find a way to honor her."

"What did you do?"

"I cried myself to sleep. I dreamed about Ashley. I saw her burning. I didn't know what to do. I got on a bus and then stayed in a cheap motel for a few nights in Colorado Springs. A woman next door saw me crying in a booth in a diner. We talked. She said she used to be a heroin addict, but she had cleaned up and made a living cleaning houses. She came back to my room with me and said she would watch over me while I kicked my cocaine habit."

Adam saw determination in her eyes. There was no lust there, no sparkle, and her mouth and face had lost the soft come-hither look that Adam remembered. As Lila, Lola had become plain, unadorned, and could easily be a choir member or a librarian. "It sounds like an angel came into your life," he said.

"Well, if she was an angel, she was one tough angel. She kept me locked in my room, fed me, bathed me, and gave me cups and cups of hot sweet tea. The cramping was unbearable, so she made sure all my screaming was into a pillow. I think we were there for three days and four nights. I was shaky and wasted. She ordered take-out, and we ate chicken and noodles while she talked about her life on the streets. "Never again," she said, and I hope 'never again' for you, too. You need to find a purpose for your life."

Sounds familiar, thought Adam. So do I. "Did you find something?"

"I went to the Colorado Springs bus station to get a ticket to El Paso or maybe Phoenix—I really didn't care where I went—just far away from here. In the bathroom at the bus station, I met a young girl, a runaway named Amy. She was about thirteen years old, abused by her mother's boyfriend. Turned out she was also from Albuquerque. I took her under my wing and pretended we were mother and daughter. I cut my hair, dyed it, threw away all my makeup. She wanted to go home again, so I promised I would bring her. I planned to just keep going once we were in Albuquerque. But then, from a woman on the street, we learned about Hope House—a battered women's shelter. They took Amy in and took care of her. In fact, they took care of twenty people regularly. Next thing I knew, I was comforting and counseling all these girls."

"That's your work now?"

"Cook, clean, and bring women and children into the community. I met Blaze Wildrunner when he inquired at Hope House about his niece. He helps me with transportation and watches over me. We ask everyone we meet about Inez and traffickers. One woman staying at Hope House recognized Inez's picture. She's likely held as a prisoner with other young girls until they're sold into the black market. We keep searching for a place where they keep the girls they abduct."

Blaze Wildrunner grimaced and took a breath. "I'm sure she's here in Albuquerque. I'm going to find her and the men who took her. I'm going to kill them." He patted the .45 on his hip. "They are some kind of evil," he said, "and they need to die."

Adam looked back over the mattress seat, drop cloths, and other painting supplies. He surmised the drop cloths were used to cover the people they were moving. "Where do you take the women and children?"

"I developed a small network of Community Angels," Lila

answered." Homes that can take in a couple of people for two weeks or so, and then we move them to another house. Along the way, people help the girls, and occasionally boys, get on their feet with clothes, money, disguises, and whatever else they need. We have Angel-homes in Santa Fe, Angel Fire, and Taos. Blaze Wildrunner has arranged for an Angel home on the Taos Pueblo."

"Wow, it sounds like an underground railroad for abused women and children. Where do they end up?"

"It all depends on where they would be safe and hard to find, usually out of state and in a busy urban environment like Denver or Salt Lake or Los Angeles."

"Well, Lila, I must admit. You are not the Lola I used to know. But why me? What can I do? I don't have much money, but you already know that."

"I was hoping that you and Maria could become a Community Angel, and we could use your home as a short-term refuge."

"Don't worry about safety," Blaze Wildrunner added. "I check on all the Community Angel houses nearly every day, either me or the police we've recruited."

"Police are involved?"

"We have a few police allies who understand trafficking and hate it. They are eager to help by patrolling Community Angel locations."

Lila put her hand to her mouth, then her chin. "I'm untraceable, Adam. Remember, I was killed. There's a death certificate on file for Lola Jenkins. Blaze helped me change my identity. He has a friend who specializes in identity work. My name is Lila Penrose now, and I'm from Taos. I have a New Mexico driver's license, a Visa, a Mastercard, and a US Passport. I don't know how he did it, but the passport is stamped by British Customs with an entry date that is the day before the fire. So, Lila Penrose was in England when Lola Jenkins was killed in the fire. I even have a Good Housekeeping and a Quilting Magazine subscription that comes to my Taos address, and both automatically renew on my Visa account."

Adam moved toward the door. "I've got to think about this. I'm just recently out of detox myself. I'm not with my wife right now, but I'm working on fixing our separation. A lot is going on. Call me in a week or so."

Lila offered a gentle smile. "Will do, Adam. Thanks. I pray to God that my behavior with you wasn't the reason you and Maria are separated."

"No, it wasn't you. Maria doesn't know about the old Lola and the time we spent together. I hope she never will."

Adam and Blaze Wildrunner got out of the painters' van and returned to Adam's truck. Blaze surveilled the area. "No cars anywhere. Looks safe."

Adam turned his truck toward his new sleeping quarters, the guest house at Dr. Warnock's place. When he arrived, his mind was trying to wrap itself around Lola's newfound dedication and her ordinary appearance. Would Maria be willing to help a woman and child in need for a few days? Maybe. But first, I need to find a way to move back home. I pray she'll take me.

Fina came out of the guest house with a vacuum in tow. "Hey, Adam, I vacuumed and left fresh towels. We're happy you are a guest."

"Thanks, Fina. But you shouldn't have to do that. You know, I am a trained husband," he said with a laugh. "I can do my own cleaning from now on. I hope it won't be for too long. Maria and I were together for one night, and I hope she'll soon make it every night. She's pleased with my detox progress. She knows I'm chasing the demons away."

"That's good to hear. I'll keep you in my prayers."

Adam carried in his backpack, work boots, and his toiletries kit. He looked over the place, made himself some hot tea, and arranged a couple of shirts from his backpack on hangers in the closet. Wow, things are changing fast, he thought. He never would have believed he would view Lola as a role model—but here she was, off the coke, cooking and cleaning and helping others, a walking-talking example of Dr. Warnock's ambitious life purpose as a healing state of mind. And what about Dr. Warnock and his care and guidance and money? And Fina, his nurse from long ago and now part of his life? What about Blaze Wildrunner and Inez—a real tragedy. And Hope House? Battered women? Losing and gaining a father? The loss of his friend Ryan? Mourning Ava?

Adam's mind felt both exhilarated and exhausted—running on a new set of tracks. It took all the energy he had just to stay focused on his recovery protocol and restoring his family, much less planning a new business.

Someone must have thrown a switch. I hear the wheels on the tracks, but I don't know where we're going.

32

Adam was up and drinking coffee when Fina knocked at the guest-house door. "Adam, come on in the house. We have breakfast ready, and we can talk about our plans."

As they walked to the house, Adam smelled bacon frying and the hint of pecans. They sat around the kitchen table to a breakfast of scrambled eggs, pecan waffles, bacon, orange juice, and coffee.

"You look good, Adam. Seems like the protocol is working," said Dr. Warnock.

"The cravings for alcohol are gone. That makes the biggest difference of all. I can think again without the constant yearning."

"The naltrexone is effective against cravings, but you still have to be motivated to quit."

"Well, I'm motivated, that's for sure."

Fina cleared the table and laid out paperwork. "We figured that a single-owner LLC would be the best business model. That way, your family is protected against any lawsuits."

"You know I'm licensed as a residential contractor, right?"

"Yes. We need to complete this form to make you the qualifying contractor for the new company. Do you have a name in mind?"

"How about 'Young and Sons Contracting'?

Dr. Warnock smiled. "How about a name with a little more punch like 'Quality Homebuilding'?

"Or maybe 'Quality Homes, LLC,'" Fina said.

Adam beamed. "I like that one. The full name would be 'Quality Homes, LLC, Adam Young Qualifying Party.'"

"That's it," Dr. Warnock said. "Quality Homes is simple, direct, and has a ring to it. So, Adam, shall we go with that?"

"Sure. I think Maria and Lucas would like that name, too."

Fina checked the Corporation Commission website and determined that 'Quality Homes' was an available name, then. completed the paperwork and prepared it for mailing. "As soon as we hear back, we can get an IRS tax number and get the application finished for the state CRS tax identification number. I know the bank will need those numbers to open your business checking account."

Dr. Warnock stood up. "Okay, guys, let's go see the land. I'm eager to get started. Adam, did you let your boss know you won't be in today?"

"Yes, I called early and left a message. When do you think I should give notice?"

"When everything's approved," Fina said. "Let's make sure."

They rode in Adam's truck to an area and went about one mile past the end of the pavement in Placitas. He slowed to five miles per hour as he avoided ruts and rocks. "Pull off over here," Dr. Warnock said. "You can park between those cedar trees. This is probably where the driveway will be."

Together they made their way about sixty yards up a slight incline to a small meadow covered with early fall wildflowers—purple asters, black-eyed susans, shasta daisies, and even a few blue cornflowers near the trees. The mountain air smelled crisp and clean, and Adam saw fluffy, white clouds drift by in the gentle breeze.

"Whoa, this is beautiful," Adam said.

"Come this way," Dr. Warnock led them about forty yards through the pinon and cedar trees to another open, flat area. "Here's another good site, don't you think?"

Adam grinned and clapped his hands. "This is perfect—Fina, pinch me. This is unbelievable." He inhaled a deep breath of crisp October mountain air. The sun streamed through the trees making dancing shadows and patches of bright light. A ground squirrel squeaked and scurried out of the way.

Fina touched his hand gently and met his eyes. Her face seemed soft and ethereal, as though she was inviting Adam into a new reality, a world without addictions where dreams come true. He felt flutters behind his heart and then his heartbeat quickened. His face flushed. He gazed up through the trees and felt taller, vigorous. Thank you, he breathed silently.

"We knew you would like it," Fina said.

"What's not to like? This is amazing. But honestly, why me?

"You're worth it, Adam. You always have been. You just haven't known it."

"Couldn't agree more." Dr. Warnock put his hands on his hips and looked around. It was quiet except for the cry of a couple of magpies. "What do you need to get started?"

Adam sat on a log and scratched his head. "This is so much more than I imagined, fantastic. Well, we'll need plans and permits, a driveway, a temporary electric meter, and a well for starters. I've got plans for a two-bedroom dream cabin. I drew them up a year ago in a fit of fantasy. I was imagining I could quit my job and escape to the mountains. I can show you this afternoon."

"Okay, what else?"

"You know, there's a lot of dirt work here. We have to build a driveway, install a culvert, create drainage ditches, move rocks, dig trenches for water lines, and bury electric lines, not to mention leveling the sites and digging footings. Then, of course, there'll be gravel to spread on the driveway as well. I think it's a good idea to buy a company backhoe. I'm a good operator, and we can find a good, used Case for twenty thousand. I can use it on future projects, too."

Dr. Warnock nodded. "I agree."

"You can look for a backhoe while you wait for the plans to be approve," said Fina.

"The project is outside any municipality," Adam said, "so all we need is the approval from the Construction Industries Division."

"We should get the permit in the name of the new company," Fina said. "So, let's wait for the approval of Quality Homes, LLC."

"Wait—waiting. I don't like waiting. Is it okay with you guys for me to bring Maria and Lucas out here to see the project?"

Dr. Warnock slapped Adam on the back. "Of course. This is the start of your new, sober life. Let's hope Maria sees it that way too. This place is magic."

"I'm sure she still loves you, Adam," Fina said. "She's still deeply in mourning, is confused about your addictions, and she isn't ready to trust you yet. It will take a while. But the longer you are sober and have a purpose, the sooner she'll take you back. Watching your competence will go a long way. In fact, I believe men are the most attractive when they have a purpose and are competent in their work."

"Thanks for that. Let's go back to your house and look at the plans I've drawn. We can make changes if you'd like, and I can finish them up while we wait for the Corporation Commission. At least I'll be working instead of waiting."

33

Tony pounded on the door. He found Hope House by intimidating a woman from the Hammer's escort service. Tony had been a money maker with the cocaine distribution, and the Hammer was integrating him into his growing trafficking operations. He used young women from the escort service to recruit runaway girls living on the street. The escorts thought they were recruiting young prostitutes, but they didn't know what happened to the girls they brought in. The Hammer and Russo kept a mobile home far out northwest of Albuquerque, past existing homes and down in a draw, barely visible from the rutted and unimproved road. They kept their girls locked in bedrooms until they had gathered a vanload. The Mexican buyer wanted to buy eight at once to minimize border crossings.

Tony pounded again. An older woman dressed in a housecoat opened the door slowly, and Tony grabbed the door and pushed himself into the foyer, nearly knocking the door off its hinges.

"I'm looking for Ashley," he said. "Do you have someone here by that name?"

"Sorry," the woman said. "I don't know anyone by that name."

Tony pushed by her and tromped down the hallway. He slammed open doors and shouted for Ashley as he searched the house.

He stormed up the stairs and continued to yell for Ashley until he'd looked in all the rooms, where women and children cowered in the corners. After he searched all the rooms, he went to the kitchen. A red-haired woman in a stained apron was stirring a large pot of onion soup.

"I need to find Ashley. Have you seen her?"

The woman raised her wooden spoon. "I don't know anyone by that name."

Tony gazed at her for a moment, slammed his hand on the counter, and headed out the kitchen door. He stopped and handed the older woman a burner cell phone. "If a woman named Ashley shows up here, push five. I'm on speed dial. If I find out she's here, and you didn't call, I'll burn this place to the ground. Do you understand?"

"Yes, sir. I understand. There's no need for violence."

"I'm the judge of that. Call if you see her. Don't screw around with me."

As he started out the door, two policemen confronted him. "You can't come in here, threaten people, and tear things up. You're under arrest."

Tony looked them up and down and then saw the second patrol car backing them up.

"Turn around," the officer said as the other officer took the gun out of Tony's waistband and slapped handcuffs on him. They hauled him off to the station and booked him for firearm possession, breaking and entering, and destruction of personal property.

The following day, Russo bailed him out.

"Thanks," Tony said as they drove away from jail.

"The Hammer put up your bail. Except for your obsession with this Ashley person, he thinks you're a good hand. He wants you more involved."

"Hey, she owes me twenty grand for a kilo of uncut cocaine."

"Yeah, she outfoxed you, but you need to let that go and look to the future. You can make up that money easily."

"How so?"

"Just wait. The Hammer will fill you in."

They stopped at a diner on Central and sat in a back booth. The Hammer got up from his stool at the counter, picked up his coffee cup, and joined them.

"Tony, you're not going to find this woman Ashley. She's long gone. Let it go."

"She tricked me. She got away with my coke."

"Let it go. You're going to make a mistake and end up doing time in the big house in Santa Fe. That's stupid. Get smart, Tony. Don't let your emotions run you."

"Do you have something in mind?"

"I need someone to help manage my other business. You might be the right guy."

"What does it involve?"

"High profit, low risk, benefits."

"What would I do?"

The Hammer folded his hands and grinned. "We help young runaway girls find a new home and good employment."

"Where do they work?"

"In Mexico, and I charge a fee of ten thousand each when I deliver them. We send eight at once or eighty thousand for a vanload. If you make a successful delivery, you get twenty thousand. Easy money, don't you think?"

Tony rubbed his hands together. "I could get all over that. And benefits?"

"Yeah, you choose your own. The girls all need training on how to make a man happy. You can pick out a couple of them and show them how."

Tony tossed his head back and laughed. "Now, those are benefits I could get used to."

"No bruises, Tony. They need to look good when you deliver them."

The Hammer tossed Russo a ring of car keys. "Take the van out front and show Tony our safe house. Then, stop at McDonald's and get a dozen Happy Meals. The girls are probably hungry."

Russo and Tony climbed in the black van and headed west.

§

Having been tipped off by one of the arresting officers, Blaze Wildrunner had been tracking Tony Giano since Lorenzo Russo had bailed him out of jail. Now he followed in the white 'Precision Restoration and Painting' van. He hung back more than two blocks, secure he wouldn't be noticed, since he'd planted a GPS tracker under the fender on the black van. They stopped at McDonald's, then drove for some time, crossing the Rio Grande River on the Montano bridge, and heading north to Rio Rancho. They continued west on Northern past Unser and a smattering of houses until the road became unmaintained. Blaze pretended to pull into a driveway and followed the progress of the black van on the GPS. He resumed his tail as they turned off on a rutted trail and drove down into an expansive draw to a rusted mobile home. Blaze parked behind some cedar trees and watched with his binoculars.

§

Tony carried the Happy Meals, and Russo unlocked the door. They walked down the hall to a locked bedroom and opened that door. Inside, five girls were sitting on mattresses, and each one wore handcuffs that were chained to the wall. The chains were long enough to allow movement to two buckets that served as toilets and a twenty-gallon water container. The room smelled like overfull portable public toilets, and the thick air burned their eyes. The girls were filthy and gaunt.

Russo took the food from Tony and tossed hamburgers and fries onto the mattresses. "There you go. Time for your feast." The girls snatched up the food and began wolfing it down.

He turned to Tony. "As soon as we have three more, it will be time for you to clean them up, dress them in fresh clothes, load them in the van, and meet the buyer in Socorro."

"That's it? Drive them to Socorro?"

"Yeah, and after you get them cleaned up—you know, showered, hair washed—then you can teach a couple of them how to please a man. That is unless you want to do that now."

Tony shook his head. "Not now. This place stinks too bad."

"I like to wait, too," Russo said. "Clean, private, young. That's what I like."

Blaze Wildrunner, concealed behind the cedar trees, watched the two men drive away. Then he drove to the mobile home, busted the lock with a sledgehammer, and walked down the hall until he heard crying. He smashed the lock and went in. Inez was huddled in a corner beside two other girls.

She gave a terrified squeak: then her eyes went wide. "Blaze, is that really you?"

She ran to him and buried her face in his chest. She sobbed and shook as tears flowed from Blaze's eyes. "The Great Spirit has been good to us today, Inez. But we've got to hurry." He took some photos on his cellphone in case they needed evidence later. "Now you girls stand up so I can cut your chains and get you out of here." He used a bolt cutter to cut the locks on the chains and the handcuffs. He helped the five girls climb into the back of his van and covered them with rumpled drop cloths. "If I get stopped, cover your heads, and stay perfectly still. I'm going to take you to the emergency room at Lovelace Hospital and get everyone checked out."

He called Lila from the road, and she arranged space at Hope House for them to stay until they could be interviewed by the police and delivered to their overjoyed parents. They had all been reported missing. After the ER visit, a shower, and clean scrubs from a medical assistant, Blaze Wildrunner drove Inez to the Taos Pueblo himself and made sure she was safely tucked away in the arms of her extended family. She was hungry and exhausted but had not been violated.

§

Carter Wilson and Antonio Romero fielded the call, drove to Hope House, and interviewed the girls in the morning. They identified Tony Giano and Lorenzo Russo from mug shots. Back from the Taos Pueblo, Blaze Wildrunner pulled the detectives aside. "Inez said she heard the men talking. They said they would be back tomorrow with three more girls, and they would bring their boss to check things out before the delivery to Socorro."

"Did they say when?" Carter asked.

"Inez said they were coming later in the day," Blaze Wildrunner said, "after five pm."

"Can you tell us the exact location?" Antonio Romero asked.

"Yes, I put a GPS tracker on their van." He handed Antonio a slip of paper. "These are the coordinates. The trailer is faded green and white. It's down in in draw, but you can see it from a hundred yards out."

Carter Wilson called in and arranged for a SWAT team to hide out nearby at four pm and await the gang's arrival. "They'll have three girls with them, so be careful."

§

The next day, at noon, well before the SWAT team would arrive, Blaze Wildrunner returned to the location. He hid in some cedar trees about two-hundred yards from the trailer. He set up behind thick branches with his .308 Winchester rifle equipped with a Lelupold VX-3i scope, covered himself with weeds, and waited.

About one hour later, a black van bounced over the dirt driveway and parked by the mobile home. Tony, Russo, and The Hammer hurried to the trailer with three weeping girls, dragging them by their chains.

"Hey," Tony said, "someone broke the lock." He rushed in. Slammed open doors. "The other girls are gone," he yelled. "Their locks have been cut. Shit, there goes fifty grand."

"Put the girls back in the van," The Hammer sad. "Let's get out of here now."

Tony pushed the girls into the back of the van and slammed the door.

Blaze Wildrunner fired his rifle rapidly. Two-hundred yards is an easy target for a .308 rifle and scope. He shot Tony in the left thigh, and he dropped, holding his leg and moaning, his femur smashed into shards. The second shot slammed into Russo's left knee and shattered it. The force spun him around as he collapsed onto the dirt, his knee folded under him. The Hammer sought cover behind the van, but he was too slow. The third shot hit him in the right hip, demolishing his hip joint and pelvis. He fell like a stone, screaming in pain. Blaze fired a fourth and fifth shot into the front tires on the van. Then he picked up his brass and raked over the dirt and tire tracks with a branch. He waved with a hand signal, and Lila drove up in a Hope House van and Blaze helped the girls out of the black van and hustled them into Lila's van. He drove to Hope House and Lila followed. The wounded men lay sprawled in the dirt, writhing, blood everywhere. They couldn't even crawl.

The SWAT van and a patrol car arrived at about four, checked with binoculars, and approached the trailer. "Hey, check this out. Looks like someone got here before us," the SWAT team leader said. "These guys are all laid out nice and neat." They cuffed Tony, Russo, and The Hammer, field dressed their wounds, and called the Fire Department. The ambulance made its way to the trailer, and the EMT's loaded the complaining men into the back. "Let's get these vermin to the hospital," the driver said.

Carter Wilson interviewed Blaze Wildrunner later that evening. The three girls had been bathed, fed, and were asleep. Lila had called their parents. Blaze told Carter he had been at Hope House all day. The staff confirmed it.

"Someone who's good with rifle shot all three traffickers earlier today," Carter said. "Probably a good Samaritan or one of the dads. Thank you, Lila, for picking up the girls. How did you know to go there?"

"One of the girls called nine-one-one from a cell phone she found on the front seat of the van. She said her kidnappers had been shot and the girls needed help. We located them from the GPS in the cell phone."

Carter nodded and put his notepad in his shirt pocket. "We'll probably never know what happened. We checked and the trailer is registered to a deceased man from Farmington. The black van is registered to a woman in New Orleans—probably stolen. But, with all the testimony from the girls and crime scene photographs, this trafficking gang will be put away for a long time."

34

Adam felt so excited that he almost forgot to vote. Proud of being a never-Trumper, he strained to keep red hats out of his mind. The previous night, he and Dr. Warnock had reviewed Adam's protocol. The naltrexone removed his cravings for alcohol, and the CBD dampened his anxiety and obsession to drink. He was down to one ten milligram OxyContin in the morning, and the pain from his burn scars was moderated by using lidocaine four times a day. The single THC gummy at night helped him get enough sleep. He felt he was benefitting from the AA meetings and counseling sessions with Dr. Warnock—both as his physician and his sponsor. His mind seemed overfull with joyful anticipation about his newfound freedom from addiction and the plans for Quality Homes, LLC. He could hardly wait to tell Lucas and Maria.

As Adam waited in the pickup line at school, he watched the vapor trail of a passenger jet that faded, the deep blue sky closing in behind. He had warm, strange feelings behind his heart. He was unnerved—perhaps even frightened—by the onrush of unexpected happiness. He took a deep breath, and two sunlit, finished cabins filled his imagination. Dreams powered him into tomorrow.

"Hey, Lucas, hop in. I've got some exciting news."

"Are you coming home?"

"Well, I don't know about that, but we're going to make a special dinner for your mom, and then we'll all talk about it."

"Come on, Dad, can't you tell me now?"

"Let's go to the grocery store. We'll get you a Klondike Bar to tide you over."

They carried in groceries, and Adam fired up the charcoal grill. Adam helped him wash the chicken breasts, and they wrapped little new potatoes mixed with chopped scallions in aluminum foil. Lucas put the chicken breasts on the grill and painted them with bar-be-que sauce. Adam set the foil package on the back of the grill to cook slowly, and they stood grinning at each other. Adam dropped to his knees and hugged Lucas, swaying back and forth. "I love you, son."

"Love you, too, Dad. Chicken breasts are Mom's favorite. She's going to be surprised."

"Let's hope so. I can hardly wait to tell you guys the news."

Maria arrived home, kissed Lucas, smiled at Adam, and went into her bedroom to shower and change. When she came out, Adam served up plates, and, surprisingly, Maria offered grace. "Thank you, Lord, for this food and for our family."

There it was again, behind his heart. A warm, strange feeling. Was he afraid? Could he trust the surge of happiness or was it fleeting? Perhaps it was gratitude that he felt?

"Okay, Dad, Mom is here, so tell us the news."

Adam smiled. "I'm quitting my job, I'm starting our own business called Quality Homes, and I have two cabins to build in the woods past Placitas. One of them will be ours."

Maria raised one eyebrow. "Have you been drinking?"

"No, I'm on a protocol from my doctor. Haven't been drinking, and I've cut way back on my pain meds."

"Where's the money coming from?"

"It's hard to believe, but Dr. Warnock and his partner Fina are loaning me all the start-up money, and they hired me to build the cabins. Guess what? One of the cabins will be ours. I'll build two, and they'll pay me by giving us one."

"Come on, Adam, what have you been smoking? Are you on some fantasy trip?"

"I promise, Maria, I am not impaired, and these people are eager to help me. Fina, remember, was my nurse twenty-some years ago in the burn unit, and Dr. Warnock is guiding my progress. He says he wants to give back from his own recovery journey and pay it forward. I've come to believe there is s spiritual force out there putting all these pieces together. Amazing."

Maria could only sit with her mouth open, shaking her head. "This is unbelievable, Adam."

"Hey, Dad. Since you're starting your own business, can we get bicycles?"

"You bet. We can go shopping next week."

"When will you quit Albuquerque Constructors? Does Ryan know?"

"My last check is at the end of next week. Don't worry about the money. As soon as we get tax ID numbers, Fina will open a business account with twenty thousand start-up money. I can pay myself from that. And Ryan? I'll tell him Monday when I put in my resignation letter. You can write Ryan off—he's no longer a friend. Like I said, he's a liar, and I can't trust him. I'm sad about it."

"Do Rocky and Jim Olander know? They've been good to you," Maria said.

"I talked with Rocky. He and Jim volunteered to write letters of recommendation for me to use with customers. I was really surprised. He said they won't tell Ryan until my letter is official. I can't believe their reaction. They wished me well, and said, if I wanted it, they would sell me their used Case backhoe for fifteen-thousand, five grand under market value."

"That will leave a clean slate. It must feel great to be encouraged by them. I'm sorry about Ryan, though. He was a good friend."

Lucas looked distressed. "Ryan helped Mom while you were in the hospital. We played Go Fish."

"I know, son," Adam said. "But some grownup things happened, so we can't be friends now."

Lucas appeared confused, but Maria patted him and changed the subject. "So, what about these cabins?"

Adam spooned a few more potatoes onto Maria's plate, along with half of another chicken breast. "Since tomorrow is Saturday, let's take a ride to the job site, and I can show you the project."

"Pardon me for being skeptical, Adam, but this is all new, like an unbelievable fantasy. Tell me about the protocol from Dr. Warnock. Do you think it will work? I'm starting to feel a little hope."

"Sure, and Lucas is old enough to hear." He explained the regimen, knowing Maria, as a nurse, would understand the dosages.

Maria pursed her lips. "Wow, that's elaborate. Do you think it's going to work?"

"Right now, I feel like it's working, and guess what? I'm not an addict."

"Well, if this works, Adam Young will be a new man with a new heart."

"Dr. Warnock added something else. He believes there is a psychological component that haunts addicts and makes them crazy. As people drink more or take more drugs, they lose any sense of ambition or purpose. They can't envision tomorrow—only the next drink or fix. Dr. Warnock thinks ambition is the magic potion that helps addicts stay clean. He says that ambition—the desire to be something, to have a purpose—is a power that moves us through recovery. He might be right. My mind is so full of hope for the future that I don't even think of drinking. My legs don't hurt as much."

"So, he thought of your dream of us owning a building company as a force? Your dream is a force?"

"Yes, but until now, we haven't had the means. That's where he's giving back—loaning money for start-up costs and giving me a job building cabins. Please, let's go tomorrow, and I can show you."

"Dad, check this out," Lucas said. He pointed to a bicycle ad in a Highlights magazine.

"Looks like a good one. Help me with the dishes, and then I'll beat you at Chutes and Ladders."

"Okay, but you won't beat me."

"You guys are doing the dishes? My Lord, gentlemen, what is happening to the men in this family?" Maria tossed a leftover chicken bite to Nacho, and he caught it in the air.

After the dishes were put away and Lucas had won at Chutes and Ladders, he brushed his teeth, put on his Star Wars pajamas, and got into bed. Maria and Adam tucked him in.

"Are you moving back home?" Lucas asked.

Maria leaned down and kissed Lucas on both cheeks. "We'll talk about that later. Good night, little man. I love you."

"Love you too, Mom. Love you, Dad."

Adam stood up, heading for the kitchen. Maria followed. He turned and held out both hands, and Maria took them in hers. A single tear appeared on Adam's cheek. Maria nuzzled into his neck and shoulder. "Why don't you stay the night," Maria said. "Then we can leave from here to go see the building site."

"Is that the reason, because it's convenient?"

"Yes, it is convenient. But I had something else in mind."

Their lovemaking was passionate and clingy, as though the feelings of warmth and the hint of happiness might simply fly away like a passing cloud. In the midst of things, Adam whispered. "Are you taking your birth control pills?"

"Not since Ava died. Please, just hush and carry on."

They laid on their backs holding hands, regaining their breath, moonlight from the window shimmering on Maria's breasts. "You're gorgeous, Maria. I love you so."

"Sometimes, I love you, too."

"Sometimes?"

"Yes, like right now."

Maria laughed softly. "And sometimes you are just too much trouble for words. Do you trust Dr. Warnock?"

"Yes. I'm filled with hope because of him—and Fina. She cares, too. I know this is all up to me—that I have to do the work. But they are like guardian angels. I can't wait for you to meet them. You'll see."

35

Adam slowed to five mph as he neared the building site. He pulled over. "Okay, we need to walk from here. This is where the driveway will begin."

Maria and Lucas followed closely behind as they threaded their way through the trees and came to an open clearing.

"The first cabin will be right about here. We'll drill a well over there to share, and the driveway will make a loop from the second cabin—the one that will be ours."

They walked about thirty yards through the trees and came upon another small clearing. "Here it is. Our little piece of heaven."

Maria stopped in a patch of sunlight. She took a deep breath and looked around, a little vague, as though she was wondering if the trees and wildflowers were about to tell her something.

"It's a beautiful spot, Adam."

"Yeah, it's great. Beautiful, isolated and just waiting for us to arrive."

"Hey, Dad, check this out," Lucas called. He was sitting on a rock under an overhanging ledge overhang that created a small cave. It was about four feet deep into the side of a pile of huge boulders.

"Wow," Adam said. He and Maria bent down, and entered the cave, where they sat down on the rock on either side of Lucas. He was grinning from ear to ear.

"This will be my fort," he said. "Maybe we can build a fire and sleep here sometimes."

Adam studied the back of the cave. Sunlight peeked through a slight break in the overhang. "Look, Lucas. If we build a fire back here, it will be safe from spreading and the smoke will go out that break above us."

Lucas clapped his hands and hopped to his feet. "Should I gather some firewood now?"

"Let's wait until we get this all situated. Then we can bring sleeping bags and curl up together."

"That would be great."

"That sounds fun," Maria said, "but I think I'll leave that to you and your father."

"Okay, Mom. Dad and I can sleep in the cave and guard the cabin."

"I love your imagination," Adam said, "but let's not get too far ahead of ourselves. I don't even have the permits yet."

A couple of stellar jays set up a racket from a nearby tree, as though they sensed that this idyllic spot in the woods was about to change. Maria smiled but crossed her arms. "When can you start?" she asked warily.

"It will take a couple of weeks for the permit, but way out here, I think I can start on the driveway, culvert, and water well right away. No one will even know. We're shopping for a used backhoe now."

Maria wrinkled her nose. "Really? You're going to buy a backhoe?"

"Dr. Warnock and Fina said they would loan me the money, and it's a piece of equipment I'll use on every project. It'll pay for itself compared to the cost of subcontracting the work."

"You're really going to do this, aren't you?"

"I'm committed. Unbelievable, right?"

Maria clasped her hands on top of her head. "I'm having a hard time absorbing all this. You come home bright and sober from detox. You share old times in our bedroom. You make breakfast and wash the dishes. You quit your job. You start our own business. You have a benefactor who provides money. It seems like something powerful is watching over us, Adam. I want to believe you're getting a second chance—we're getting a second chance."

"Like Dr. Warnock says, when you quit drinking and surrender to a power greater than yourself, good things begin to happen. I couldn't do any of this by myself. It takes a push from benevolent forces I don't understand. But, hey, let's go with it. Right now, I'm filled with purpose and hope for the future. My dream is coming true, and if you are with me on this, I don't see how we can fail. God is good, the stars are aligned, and we're in love."

Maria walked over to Adam and took both of her hands in his. She gazed warmly into his eyes. "It will take me a while to forgive you, Adam, and to fully trust you again. But I'm with you in your dream."

36

As Adam parked by their home, his cell phone rang.

"Hey, Adam. Russell Kramer here." His voice sounded as if he was smiling through the phone. "Your father, remember?"

Adam gestured to Maria and Lucas to go on in the house. "It's Russell. This will take a few minutes."

"Of course, I remember. What's happening? Are you in Albuquerque?"

"Yes, can you meet me for coffee? I have some news from my home front."

"Okay, I can meet you at Starbucks."

The day had turned warm, and they sat outside at a sunlit table.

"So did you talk with your wife and daughters?" Adam asked.

"Yes, I told them the whole story. Said I found you in Albuquerque. My wife was angry and shaken, but Maggie and Melody were intrigued. They said they want to meet their half-brother. I thought about bringing them here for Christmas—you know, to visit for a few days."

"And your wife?"

"My guess is she won't want to be involved. Sorry Adam. She's hurt and angry. That's beyond my control."

"I need to check with Maria. I think she'll be supportive. She believes in the strength and support that comes from and extended family, especially since she didn't have one."

"This is weird, Russell, but new things are happening every day around here—almost too fast to understand."

"How so?"

Adam told Russell about his medical protocol, his new business, and the contract to build two cabins in Placitas. "The best part is that Maria is excited about her new man and her new future. I have some hope that we'll be back together soon."

"Adam, that's amazing. I'm proud of you. I feel privileged that I can watch the miracle of your recovery and a new future for your family. What a blessing."

"I'll talk with her later tonight. In fact, why don't you come by for coffee and dessert. I told Lucas I was going to make chocolate sundaes. Say about seven?"

"I'll be there. Should I bring anything?'

"No, I've got it covered."

On the dot of seven, a smiling Russell handed Maria a bouquet of roses when she answered the door. "These are for you." Then he took a small light out of his pocket and handed it to Lucas. "Your dad told me you would be getting a bicycle. Here's a flashing light for the back. It goes under the seat, and you can turn it on when it gets dark. That way, people can see you better."

Maria put the roses in a vase and Lucas flipped on the light. "Wow, it's bright. I'll be you can see this a block away. Thank you."

"You're welcome. I am thrilled to have a grandson. You can call me Grandpa if you want."

"Okay. Thanks, Grandpa."

"These roses are beautiful," Maria said. "Thank you. Adam has shared most everything about you, so I guess I'm your daughter-in-law... technically your half daughter-in-law. How about I just call you Russell and you call me Maria."

"Sounds fine with me."

They sat at the kitchen table and Adam made sundaes using chocolate chip ice cream with chocolate fudge topping.

"Adam said you've shared the facts with your wife and daughters," Maria said. "I gather it didn't go over too well."

"My daughters, Maggie, and Melody, seem intrigued, but my wife—even after thirty-some years, it's a surprise, and she sees it as a violation of our wedding vows."

"Given some time, she may warm up to the idea," Maria said.

"Lucas can be charming. She may not be able to resist him. There are no other grandchildren, right?"

"Yes, Lucas is the only one. Our daughters have never married. Maria, I'm deeply sorry for your loss of Ava. A sudden infant death is so devastating." He looked at Adam, then fixed his gaze on Maria. She had raised her ring to her lips. "Is there anything at all I can do to relieve your suffering?"

Maria shook her head and idly stirred her sundae into a melted mush.

Adam stood up. "Anyone want more ice cream?"

"Maria," Russell said, breaking the tension. "Can I please ask you about an idea? I was thinking about bringing Maggie and Melody to Albuquerque for Christmas. They are eager to meet you and we could have a Christmas dinner somewhere nice. My treat. What do you think?"

Adam turned toward Maria and raised his eyebrows. "Sound okay with you? It would be fine with me. Lucas can meet his aunts and I can meet my sisters. What do you think?"

"I think it's the right thing to do," Maria said. "God seems to be moving us into a new place, and we should follow the spiritual leading."

Adam put his hands on his hips. "Okay, we are agreed, but I've got to insist on one thing—it will be my treat, not yours Russell."

Russell gave Maria a gratified smile. "All right, then, I'll get the plane tickets and make reservations at the Hilton in the name of Adam Young. In the meantime, I'll be around for a few days. Adam, can I help you with paperwork or anything?"

"Sure. I'll be doing some preliminary survey work at the cabin site. You can hold the stick for me. I need to set some grade stakes and layout the driveway. Once we get the sites leveled, I'll layout the foundations."

"Where can I meet you?"

Adam looked at Maria with a slight grin. "Well, I guess you could come by in the morning and leave your car here. We can drive together."

Maria stood up, took her dish to the sink, and turned back to Russell. "That sounds fine. I'm sure Adam will have coffee ready."

Russell stood up. "Thanks for the ice cream. I'm glad we had this chance to visit." He headed toward the door.

"And thank you for the roses," Maria said, "and the bicycle light for Lucas."

Later, Maria sat on the edge of the bed next to Adam. "There is so much going on that I feel dazed, unmoored. I guess we're going to be okay, right?"

"There's something else," Adam said.

"Something else?"

"Yes, I want you to meet Dr. Warnock and Fina."

"Okay, I want that too. You can invite them for coffee. If we meet in the hospital cafeteria, I can be there over my lunch hour, and no one has to drive anywhere."

"Great. Sometimes I forget how practical you can be."

"Let me know when. Like it or not, I guess I'm supposed to be part of your support group."

"Okay, and there's something else."

"Adam, I don't know if I can handle anything else, unless it's more chocolate or your sweet lips."

"I'll spread more chocolate on my lips in a minute," he said with a wink. "But the one more thing is a good thing, and just something to think about. There's this woman, Lila, who is a friend of Fina's, and she helps operate Hope House, a safe house for runaway girls and abused women. She has asked Dr. Warnock and Fina to become Community Angels, and she also asked me to see if you are interested."

"What in the world is a Community Angel?"

"There is a risk that after a few days an angry man can track down his runaway wife at Hope House, so Lila arranges for them to leave after four or five days, once their wounds are attended to, and they are fed, clothed, and disguised."

"Disguised?"

"You know, their hair is cut, dyed a different color, and they're dressed in overalls and work boots. If a woman has a child with her, the child is also disguised with new hair color and baggy, nondescript clothes."

"And then?"

"That's where the Community Angels come in. A woman and, let's say, her daughter are taken to another residence and they stay about a week, maybe two. Then they go to a different residence for another week, and so on, until they can be placed in a different city."

"Sort of like an underground railroad?"

"Exactly, and the people who take them in for a week are called Community Angels. Lila asked if we might become a Community Angel home and give it a try. She has dedicated her life to this higher purpose and looks every day for allies. Seems like a worthy cause, don't you think?"

Maria took a breath and clasped her hands in her lap, lips tightened into a slight frown. "What in the world has come over you?"

"Nothing really. I'm just responding to folks who have been helping me."

"But you've never been especially charitable. This is a big change, and a scary reach outside our home. You want to do this?"

"Only if you do, too. I will want us to both be here if we have a guest. And your skills as a nurse would surely be welcome."

"Can we just dip our toe in the water? You know, try it once and see how it goes?"

"I'm sure that would be fine. I could tell her we're up for a test drive, and that we can't commit beyond that."

"Okay, Adam. We can try it once. It could be dangerous. We need to be careful."

"There's something else."

"Oh God, no. Something else?"

"Yes, and this is the most important one of all."

"What's that?"

"Please take off your pajamas."

36

Adam and Russell worked most of the day at the building site. As Adam was packing up his tools, his cell phone rang.

"Adam, this is Lila. I need an angel for tonight. A woman named Sarah and her daughter Elisa are at Hope House, and they're in a bad way—scared to death. They're ready to be moved, but I don't have a place to take them. Can they come to your house?"

"This is a surprise, Lila. I just talked with Maria about it last night."

"Sorry, but I'm desperate. They are from Grants, and her husband is in Albuquerque searching for them. Sarah filed a domestic abuse complaint, and he's angry as a hornet. If he finds Hope House and she's still here, I'm afraid he'll kill her and take her daughter to God knows where. Elisa is only seven, and she's essentially shut down and depressed, and Sarah needs regular medical attention for her wounds and the stitches in her lip and over her eyebrow, so we thought maybe Maria…."

"I'll be home in an hour, and I'll call you back. Is this a good number?"

"It's a burner phone, but I'll be using it until tomorrow. I need to place them somewhere tonight. I know it's short notice but see what you can do."

On the way home, Adam talked with Russell about the Community Angel network. Russell said he would be eager to help Adam and Maria however he could, and he thought it was a great way to serve other people. "Removing people from fearful circumstances and giving them hope is always a higher calling. You should go ahead if you can, don't you think?"

"Yes, and Maria said we could give it a try, but she won't be expecting anyone to come this soon."

Adam dropped Russell at his car, and then called Fina.

"Hey, remember that conversation we had about Lila and her idea of Community Angels?"

"Yes, I remember."

"I haven't told you this before, but I knew Lila in a different context. As Lola, she was a drug was a drug rep who hustled doctors. We spent a little time together. But now she is dedicated to helping battered women and children. So, I told Maria a harmless lie, and I hope you will cover for me."

"That depends, Adam. We have to stay in the truth."

"I know. I told her that you knew about Lila's idea and admired her for it."

"That's true enough."

"And I told her you thought it might be a good idea to be involved."

"Okay so far."

"Adam, if you and Maria are thinking about becoming a Community Angel, then I'll stand by and answer appropriately. The Lola that you knew before was killed in a fire, remember? So, this Lila must be someone else. As you said, this Lila is not that Lola. We don't have to lie."

"Thanks. I've learned in AA, when making amends, we're told to make direct amends to people except when it would injure or bring harm to others. I worry that telling Maria would hurt her deeply and blow up our marriage. That's a sleeping dog I would prefer to let lie."

"I agree, Adam. You've moved way beyond the old Lola, and Lila says the old Lola no longer exists."

§

Adam headed to school to pick up Lucas and to get a couple of pizzas. Soon after they got home, Maria came in.

"Pizza smells good. Give me a minute to shower and change clothes."

"Okay, Mom. We had the pineapple put on one side so you wouldn't have to eat it."

"Thanks, little man. You are thoughtful"

She came to the table in her terrycloth robe. "Can you guys bow your heads please? Dear God, thank you for this food and for my husband and son. Amen."

After they ate, Lucas excused himself and turned on the TV.

Adam took care of the few dishes, and then sat back down with two cups of chai. "I need to talk with you about something."

"Oh, no. Something else?"

"No, not something else, just something. Lila called me this afternoon. She's worried about a woman named Sarah and her seven-year-old daughter Elisa." He explained Lila's concerns. "She apologized that it's so sudden; but it's urgent."

"Urgent—You mean tonight?"

"Afraid so."

Maria sighed and crossed her arms. "Are we up for this? I want to help, but this is a small home. I guess we could put them on the couch. Did Lila say the wounds were bad?"

"Yes, Sarah will have scars, and Elisa's heart will be scarred for life. I mean, how would you feel at age seven to watch your father go crazy with rage?"

"Okay, we can give it a try. But ask Lila to find an alternative in case this doesn't work out."

Adam called Lila. "We're on. I'm on the way to the store to get some groceries."

"Could you get some Fruit Loops? That's Elisa's favorite breakfast."

"Will do. When will you be here?"

"I'm not coming. My friend Blaze Wildrunner will bring them by in the white van that says 'Perfection Restoration and Painting' on the side. He'll be there by eight."

"We'll look for him then."

"Close your curtains and keep the porch light off. Do you have a gun?"

"I've got a thirty-eight-caliber revolver."

"Better keep it handy. I don't expect anything but be prepared to call nine-one-one if a strange man comes around. Keep your phones nearby."

Adam related his call with Lila to Maria and headed to the store.

He came in with groceries an hour later and started putting them away. He noticed that the couch was not made up. "Maria, should I help you make up the couch?"

"No, Adam, I'm in here."

Adam found Maria in Ava's nursery. She had moved all the baby things out, dragged a futon in from the living room, made up the bed, and cleared out the dresser drawers.

"We have the space, and these poor folks are going to need it, so we'll put them here in Ava's old room."

Adam wiped his wet eyes with his sleeve. "Are you sure?"

Maria sniffed, blew her nose into a tissue, and took Adam's hand in hers. "I guess I'm sure enough. That was then and this is now, and they need someone to care for them. I told Lucas we would be having special guests from time to time who need a quiet place for a little while."

Adam heard a soft knock at the door. He swung the door open and recognized the very large man with a black ponytail and a scarred face. Blaze scooted past him with a slender woman and a young girl in tow. Both had matching chocolate-brown hair cut short.

"This is Sarah and Elisa. I'm Blaze Wildrunner," he told Maria politely. "This small suitcase is all they have. I'll keep in touch and be back in a week. They should stay inside. You should continue with your normal routines. Here's my phone number."

He slipped out as quickly as he'd come in.

Maria greeted the newcomers. "I'm Maria, and welcome. We understand that you need a safe place, and for now, it will be here. Come with me and we'll get you settled in your room."

Lucas turned away from the TV. He approached Elisa. "Hello, I'm Lucas. I can show you how to play Chutes and Ladders. Would you like that?"

Elisa put her thumb in her mouth and nodded yes.

"And I'm Adam. I'll be cooking and shopping for groceries, so please make a list of food you like." He handed Sarah a small notepad and pen. She took it with a grateful nod, appearing exhausted and older than her likely age.

"Both Maria and I work in the daytime, but I'll check in at noon, and then I pick up Lucas from school at three-thirty. Maria is a nurse at the hospital and gets home a little after four-thirty. You can have the run of the house while we're gone, but Lila and that man Blaze both say you should stay in the house and out of sight. I think they plan on moving you to another safe house in about a week."

Maria showed them their room. "Sarah, I'm going to get some first aid supplies from the bathroom, and I'll clean and dress your stitches. Are you in much pain?"

"Oh, it's not so bad, actually. I'm healing well. I'm mostly just scared." Elisa moved near her mother and held onto her leg. "My husband is unemployed and drinks a lot. He's turned out to be mean as sin."

"You'll be safe here," Maria said. "At least you can relax for a week."

"We don't know how to thank you."

Adam poked his head into the room. "I made some blueberry pancakes. Come, sit down, and have something to eat."

Elisa brightened and looked up. They were hungry.

Later, at about midnight, Adam and Maria were in bed. Maria turned off the light on the nightstand. "Adam, I'm glad you said we would do this. I feel like a new, fresh breeze is blowing through the house. We've had our problems, but so does everyone else." She snuggled into Adam's neck and shoulder as he wrapped his arm around her.

"I got Fruit Loops for breakfast," he said.

"I can hardly wait."

37

After the building permits arrived, Adam hired a couple of men from his old framing crew. He rented an RV for a month and set it up at the building site so at least a couple of workers could stay overnight. The work went quickly. He built the driveway and installed the culvert with his new, used backhoe he'd bought from Rocky and Jim, and dug the foundations for both cabins. He hired his old cement crew for a couple of weekends, and they poured both foundations and slabs. He had lumber delivered and laid out the framing. They had installed windows and doors and fortunately had the green metal roofs on just two days before a snowstorm that shut down the road.

Adam had installed pellet stoves in both cabins. Now, all that was left was inside work—insulation, sheet rock, final plumbing, painting, installing kitchen cabinets, and finished electric. He had run temporary electrical service to both cabins, so he had lights and heat. With a small grill on the pellet stove, he could make coffee and cook. He felt warm, successful, and even happy when he was there. The crisp smell of cedar and pinon and the call of the stellar Jays and magpies made him feel that he was part of things. On Saturdays, he brought Lucas with him and spent time teaching him about measurement, framing, window installation, and door sizes. Lucas was smart and seemed to enjoy the process. Someday he would be a good hand.

Much to his chagrin, Trump was elected even though Hillary Clinton had garnered three million more votes. Everyone was surprised. Trump's remarks about women, his coarse treatment of Latinos, his questionable bankruptcies and business practices, and his general disrespect for government had not been enough to keep him out of public office. Adam remembered that in his old state of mind, the election outcome would've angered him and served as a good excuse to drink. But now, with his mind full of dreams and plans, he was able to detach his emotional life from political disappointments. Adam knew better than to give Trump free rent in his mind.

Determined to stay on his protocol, Adam focused on his success with Quality Homes, LLC. He checked in regularly with Dr. Warnock, and Fina helped him set up his bookkeeping, banking, and bill paying. Maria had told him he could move back home permanently. It was early December and he and Maria had hosted several women as a Community Angel safe house. Lila sent Maria the women who needed the most medical care because she was a nurse, and her talents and empathy continued to grow.

§

Maria felt deep changes as well. One night she told Adam that she may have found her purpose in life. She loved being a nurse, but she said that helping downtrodden and abused women was a higher calling. She added that she was grateful that Ava's old room was full of life and hope. Ava would be proud of the family's life-giving compassion that filled the room and spilled out the window onto the apricot tree nearby.

However, Maria was worried—perhaps frightened with a mixture of excitement, but certainly worried. Her period was three weeks late and her breasts were tender. She had bought two home pregnancy tests on the way home, and tonight she was going to find out. She had put it off for a week but needed to know even though the outcome could be momentous. The gray, shadowy presence of Ryan lurked, curled up like a worm deep in her worries. Adam insisted that Ryan was a liar. Was he? Did he for sure have a vasectomy? She thought of the many times she and Adam had made love, so her worry was probably silly.

She went into the bathroom as soon as she got home. The test was positive. She tossed the urine stick in the trash. Then she called Adam into the bedroom. "I'm three weeks late and my breasts are tender."

Adam grinned, spread his arms out and raised his hands above his head. "All right, this could be good."

"You stay here," Maria said. She went in the bathroom, sat on the toilet, and peed on the second test stick. It was also positive. She shook off the stick and walked out of the bathroom. "Check it out, Adam. We're going to have a baby."

"Hallelujah," Adam said, beaming. "Are you happy?"

"I think so. I'm scared and excited at the same time. It's so soon after—everything. Are we ready for this?"

"It seems like a new little someone is ready, whether we are or not." Adam smiled. "It's going to be okay. I'm committed to staying still clean and sober, Dr. Warnock and Fina and you are in support; and our business is thriving. We have a custom home to build for a friend of Fina's and soon we'll soon have enough money for me to build us our own house. We can add a guest house so we can use it for Community Angel folks. Life is good."

"This is all happening so fast, Adam. It wasn't that long ago that we were having a memorial for Ava—just seven months ago." She kissed her sapphire ring. "I miss her so. I know you did your best."

"I miss her, too. Sometimes I see her little smile in the night, as though she has come to visit. She has that little blue bow on her forehead. Sometimes I wake up crying."

"So fast. Everything is so fast. I can barely gather my wits, let alone find them."

"You're right. Things are moving way too fast." He gathered Maria up in his arms and gently rocked back and forth. They could see the moon coming up through the window, and together they made a dancing shadow on the bed. "But we'll be able to handle it. We can handle most anything together, don't you think?"

"I love you, Adam. Do you think it's a boy or a girl?"

"I don't even want to guess. I'll love whoever it is."

"Please, let's not tell anyone until after the first trimester. I'm still enough of a nurse to know the first three months are the riskiest for a miscarriage. And we've had so much stress lately, even if most of it is good stress."

"We need to take good care of you. You know I will do my part."

"Now, why in the world would you do that?"

"Because you're worth it."

38

The second week in December, Russell introduced Adam and Maria to his daughters, Maggie and Melody, at a nearby Starbucks. They were all wary and curious, but open. After a short visit, Adam invited them all for dinner at their home. Russell, perhaps in a fit of wisdom, begged off. "You guys should have the chance to get to know each other without me there. I don't want to bring any discomfort from the past. It's not about me. It's about your future." Maggie and Melody looked at each other with eyebrows raised, but then smiled. "We'll look forward to an evening together," Melody said. With a mischievous grin, Maggie put her hand on Russell's hand. "We don't need him anyway."

Adam barbecued chicken breasts on the grill, and Maria made a tasty potato salad. Lucas took charge of the chocolate chip ice cream for dessert. Maria talked about her nursing career, and Adam shared his excitement about their new company and their project in Placitas. Both Maggie and Melody warmed up right away, and Maria was a gracious hostess. They all made plans to spend Christmas dinner together. Sadly, they explained that their mother was unforgiving and would not attend.

Maria and Carolyn spent the day Christmas shopping together, and they went to Applebee's for coffee. They were both eager to talk privately before the Christmas dinner.

Maria took Carolyn's hand. "I've got something to tell you. You can't say anything to anyone, ever."

Carolyn leaned in. "I've got things to tell you, too. There's a lot going on in my house. You go first."

"I'm pregnant Carolyn, about six or seven weeks."

"Wow, that's a surprise. Is Adam happy about it?"

"He's on cloud nine, excited beyond words. Since I told him, he hasn't stopped smiling. It's great to see him so happy."

"And you?"

"About the same as Adam, but I have a worry."

"What's that?"

Maria's voice dropped to a whisper. "When Adam was in detox, Ryan was helping with Lucas. He stayed over one night and, well, I slipped, but it was just once."

"Ryan stayed over one night?"

"Actually, it was two. He was comforting me, you know, giving me a massage, and things got a little out of hand. I felt bad in the morning and took long shower. Ryan said he had a vasectomy years ago, so I shouldn't be concerned."

"Do you believe him?"

"I did, but Adam and Ryan had a fight and Adam told me Ryan was a liar. Adam found a pair of my blue panties in Ryan's laundry—almost like a trophy. I think he took them from my laundry basket. Weird, huh?"

"And Adam? Have you been sexually active?"

Maria smiled and dropped her head slightly. "Very active, almost like we're making up for lost time. I've always enjoyed making love with Adam, and I think I've forgiven him, at least when we're in bed."

"Any protection?"

"No, I haven't taken any birth control pills since Ava died."

"Let me see if I understand. So, either Adam or Ryan could be the father?"

"That's about right."

"I think you should go with the vasectomy and forget about it. You and Adam deserve the happiness that will come from this. You don't have time for regrets. Neither do I."

"You're probably right. I need to focus on the future. If I say anything to Adam about this, I'm afraid it will end our marriage or at least his sobriety."

"I agree," Carolyn said. Sometimes it's best to let things be. Making amends does not mean harming others."

Maria sighed. "Now tell me what's been going on at your house?"

Carolyn clasped her hands together on the table. "Doug's drinking is out of control, and he lost his job. He's angry all the time, and he's getting, well, mean."

Maria frowned. "Has he hurt you?"

"No, but sometimes I'm afraid. I told him he needed to leave until he gets his drinking under control. He threw a chair against the wall and stormed out of the house. I checked our joint account the next day, and he had cleaned it out and closed it—nearly four thousand dollars."

"Have you seen him since?"

"No, and I've talked with a lawyer about a divorce. Doug has clearly gone off the deep end. I don't love him anymore, and I live in fear. Life is too short. Why stay married?"

"You're right about that. But I'm sorry you have to go through this. You know, if you need to, you can come and stay with us for a while. I know Adam would help keep you safe."

"Thanks for that. I may take you up on it."

"I don't want to get all schmaltzy about it, but Carolyn, you are my best friend in the whole world. Our friendship helps keep me sane, and I love you so much."

"I love you, too. What would life be like without our friendship?"

"Life would suck, that's what. Friends keep our hearts going. You're welcome to have Ava's room for a week or two if Doug threatens you—or even if you just need some time away. Oh, did I tell you that Adam and I have become a Community Angel household?"

"No, what in the world is that?"

Maria explained the "underground railroad" model they had joined

"Adam is okay with this?"

"He's the one who brought us the invitation, and he thinks it might be a calling for me, a level above my nursing skills."

"Do you know why he thinks that?"

"He said that seeing me make up Ava's room for a mother and her daughter lighted up my calling—kind of like an aura he can see. Plus, he said he hasn't felt any psychic pain coming from me since that night. Sarah and Elisa stayed for eight days. Lucas taught the girl how to play Chutes and Ladders, and Adam bought groceries and cooked. I helped Sarah by dressing her wounds and listening to her story."

"Offering Ava's room—I agree, that sounds like a calling. How did you feel about it?"

"I felt warm, energetic, and, well, grown up. Seemed like I was in a new future for a few days. It was exciting and strange, like putting on a new formal gown for the first time."

"I guess neither of us lacks for drama in our lives."

"You've got that right. I'm glad you are coming to Christmas dinner with us. It is a big deal because Adam's father and his half-sisters will be there, and I want you to meet them. Dr. Warnock and his partner Fina will be there, too. They've saved Adam's life—led him through detox and loaned him money to start his own business. Not many people know that."

Carolyn smiled, her eyes moist. "Sounds like you have wonderful new friends."

Then Carolyn swung her hand around in a circle. "This old world keeps on turning. I knew a lot was going on, but Lord help us, I had no idea how much. It is almost as though you and Adam have a new life."

"I know, and it's a little scary. I want to trust happiness, but it seems like it might slip away. It's going to take time for me to get used to it. I never have been able to trust. I hope this is a turning point for me. At least I've forgiven Adam."

"You mean about Ava?"

"Yes. I've come to believe he did the best he could. His heart was in the right place. It always has been, except it's been shrouded in his addictions."

"That's great, Maria. I believe forgiveness clears things out, so you have a fresh start, a second chance."

"God, I hope so. Adam has a dream and a purpose. He's always wanted to have our own business. He's pumped and full of ambition every day. This morning he hugged me and said, 'be of good cheer. A good marriage is hard won, and we have a good marriage.'"

"And you're a Community Angel—a high calling if I've ever seen one—and you support each other. I'm so happy for you guys."

Maria stood up. "I guess we'd better get on with our shopping. I want to find something to give Adam after the Christmas dinner. It'll be a large group," Maria said. "Adam said Russell invited Jane. They have had coffee a couple of times, and I think Jane likes the idea of knowing Adam's real father. She didn't like Edward at all, even before the fire. Russell is interested in Adam's early life, and Jane has been sharing the events of their life together as his mother.

"She's a saint," Carolyn said. "She gathered up her sister's injured child, loved him and stood by him through all his surgeries, helped him with school, and gave him a home any young boy would admire. She taught him about money and business. She taught him compassion with animals. She essentially dedicated her life to him—even more than anyone would imagine."

"Have you seen her lately?" Maria asked.

"No, why?"

"She's had a makeover. Fresh hair style, make up, Botox, stylish clothes, sexy shoes, you know, the works."

"Does she look good?"

"Oh, yes, and younger, too. I barely recognize her. She used to be plain," Maria said.

"Do you think she has a thing for Russell?"

"I can't think of another reason she would put herself through all that. Her appearance never really mattered to her before."

"But I've heard he's a married man on a short leash."

Maria grinned and gathered up her purse. "I think the leash is gone, and I think he's searching for a new life. He's been in a loveless marriage for over thirty years. Both his daughters told me he's tired of it. I can see the loneliness in his eyes. And Jane must surely remind him of Margaret. I don't think he ever quite got over losing Adam's mother."

Carolyn waived her hand in a circle again. "Oh, my Lord. What a life. Next thing you know, he'll be helping Jane sweep out the pet store, just like Adam used to do."

"I'm going to go home and change. I'll see you at the Hilton at six-thirty."

"Okay, see you there. Let's sit together."

§

Russell had promised Adam that this would be a Christmas dinner like no other. Adam had reservations at the Hilton in a private dining room, and Russell had ordered two small Christmas trees with white lights for the centerpieces and selected the menu. Russell sat at the end of the table with Maggie and Melody on his right, followed by Dr. Warnock, Fina, and Lila Penrose. Adam sat at the head of the table. Maria sat to Adam's left, followed by Lucas, Carolyn, Adam's mother Jane, and Blaze Wildrunner. Everyone was drinking sparkling apple juice.

The lights were dimmed, and the Christmas carol "Do You Hear What I Hear" played quietly in the background. Adam tapped on the table with his spoon and stood up, a huge grin on his face. "Welcome everyone to our Christmas celebration. You are here because each of you is important to the rest of us. This group may be one of the finest gatherings of people I have ever seen. Now, let me offer a toast. Please raise your glasses."

Do you see what I see? A star, a star, dancing in the night.

Adam held his glass aloft. "I have a real father here with us, and I want to celebrate his presence. Let's offer a toast to Russell Kramer, my father for the rest of my life."

Russell stood next to his chair. His lips quivered as he took a breath. "For years I've dreamed of being a real father to Adam. For years I've wondered if it could ever happen. And now, in this Christmas season, I've shared the truth, brought my daughters to meet their brother, seen my son battle his demons in recovery, and found a new faith in God—my prayers have been answered. I want to thank each one of you for your love and care for my son. Thanks to you, this is the happiest day of my life." He smiled at each person, lingering with his smile when he looked at Jane. Her face flushed as she raised her glass. Russell paused for a quiet moment. "Let's drink to the celebration of new friends."

A song, a song high above the trees, with a voice as big as the sea.

Adam waved and stood up again. He looked at Dr. Warnock and Fina, then Lila, and then Lucas and Maria. "Thanks to people who care about me, a new life has come upon me. I am no longer controlled by addiction. My love has been released from heavy darkness. I have a new future. As Dr. Warnock has said, when we surrender ourselves to a higher power, then we learn to put one foot in front of the other, embrace our dreams with passion, and leave the outcome up to God. Each of you has had a hand in my new life, and I thank you for that. I could not have done this alone."

Adam looked at Lila and then at Blaze Wildrunner. "Thanks to Lila and Blaze, our home has become a Community Angel home and Maria as emerged as the angel. I offer this toast to all of you, but especially to Maria and Lucas, my very life blood."

Everyone raised their glasses. Lila wiped away a tear, and Maria put her arm around Lucas and pulled him close.

Said the shepherd boy to the mighty king, Do you know what I know?

The waiters brought ham, turkey, dressing, cranberry sauce, cornbread, a medley of vegetables, and then later, pumpkin pie with ice cream. They presented Lucas a Klondike Bar on a dessert plate. Blaze Wildrunner tapped on his water glass with a spoon. Smiled, and stood up. "I have an announcement. Lila and I are getting married." Then he sat down.

Lila's face turned pink, and then she broke out in an excited smile. "Probably next month, and you will all be invited."

Pray for Peace, people, everywhere. Listen to what I say!

Russell stood up again. "I have something else to say. I've decided to buy a condo here in Albuquerque and to live here most of the time. It's three-bedroom, so Maggie and Melody and come and stay with me whenever they want. My calling now is to help Adam and Maria stand up their new business, help Maria with the Community Angels, be Adam's father in a real way, and to be a worthy grandfather to Lucas." He paused and smiled at Lucas. "This whole thing has been under wraps for way too long, and I believe it is never too late to be a family. Shame can no longer exist around here, understood? There is no room for shame among people who love each other."

The Child, the Child sleeping in the night,
He will bring us goodness and light.
He will bring us goodness and light.

Adam stood again and allowed his tears to flow freely over his joy-filled face. "My heart could not be fuller. My love overflows. Merry Christmas, everyone!"

READERS GUIDE

1. The story of Adam Young illustrates his transformation from an angry addict to a gentle, resolute husband and father. What were the turning points in his life?
2. Except for occasional doubts, Adam thought he did everything he could to save Ava. Would it have mattered if he had not been impaired?
3. Adam falls into unruly behavior with Lola and with a homebuying customer. What brought about his actions? Are his mistakes forgivable?
4. The irony in Adam's treatment program by Dr. Warnock was that they used drugs to escape addiction to drugs and alcohol. Is this an acceptable treatment?
5. Dr. John Warnock was drawn to helping Adam. What motivated him to be so involved?
6. Edward Young was mean to Adam. Why did he behave that way?
7. Maria fell into a short tryst with Ryan. Why did she become unfaithful? Did it mean anything to her?
8. Addicts often give up hope for recovery. What was the power of hope in Adam's journey?
9. What does it mean "to surrender?" What was the role of surrender in Adam's journey?
10. People often search for purpose in their lives. What was Maria's purpose? What was Adam's purpose? How did having a purpose contribute to their health and marriage?
11. What was the theme of the novel?

www.ingramcontent.com/pod-product-compliance
Lightning Source LLC
Chambersburg PA
CBHW010746310726
48980CB00004B/379

* 9 7 8 1 6 3 2 9 3 4 7 0 3 *